DAY OF JUDGMENT
Amid the frenzied cheering of hundreds of people, President Kennedy steps out onto the balcony of West Berlin's town hall, unaware that he is the centerpiece of a . . .

DAY OF JUDGMENT
Higgins surpasses Higgins in an action thriller, his most stunning suspense novel yet . . .

DAY OF JUDGMENT
"Higgins . . . is a master at involving his readers in the fate of his characters and in the story-teller's most basic art—keeping alive the eagerness to see what happens next."
—Washington Post

DAY OF JUDGMENT
"Higgins can always be counted on for a high-tension performance . . . **Day of Judgment** possesses a solid moral core that transcends mere expertise. There is more at stake here than the deft resolution of a clever plot."
—Cosmopolitan

DAY
OF
JUDGMENT

Jack Higgins

BANTAM BOOKS
TORONTO · NEW YORK · LONDON

DAY OF JUDGMENT

*A Bantam Book | published by arrangement with
Holt, Rinehart and Winston*

PRINTING HISTORY

*Holt, Rinehart and Winston edition published March 1979
3 printings through April 1979
Literary Guild edition May 1979
Serialized in* EAST/WEST NETWORK *Magazine May 1979,*
TEXAS FLYER *Magazine May 1979 and* SUNDANCER
*Magazine May 1979
Bantam export edition/October 1979*

Bantam edition | June 1980

For Mike Green,
With Thanks

Freedom has many difficulties and democracy is not perfect, but we never had to put up a wall to keep our people in.

—*President John F. Kennedy,*
June 26, 1963

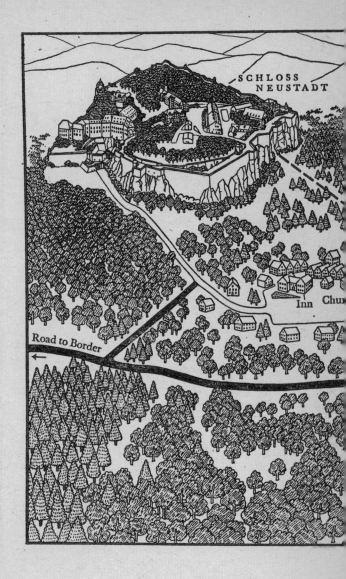

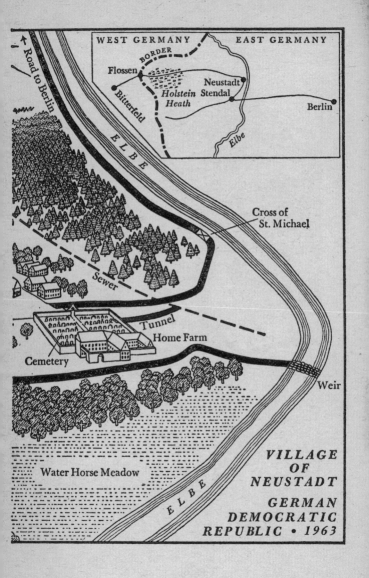

VILLAGE
OF
NEUSTADT

GERMAN
DEMOCRATIC
REPUBLIC · 1963

ONE

As Meyer turned the corner in the old hearse, he reduced speed, his hands slippery with sweat as they gripped the wheel, his stomach tightening as he drove toward the checkpoint, clear in the night under the harsh white light of the arc lamps.

"I must be mad," he said softly. "Crazy. The last time, I swear it."

There were two Vopos at the red-and-white barrier wearing old-fashioned Wehrmacht raincoats, rifles slung. An officer lounged in the doorway of the hut, smoking a cigarette.

Meyer braked to a halt and got out as one of the sentries opened the door. The street ran through an area in which every house had been demolished, to the wall itself. Beyond, in a patch of light, was the Western Zone checkpoint.

He fumbled for his papers, and the officer came forward. "You again, Herr Meyer. And what have we this time? More corpses?"

Meyer passed his documents across. "Only one, Herr Lieutenant." He peered anxiously at the officer through steel-rimmed spectacles. With his shock of untidy gray hair, the fraying collar, the shabby over-

1

coat, he looked more like an unsuccessful musician than anything else.

"Anna Schultz," the lieutenant said. "Age nineteen. A trifle young, even for these hard times."

"Suicide," Meyer explained. "Her only relatives are an uncle and aunt in the Western Zone. They've claimed her body."

One of the Vopos had the back of the hearse open and was starting on the brass screws of the ornate coffin lid. Meyer hastily grabbed his arm.

The lieutenant said, "So, you don't want us to look into the coffin? Now why should that be, I wonder?"

Meyer, wiping sweat from his face with a handkerchief, seemed at a loss for words.

At that moment, a small truck pulled in behind. The driver leaned out the window, holding his documents. The lieutenant glanced over his shoulder impatiently and said, "Get rid of him."

One of the Vopos ran to the truck and examined the driver's papers quickly. "What's this?"

"Diesel engine for repair at the Greifswalder Works."

The engine was plain to see, roped into position on the truck's flat back. The Vopo returned the documents. "All right—on your way."

He raised the red-and-white pole; the truck driver pulled out from behind the hearse and started toward the gap in the wall.

The lieutenant nodded to his men. "Open it."

"You don't understand," Meyer pleaded. "She was in the Spree for a fortnight."

"We shall see, shall we?"

The Vopos got the lid off. The stench was immediate and all-pervading so that one of them vomited at the side of the hearse. The other flashed his torch for the lieutenant to peer inside. He moved back hurriedly.

"Put the lid on, for God's sake." He turned to Meyer. "And you get that thing out of here."

The truck passed through the barriers on the other side and pulled in at the checkpoint hut. The driver got out, a tall man in a black leather jacket and flat cap. He produced a crumpled packet of cigarettes, stuck one in his mouth, and leaned forward to accept a light from the West German police sergeant who had moved to join him. The match, flaring in the sergeant's hands, illuminated a strong face with high cheekbones, fair hair, gray eyes.

"Don't you English have a saying, Major Vaughan?" the sergeant said in German. "Something about taking the pitcher to the well too often?"

"How do things look back there?" Vaughan asked.

The sergeant turned casually. "There appears to be a little confusion. Ah, yes, the hearse is coming now."

Vaughan smiled. "Tell Julius I'll see him at the shop."

He climbed into the cab and drove away. After a while he kicked one heel against the front of the bench seat. "Okay in there?" There was a muffled knock in reply, and he grinned. "That's all right then."

The area of the city into which he drove was one of mean streets of old-fashioned warehouses and office blocks, alternating with acres of rubble, relic of the wartime bombing campaign. Some fifteen minutes after leaving the checkpoint, he turned into

Rehdenstrasse, a dark street of decaying warehouses beside the Spree River.

Halfway along, a sign lit by a single bulb read JULIUS MEYER AND COMPANY, UNDERTAKERS. Vaughan got out, unlocked the large gates, opened them, and switched on a light. Then he got into the truck and drove inside.

The place had once been used by a tea merchant. The walls were of whitewashed brick, and rickety wooden steps led up to a glass-walled office. Empty coffins were stacked on end in one corner.

He paused to light a cigarette, and the hearse drove in. Vaughan moved past it quickly and closed the doors. Meyer switched off the engine and got out. He was extremely agitated and ceaselessly mopped sweat from his face with the grimy handkerchief.

"Never again, Simon, I swear it. Not if Schmidt doubles the price. I thought the bastard was on to me tonight."

Vaughan said cheerfully, "You worry too much." He leaned into the cab of the truck, fumbled for a hidden catch so that the front of the bench seat fell forward. "All right, you can get out now," he said in German.

"This is a life, this life we lead?" Meyer said. "Why do we have to live this way? What are we doing this for?"

"Two thousand marks a head," Vaughan said. "Paid in advance by Heini Schmidt, who's got so many of the poor bastards lined up over there that we can do it every night if we want to."

"There's got to be an easier way," Meyer told him. "I know one thing. I need a drink." And he started up the steps to the office.

The first passenger, a young man in a leather

overcoat, crawled out of the hidden compartment and stood blinking in the light, clutching a bundle. He was followed by a middle-aged man in a shabby brown suit whose suitcase was held together by rope.

Last of all came a girl in her mid-twenties with a pale face and dark, sunken eyes. She wore a man's trench coat and a scarf tied peasant fashion around the head. Vaughan had never seen any of them before. As usual, the truck had been loaded in advance for him.

He said, "You're in West Berlin now and free to go anywhere you please. At the end of the street outside you'll find a bridge across the Spree. Follow your nose from there and you'll come to an underground station. Good night and good luck."

He went upstairs to the office. Meyer was sitting at the desk, a bottle of Scotch in one hand, a glass in the other, which he emptied in one quick swallow.

He refilled it, and Vaughan took it from him. "Why do you always look as if you expected the Gestapo to descend at any moment?"

"Because in my youth, there were too many occasions when that was a distinct possibility."

There was a tapping at the door. As they both turned, the girl entered the office hesitantly. "Major Vaughan, could I have a word with you?"

Her English was almost too perfect, no trace of any accent there at all. Vaughan said, "How did you know my name?"

"Herr Schmidt told me when I first met him to arrange the crossing."

"And where was that?"

"In the restaurant of the old Hotel Adlon. Herr Schmidt's name was given to me by a friend as a reliable man to arrange these matters."

"You see?" Meyer said. "Every minute it gets

worse. Now this idiot hands your name out to strangers."

"I need help," the girl said. "Special help. He thought you might be able to advise me."

"Your English is really very good," Vaughan told her.

"It should be. I was born in Cheltenham. My name is Margaret Campbell. My father is Gregory Campbell, the physicist. You've heard of him?"

Vaughan nodded. "Between them, he and Klaus Fuchs handed the Russians just about every atomic secret we had back in 1950. Fuchs ended up in the dock at the Old Bailey."

"While my father and his twelve-year-old daughter found sanctuary in East Germany."

"I thought you were supposed to live happily ever after," Vaughan said. "Socialist paradise and all that. Last I heard your father was professor of nuclear physics at Dresden University."

"He has cancer of the lung," she said simply. "A terminal case. A year at the most, Major Vaughan. He wants out."

"I see. And where would he be now?"

"They gave us a place in the country. A cottage at a village called Neustadt. It's near Stendal. About fifty miles from the border."

"Why not try British Intelligence? They might think it worth their while to get him back."

"I have," she said. "Through another contact at the university. They're not interested—not any longer. In my father's field, you're very quickly yesterday's news, and he's been a sick man for a long time now."

"And Schmidt? Couldn't he help?"

"He said the risk involved was too great."

"He's right. A little border hopping here in Berlin is one thing, but your father—that's Indian territory out there."

Whatever it was that had kept her going went out of her then. Her shoulders slumped; there was only despair in the dark eyes. She seemed very young and vulnerable in a way that was curiously touching.

"Thank you, gentlemen." She turned wearily, then paused. "Perhaps you can tell me how to get in touch with Father Sean Conlin."

"Conlin?" Vaughan said.

"The League of the Resurrection. The Christian Underground movement. I understood they specialize in helping people who can't help themselves."

He sat staring at her. There was silence for a long moment. Meyer said, "So what's the harm in it?" Vaughan still didn't speak, and it was Meyer who turned to her. "Like Simon said earlier, cross the bridge at the end of the street and straight on, maybe a quarter of a mile, to the underground station. Just before it, there's a Catholic Church—the Immaculate Heart. He'll be hearing confessions round about now."

"At four o'clock in the morning?"

"Night workers, whores, people like that. It makes them feel better before going to bed," Vaughan said. "He's that kind of man, you see, Miss Campbell. What some people would term a holy fool."

She stood there, hands in pockets, a slight frown on her face, then turned and went out without a word.

Meyer said, "A nice girl like that. What she must have gone through. A miracle she got this far."

"Exactly," Vaughan said. "And I gave up believing in those long ago."

"My God," Meyer said. "Have you always got to

look for something under every stone you see? Don't you trust anybody?"

"Not even me," Vaughan said amiably.

The judas gate banged. Meyer said, "So you're just going to stand there and let a young girl walk all that way on her own and in a district like this?"

Vaughan sighed, picked up his cap, and went out. Meyer listened to the echo of his footsteps below. The door banged again.

"Holy fool." He chuckled to himself and poured another glass of Scotch.

Vaughan could see Margaret Campbell pass through the light of a streetlamp thirty or forty yards in front of him. As she crossed the road to the bridge and started across, a man in slouch hat and dark overcoat moved out of the shadows on the far side and barred her way.

The girl paused uncertainly, and he spoke to her and put a hand on her arm. Vaughan took a .38 Smith & Wesson from his inside pocket, cocked it, and held it against his right thigh.

"No way to treat a lady," he called in German as he mounted the half-dozen steps leading to the bridge.

The man was already turning very fast, his hand coming up holding a Walther. Vaughan shot him in the right forearm, driving him back against the rail, the Walther jumping into the dark waters below.

He made no sound, simply gripped his arm tightly, blood oozing between his fingers, lips compressed, a young man with a hard, tough face and high Slavic cheekbones. Vaughan turned him around, rammed him against the handrail, and searched him quickly.

"What did he say to you?" he asked Margaret Campbell.

Her voice shook a little as she replied. "He wanted to see my papers. He said he was a policeman."

Vaughan had the man's wallet open now and produced a green identity card. "Which, in a manner of speaking, he is. SSD. East German State Security Service. Name of Röder, if you're interested."

She seemed genuinely bewildered. "But he couldn't have followed me. Nobody could. I don't understand."

"Neither do I. Maybe our little friend here can help us."

"Go to hell," Röder said.

Vaughan hit him across the face with the barrel of the Smith & Wesson, splitting flesh, and Margaret Campbell cried out and grabbed him by the arm.

"Stop it!"

She was surprisingly strong, and during the brief struggle, Röder ran to the end of the bridge and stumbled down the steps into the darkness. Vaughan finally managed to throw her off and turned in time to see Röder pass under a lamp at the end of the street, still running, and turn the corner.

"Congratulations," he said. "I mean, that really does help a lot, doesn't it?"

Her voice was the merest whisper. "You'd have killed him, wouldn't you?"

"Probably."

"I couldn't stand by and do nothing."

"I know. Very humanitarian of you and a great help to your father, I'm sure." She flinched at that, her eyes wide, and he slipped the Smith & Wesson into his inside pocket. "I'll take you to see Father Conlin now. Another one big on the noble gesture. You and he should do rather well together."

He took her arm, and together, they started across the bridge.

Father Sean Conlin had, with Pastor Niemöller, survived the hell of both Sachsenhausen and Dachau. Afterward, five years in Poland had made him realize that nothing had really changed. That he was still fighting the enemy under a different name.

But a tendency to do things in his own way and a total disregard for any kind of authority had made him a thorn in the side of the Vatican for years, on one famous occasion censured by the Pope himself, which perhaps accounted for the fact that a man who was a legend in his own lifetime should still be a humble priest at the age of sixty-three.

He sat in the confessional box, a frail, white-haired man in steel-rimmed spectacles, dressed in an alb, a violet stole about his neck, tired and cold, for there had been more than usual that morning.

His last client, a local streetwalker, departed. He waited for a while, then started to get up.

There was a movement on the other side of the screen, and a familiar voice said, "You know, I've been thinking. Maybe people decide to give themselves to God when the devil wants nothing more to do with them."

"Simon, is that you?" the old man replied.

"Together with a true penitent. A young woman whose confession runs something like this: Forgive me, Father, for I have sinned. I am Gregory Campbell's daughter."

Conlin said quietly, "I think you'd better bring her into the sacristy and we'll have a cup of tea and see what she's got to say for herself."

The sacristy was almost as cold as the church itself. Conlin sat at the small deal table with a cup of tea, smoking a cigarette, while the girl told him about herself. She was, it seemed, a doctor by profession; had only taken her finals at Dresden the previous year.

"And your father? Where is he now?"

"Near Stendal, in the country. A village called Neustadt. A very small village."

"I know it," he told her. "There's a Franciscan monastery there."

"I wouldn't know about that, but then I don't know the place well at all. There is an old castle by the river."

"That will be Schloss Neustadt. It was presented to the Franciscans by some baron or other at the beginning of the century. They're Lutherans, by the way, not Catholic."

"I see."

He said to Vaughan, "And what do you have to say?"

"I'd give this one a miss."

"Why?"

"The SSD man at the bridge. What was he doing there?"

"It could be that they are on to you and Julius. Bound to happen after a while."

"Excuse me, but is Major Vaughan's opinion relevant?" Margaret Campbell asked.

The old man smiled. "You could have a point there."

Vaughan got up. "I think I'll take a little walk, just to see how things stand."

"You think there could be others?" she asked.

"It's been known."

He went out. She said to Conlin, "He scares me, that one."

Conlin nodded. "A very efficient and deadly weapon, our Simon. You see, Miss Campbell, in the kind of game he plays he has a very real advantage over his opponents."

"What is that?"

"That it is a matter of supreme indifference to him whether he lives or dies."

"But why?" she demanded. "I don't understand."

So he told her.

When Vaughan went back into the sacristy, they were talking quietly, heads together. The old priest glanced up and smiled. "I'd like you to see Miss Campbell safely back into East Berlin later today. You'll do that for me, won't you, boy?"

Vaughan hesitated. "All right," he said, "but that's as far as I go."

"No need for more." Conlin turned to Margaret Campbell. "Once back on their side, return to Neustadt and wait for me. I'll be there the day after tomorrow."

"Yourself?"

"But of couse." He smiled almost mischievously. "Why should others have all the fun?" He stood up and put a hand on her shoulder. "Never fear, my love. The League of the Resurrection has something of a reputation in this line of work. We won't let you down."

She turned and went out. The old man sighed and shook his head. Vaughan said, "What are you thinking about?"

"A child of twelve who, with only her father's hand to hold on to, was suddenly spirited away by night from everything warm and secure and recognizable to a strange and rather frightening country with an alien people whose language she didn't even understand. I think now that in some ways she is still that lost and frightened little girl."

"Very touching," Vaughan said. "But I still think you're wrong."

"O ye of little faith."

"Exactly."

Margaret Campbell was at the church gate when Vaughan caught up with her.

The street was deserted, grim and forbidding in the gray morning light. As they started along the pavement, she said, "Why do you live like this, a man like you? Is it because of what happened out there in Borneo?"

"Conlin and you *have* been improving the shining hour," he said calmly.

"Do you mind?"

"I seldom mind anything."

"Yes, that was the impression I got."

He paused in a doorway to light a cigarette, and she leaned against the wall and watched him.

Vaughan said, "The old man was very taken."

He very carefully tucked a wet strand of hair under her head scarf. She closed her eyes and took a hesitant step forward. His arm slipped around her waist, and she rested her head against his shoulder.

"I'm so tired. I wish everything would stand up and walk away and leave me alone to sleep for a year and a day."

"I know the feeling," he said. "But when you open those eyes of yours, you'll find nothing's changed. It never does."

She looked up at him blankly. "Not even for you, Vaughan? But I thought from what Father Conlin said you were the kind of man for whom the impossible only takes a little longer."

"Even the devil has his off days, didn't he tell you that as well?"

He kissed her gently on the mouth. She was suddenly filled with a kind of panic and pulled away from him, turned, and continued along the pavement. He fell in beside her, whistling cheerfully.

There was an all-night café by the bridge. As they neared it, it started to rain. He reached for her hand, and they ran, arriving in the entrance slightly breathless and very wet.

The café was a small, sad place, a half-dozen wooden tables and chairs, no more. A man in a dark blue overcoat was fast asleep in a corner. He was the only customer. The barman sat at the zinc-topped counter reading a newspaper.

She waited at a table by a window overlooking the river. Behind her, she could hear Vaughan ordering coffee and Cognac.

As he sat down, she said, "You speak excellent German."

"My grandmother came from Hamburg. She grew up by the Elbe, I was raised on the Thames. She lived with us when I was a boy. Raised me after my mother died. Made me speak German with her all the time. Said it made her feel at home."

"And where was this?"

"Isle of Dogs near the West India Docks. My old man was captain of a sailing barge on the Thames for years. I used to go with him when I was a kid. Down to Gravesend and back. Even went as far as Yarmouth once."

He lit a cigarette, his eyes dark, as if looking back across an unbridgeable gulf. She said, "Where is he now?"

"Dead," he said. "A long time ago."

"And your grandmother?"

"Flying bomb, November '44. There's irony for you."

The barman appeared with a tray, placed a cup of coffee and a glass of Cognac in front of each of them, and withdrew. Vaughan took his Cognac down in one easy swallow.

"A little early in the day, I should have thought," she commented.

"Or too late, depending on your point of view."

He reached for her glass; she put a hand on his. "Please?"

There was something close to surprise in his eyes, and then he laughed softly. "Definitely too late, Maggie. You don't mind if I call you that, do you? In fact, very definitely far too far gone. You know that poem of Eliot's where he says that the end of our exploring is to arrive where we started and recognize the place for the first time?"

"Yes."

"He was wrong. The end of our exploring is to recognize the whole exercise for what it's been all along. One hell of a waste of time."

He reached for the glass again, and she knocked it over and sat staring at him, her face very white.

"And what's that supposed to prove?"

"Nothing," she said. "Just take it as sound medical advice."

He sighed. "All right. If you're ready, we'll move on. I'm sure you can't wait to get back on your side of the fence anyway."

As they started toward the bridge she said, "You still don't trust me, do you?"

"Not really."

"Why?"

"No particular reason. Instinct, if you like. A lifetime of bad habits."

"Yet you'll take me back across the wall because Father Conlin asked you to. I don't understand."

"I know. Confusing, isn't it?"

He took her arm, and they started across the bridge, footsteps hollow on the boards.

TWO

It was two o'clock on Tuesday evening when the old army truck loaded with turnips pulled up the hill out of the village of Neustadt. About a quarter of a mile farther on, it turned onto the side of the road under pine trees.

Father Conlin wore a corduroy jacket and peaked cap, a grimy blue scarf knotted around his neck. His companion, the driver of the truck, wore an old army tunic and badly needed a shave.

"This is it, Karl, you are certain?" Conlin asked in German.

"The cottage is a couple of hundred yards from here at the end of the farm track through the woods, Father. You can't miss it; it's the only one," Karl told him.

Conlin said, "I'll take a look. You wait here. If everything's all right, I'll be back for you in a few minutes."

He moved away. Karl took the stub of a cigar from behind his ear and lit it. He sat there smoking for a while, then opened the door, got down, and stood at the side of the truck to relieve himself. There was no sound at all, so that the blow that was de-

17

livered to the back of his head came as a total surprise. He went down with a slight groan and lay still.

There was a light at one of the cottage windows, for the curtains were partially drawn. When Father Conlin approached cautiously and peered inside, he saw Margaret Campbell, dressed in sweater and slacks, sitting in front of a blazing log fire, reading a book.

He tapped on the pane. She glanced up, then crossed to the window and peered out at him. He smiled, but she did not smile in return. She simply went to the door and opened it.

Conlin moved into the warmth of the room, shaking rain from his cap. "A good night for it."

"You came," she said in a choked voice.

"Didn't you think I would?" He was warming himself at the fire and smiled at her. "Your father—how is he?"

"I wouldn't know," she said tonelessly. "I haven't seen him for weeks now. They wouldn't allow me."

He saw it then, of course, saw all of it, now that it was too late. "Oh, my poor child," he said, and there was only concern for her in his voice, compassion in his faded blue eyes. "What have they made you do?"

The kitchen door creaked open behind, a draft of air touched his neck coldly, and he turned. A man was standing there, tall, rather distinguished-looking, dark hair turning to silver, a strong face—a soldier's face. He wore a heavy overcoat with a fur collar and smoked a thin cheroot.

"Good evening, Father Conlin," he said in German. "You know who I am?"

"Yes," Conlin said. "Helmut Klein. I believe you once enjoyed the dubious distinction of being the youngest full colonel in the Waffen SS."

"Quite right," Klein said.

Two men in raincoats emerged from the kitchen to stand beside him. At the same moment, the outside door opened, and a couple of Vopos entered, armed with machine pistols, followed by a sergeant.

"We got the truck driver, sir."

"What, no comrade?" Father Conlin said. "Not very socialistic of you, Colonel." He turned to Margaret Campbell. "Colonel Klein and I are old adversaries, at a distance. He is director of Section Five, Department Two of the State Security Service, which is charged with the task of combating the work of refugee organizations in Western Europe by any means possible. But then, you'd know that."

Her eyes were burning; her face was very pale. She turned to Klein. "I've done what you asked. Now can I see my father?"

"Not possible, I'm afraid," Klein said calmly. "He died last month."

The room was very quiet now, and when she spoke, it was in a whisper. "But that can't be. It was only three weeks ago that you first sent for me. First suggested that I . . ." She gazed at him, total horror on her face. "Oh, my God. He was dead. He was already dead when you spoke to me."

Father Conlin reached out for her, but she pulled away and launched herself on Klein. He struck her once, knocking her back into the corner by the door. She lay there dazed. As Conlin tried to move toward her, the two men in raincoats grabbed him and the Vopos advanced.

"Now what?" the old priest asked.

"What do you expect, whips and clubs, Father?" Klein asked. "Nothing like that. We have accommodations reserved for you at Schloss Neustadt. Comfortable or otherwise—the choice is yours. A change of heart is what I seek. As publicly as possible, naturally."

"Then you're wasting your time entirely," the old man said.

Behind them, the door banged as Margaret Campbell slipped out into the night.

She had no idea where she was going, her brain unable to focus properly after the stunning shock she had received. Klein had lied to her. Used her love for her father to betray a remarkable man.

Her mind rejected the idea totally so that she ran as if from the consequences of her action, blundering through the trees in the darkness, aware of the cries of her pursuers behind. And before her was only the river, its waters swollen by heavy rain, flooding across the weir.

One of the Vopos loosed off a burst from his machine pistol, and she cried out in fear. Running even faster, one arm raised against the flailing branches, she tripped over a log and rolled down the steep bank into the river.

The Vopos arrived a moment later, and the sergeant flashed his torch in time to see her out there in the flood, an arm raised despairingly, and then she went under.

It was just after eight o'clock on the following evening when the black Mercedes saloon drew up to the entrance of the Ministry of State Security at

22 Normannenstrasse in East Berlin. Helmut Klein got out of the rear and hurried up the steps to the main entrance, for he had an appointment to keep—probably the most important appointment of his entire career—and he was already late.

Section Five was located on the third floor. When he went into the outer office, his secretary, Frau Apel, rose from her desk, considerably agitated.

"He arrived ten minutes ago," she whispered, glancing anxiously at the three men in dark overcoats who stood by the inner door. Hard, implacable faces, ready for anything and capable of most things from the look of them.

There was a fourth man, lounging in the window seat, reading a magazine. Small, with good shoulders, dark hair, and gray eyes that had a transparent look to them. The left-hand corner of his mouth was lifted into a slight ironic half smile that contained no humor, only a kind of contempt directed at the world in general. He wore a dark trench coat.

Klein gave his coat to Frau Apel and moved toward him, hand outstretched. He spoke in English. "Well, we got him, Harry. It worked, just like you said. The girl did exactly as she was told."

"I thought she might." The voice was soft and pleasant. Good Boston-American. "Where is she now?"

"Dead." Klein explained briefly what had happened.

"What a pity," the small man said. "She was rather pretty. You've got the man himself in there, by the way. I almost got to touch the hem of his garment as he swept by."

Klein glanced quickly at the security men by

the door and dropped his voice. "Exactly the kind of remark we can do without. When I call you in, try to behave yourself."

He opened the door to his office and entered. The man in the trench coat stuck a cigarette in the corner of his mouth but didn't bother to light it. He smiled down at Frau Apel, and for some reason she was aware of a slight flutter of excitement.

"Big night, eh?" he said in German.

"A great honor." She hesitated. "They may be a while. Perhaps I could get you a cup of coffee, Herr Professor?"

He smiled. "No, thanks. I'll just go back to the window seat and wait. I get an excellent view of your legs from there under the desk. You really are a very disturbing person, did anyone ever tell you that?"

He returned to the window. She sat there, her throat dry, unable to think of a thing to say, and he stared at her with those gray, dead eyes that gave nothing away, the perpetual smile as if he were laughing at her. She reached for a sheet of typing paper quickly. As she put it into the machine, her hands were shaking.

When Klein entered his office, the man behind the desk glanced up sharply. His suit was neat, conservative, his beard carefully trimmed, his eyes behind the thick lenses of glasses apparently benign. Yet this was the most powerful man in East Germany —Walter Ulbricht, chairman of the Council of State.

"You're late," he said.

"A fact which I sincerely regret, Comrade Chairman," Klein told him. "Several main roads leading into the city from the west are flooded. We were obliged to make a detour."

"Never mind the excuses," Ulbricht said impatiently. "You got him?"

"Yes, Comrade."

Ulbricht showed no particular emotion. "I fly to Moscow in the morning, and as I shall be away for a week at least, I want to make sure this thing is fully under way. The man you have chosen to accomplish the task, the American, Van Buren. He is here?"

"Waiting outside."

"And you believe he can do it?"

Klein opened his briefcase, took out a folder which he placed on the desk before Ulbricht. "His personal file. If you would be kind enough to have a look at it before seeing him, Comrade, I think it speaks for itself."

"Very well." Ulbricht adjusted his glasses, opened the file, and began to read.

In the early months of 1950 Senator Joseph McCarthy charged that he had evidence that a number of employees of the American State Department were Communists. Arthur Van Buren, a professor of moral philosophy at Columbia University, was injudicious enough to write a series of letters to *The New York Times* in which he suggested that in this new development the seeds of a fascist state were being sown in America.

Like others, he was called to Washington to stand before a Senate subcommittee in the greatest witch-hunt the nation had ever seen. He emerged from it totally discredited, branded a Communist in the eyes of the world, his career in ruins. In March 1950 he shot himself.

Harry Van Buren was his only son, at that time twenty-four years of age. He had majored in psychology at Columbia, researched in experimental psychiatry at Guy's Hospital in London, taking his doctorate at London University in February 1950.

He arrived home in time to stand beside his father's grave when they buried him. He didn't really know what to make of it all. His mother had died when he was five.

His father's brother was in the machine-tool business and almost a millionaire; his Aunt Mary, married to a man who owned forty-seven hotels. They seemed more concerned with the possibility that the senator from Wisconsin had been right. That his father was, indeed, a Red. It was up to Harry to restore the family honor, which he did by joining the Marine Corps the moment the Korean War started.

Nonsensical behavior, of course. As a professional psychologist he could see that. He could even understand the reasons for it, and yet he went ahead, lying on his enlistment papers about his education, a need, he told himself, to purge some kind of guilt.

He pulled mess duty, swabbed out the heads, endured the close proximity of companions he found both brutal and coarse, and kept to himself. He took everything they handed out to him and developed a kind of contempt for his fellows that he would not have thought possible.

And then came Korea itself. A nightmare of stupidity. A winter so cold that if the M-1 was oiled too much, it froze. Where grenades did not explode, where the jackets of the water-cooled heavy machine guns had to be filled with antifreeze.

In November 1950 he found himself part of the First Marine Division facing northward to Koto-ri to end the war at one bold stroke as General Douglas MacArthur intended. Except that the Chinese army had other ideas, and the marines walked into a trap that was sprung at the Chosen Reservoir and led to one of the greatest fighting retreats in the history of war.

For a while he played his part with the others who fought and died around him. He killed Chinese with bullet and bayonet, urinated on the bolt mechanism of his carbine when it froze, and staggered on with frostbite in his left foot and a bullet in the right shoulder. And when a boot in the side stirred him into waking one misty morning, it was something like a relief to look up into a Chinese face.

It was at the camp in Manchuria that he'd decided he'd had enough after the first month in the coal mine. The indoctrination sessions had given him his opportunity. The chief instructor was crude in the extreme. Easy enough not to contradict, but to reinforce, the points he was making. A few days of that, and Van Buren was sent for special interrogation, during which he made a full and frank confession of his background.

He was used at first to work as a missionary among his fellow prisoners until he came to the attention of the famous Chinese psychologist Ping Chow, of Peking University, who at that time was making a special study of the behavior patterns of American prisoners of war. Ping Chow was a Pavlovian by training, and his work on the conditioning of human behavior was already world-famous at an academic level.

In Van Buren he found a mind totally in tune

with his own. The American moved to Peking to do research in the psychology department of the university there. There was no question in his own mind now of any return to America.

Soon enough both the Pentagon and the State Department became uncomfortably aware of his existence but kept quiet about it for obvious reasons, so that he remained on that list of those missing, presumed dead, in Korea.

By 1959 he was an expert in thought reform and by special arrangement moved to Moscow to lecture at the university there. By 1960 his reputation in the field of what the press popularly termed brainwashing was already legendary. There was not a security department in any iron curtain country which had not called upon his services.

And then, in April 1963, while lecturing at the University of Dresden in the German Democratic Republic, he had received a visit from Helmut Klein, head of Section Five in the State Security Service.

Walter Ulbricht closed the file and looked up. "There is one flaw in all this."

"Which is, Comrade Chairman?"

"Professor Van Buren is not, and never has been, a Communist."

"I agree entirely," Klein said. "But for our purposes he is, if I may say so, something far more important—a dedicated scientist. He is a man obsessed by his work to an astonishing degree. I have every faith in his ability to accomplish the task we set him."

"Very well," Ulbricht said. "Show him in."

Klein opened the door and called, "Harry, in here."

Van Buren entered, hands in the pockets of his coat. He stood in front of the desk, that slight, mocking smile set firmly in place.

"You find something amusing?" Ulbricht inquired.

"My deep regrets, Comrade Chairman," Van Buren said. "But the smile is beyond my control. A Chinese bayonet in the face at Koto-ri in Korea in the winter of 1950, when I was serving with the American marines. Eight stitches, very badly administered by a medical orderly who didn't really know much better. He left me looking on the bright side permanently."

"This Conlin affair," Ulbricht said impatiently. "You understand the implications?"

"They've been explained to me."

"Then allow me to refresh your memory. Conlin, as you know, stood beside Niemöller in opposition to the Nazis. Went to Dachau for it."

"And survived," Van Buren said. "Which means he must be quite a man. I've been looking him up. At his trial in 1938 the Nazis were able to prove that his organization had helped more than six thousand Jews to escape from Germany over a two-year period. The Israelis gave him honorary citizenship two years ago."

"None of which is material to the present issue," Ulbricht said. "We have a situation in which thousands of misguided comrades persist in attempting to cross over to West Germany. In the main, they have to rely on the help of organizations based on the other side that operate purely for financial gain."

"Or try Conlin?"

"Exactly. This League of the Resurrection of his asks for nothing."

"Very charitable of them."

"Which unfortunately makes for excellent publicity," Klein said. "It has made Conlin a celebrity again. He was featured on the cover of *Life* magazine in America only four months ago. Last year he was recommended for a Nobel Peace Prize and had to turn it down because the church didn't approve."

"I should imagine that must have been the first time in years he took any notice of the Vatican," Van Buren commented.

Ulbricht said, "You know that President Kennedy visits Berlin next month?"

"I had heard."

Ulbricht was angry now; he removed his glasses and polished them vigorously. A dedicated Communist of the old school, he had managed to prevent, in East Germany at any rate, the de-Stalinization movement which had swept Eastern Europe after the death of the Russian dictator. There was no one he hated more than the current American President, especially since his triumph in the Cuban crisis.

"If it could be proved in a public trial that Father Conlin's actions were motivated not so much by Christian ideals as by political ones, if he could be made to admit to the world his involvement with the American CIA and their espionage activities directed against our republic, this would have the most damaging effect on Kennedy's visit to Berlin. It would, in fact, make it totally worthless as a diplomatic gesture."

"I understand."

"For God's sake, man." Ulbricht was almost angry now. "Rats in cages, dogs oozing saliva at the sound of a bell. I know as much of this Pavlovian psychology as anyone, but can you really change a man? Make him act like a different person, because that's what we need. Conlin to stand up in court before the cameras of the world and freely admit to having been a political agent acting for the Western powers."

"Comrade," Harry Van Buren said crisply, "I could make the devil himself think he was Christ walking on the water, given enough time."

"Which is exactly what we don't have," Klein said. "The problem of the Campbell girl and her knowledge of the affair has solved itself, but there will be others. Conlin's associates in this League of Resurrection will be aware, within a matter of days, that something has gone badly wrong." He hesitated, then said carefully to Ulbricht, "And then, of course, Comrade, there are certain traitors in our own ranks still . . ."

"I know that, man, I'm not a fool," Ulbricht said impatiently. "What you are saying is that there are those in the West who will discover what's happened and attempt to do something about it." He shook his head. "Not officially, believe me. The Americans are heavily concerned to improve relations with Russia at the moment, and Pope John's attempts to come to terms with the Eastern bloc speak for themselves. And what can they say? Conlin has simply ceased to exist. After all, he shouldn't have been here in the first place, should he?"

He actually permitted himself a smile.

"Of course, Comrade," Klein said.

"I have every confidence in your ability to deal with any such attempts with your usual efficiency, Colonel."

There was a slight silence. Ulbricht adjusted his glasses and said to Van Buren, "You have a month.

One month, that's all, before Kennedy's visit. You have those papers, Colonel Klein?" Klein produced a sheaf of documents instantly and laid them before Ulbricht, who took out his pen and signed them, one after the other.

"These give you full authority, civil and military, in the district of Neustadt, where Conlin is being held at the schloss. Power of life and death, total and complete, Comrade. See that you use it wisely."

Van Buren took the papers from him without a word, and Klein came forward with the chairman's coat as Ulbricht stood up. He helped him into it, then escorted him to the door.

Ulbricht turned, looking from one to the other. "When I was a boy, my mother was very fond of reading the Bible to me. 'Well done, thou good and faithful servant.' I remember that phrase particularly. The Council of State feels exactly like that, Comrades, towards those who succeed, but for the failures . . ."

He put on his hat and went out, closing the door behind him.

Klein turned to Van Buren. "So, my friend, it begins," he said.

THREE

For Margaret Campbell rebirth was a nightmare. Of suffocation, freezing cold, and then a long darkness, from which she finally surfaced to find a middle-aged gray-haired man at her side. He wore a brown habit, a knotted cord at his waist from which a large crucifix was suspended.

Her mouth was dry so that she found it impossible to speak, and he got an arm around her shoulders and put a glass to her lips.

"Easy now," he said in German.

She coughed a little and said hoarsely, "Who are you?"

"Brother Konrad, of the Franciscan Order of Jesus and Mary. This is our house at Neustadt."

"How did I come here?"

"One of my brothers found you this morning, caught on the weir, draped across the trunk of a tree. The Elbe is in flood because of the heavy rains."

She tried to move and was aware of an excruciating pain in her left leg. Her hand, moving instinctively to the spot, encountered heavy bandages. "Is it broken?"

"I think not. Very badly sprained. A torn thigh muscle."

"You seem very sure."

"I'm not without experience in these matters, Fräulein. During the war, I served as a volunteer with the Medical Corps, mainly on the Russian front. Unfortunately, the nearest doctor is at Stendal, but if you think it necessary . . ."

"No," she said. "The nearest doctor is here."

"I see." He nodded calmly. "On the other hand, although our Lord said, 'Physician, heal thyself,' this is not the easiest of precepts to follow."

"I am in your hands, it would seem."

"Exactly." He gave her two white tablets and a glass of water. "Take these, they will help with the pain." He arranged the pillow behind her head to make her more comfortable. "Sleep now. We will talk again later, Fräulein . . . ?"

"Campbell," she said. "Margaret Campbell."

"Is there someone I can notify of your safety?"

"No." She leaned back, staring up at the ceiling. "There is no one."

It was toward evening, and she was wide awake, her head turned to one side, trying to look over the sill out the window, when he came in.

He put a hand to her forehead. "Better," he said. "The fever has gone down. A miracle when one thinks how long you were out there in the water."

His face was full of strength, firm, aesthetic, and touched with a tranquillity that she found completely reassuring.

"The Society of Jesus and Mary?" she said, and

remembered her first meeting with Conlin. "You're Lutherans, isn't that so?"

"That's right," he told her. "Our movement started in England in the closing years of the last century. There was a great interest at that time in the work of St. Francis and a desire, by some people, to continue his mission within the framework of the Church of England."

"And how did you end up in Neustadt?"

"A lady called Marchant married the Graf von Falkenberg, the greatest landowner in these parts. On the death of her husband, she offered Schloss Neustadt to the order. They came here in 1905, led by Brother Andrew, a Scot. There were twelve friars then, just like the disciples, and eight nuns."

"Nuns," she said blankly. "There are nuns here?"

"Not anymore."

"But this is not Schloss Neustadt," she said. "It can't be."

He smiled. "We were moved out of the castle in 1938. The army used it as a local area headquarters for a time. Towards the end of the war it served to house prominent prisoners."

"And since then?"

"The state has failed to find any particular use for it but, on the other hand, has never shown any great desire to return it. This house, in which we have lived for some years now, is called the Home Farm. If I raise you against the pillows, you can see the river and the schloss on the hill above."

He sat beside her, an arm about her shoulders, and now she could see a pleasant garden surrounded by a high wall. On the other side there was a cemetery. To the right, the Elbe River raced between trees, a brown, swollen flood. Beyond, on the hill above the village, stood Schloss Neustadt behind its massive walls, pointed towers floating up there in the light mist, the approach road zigzagging up the face of the hill toward the great gate of the entrance tunnel.

The door opened, and another middle-aged man entered, carrying a tray. "And this," Konrad said, "is Brother Florian who fished you out of the river."

Florian placed the tray across her knees. There was soup in a wooden bowl, black bread, milk. She put a hand on his sleeve. "What can I say?"

He smiled again and went out without a word. "He cannot speak." Konrad told her. "He is under vow of silence for a month."

She tried a little of the soup and found it excellent. "The nuns," she said. "What happened to them?"

His face was grave now, something close to pain in his eyes. "They left," he said. "The last of them about two years ago. There are only six of us here now, including myself. A year from now I should imagine we'll all be gone if the state has its way."

"But I don't understand," she said. "It states quite clearly in the constitution that no individual shall be prevented from practicing whichever religion he chooses."

"True. The youngest amongst us, Franz, joined our order only six months ago in spite of every obstacle that officialdom tried to put in his way. Are you a Christian, Fräulein Campbell?"

"No," she said. "When it comes right down to it, I don't suppose I'm anything."

"The state is rather more equivocal. The rights to religious free expression, as you have said, are enshrined in the constitution. At the same time Walter Ulbricht himself has told the country in more than one speech that church membership is not compatible with being a good party member."

"But the constitution remains. What can they do?"

"Provide state services as a substitute for Christian ones. Marriage, baptism, funeral—all taken care of. To go to church is to deny the state, which explains why there hasn't been a Catholic priest here for five years and in what has always been a mainly Catholic area, the church door remains barred."

Her mind was full of disturbing emotions. Religion had never interested her. There had been no place for it in her home background, for her father had been an atheist for most of his adult life. Her education had followed the path set for the children of all important officials in the Socialist Democratic Republic. Privileged schooling and an open door to the university. A private, enclosed world in which all was perfection. What Brother Konrad was saying was new to her and difficult to take in.

"Why did the nuns go?" she said.

"There was an article in *Neues Deutschland* implying that orders such as ours were immoral. Old wives' tales, common for centuries. That in pools near convents, the bodies of newborn infants had been discovered. That sort of nonsense. Then the state medical authorities started monthly inspections for venereal disease." He smiled sadly. "It takes great strength of will to stand up to such ceaseless pressure. The nuns of our order, one by one, gave in and returned to life outside, as did most of our brothers."

"But you hang on," she said. "A small handful, in spite of everything. Why?"

He sighed. "So difficult to explain." And then he smiled. "But perhaps I could show you."

He brought an old wheelchair, a robe to put about her shoulders, and took her out and along the stone-flagged corridor, into the courtyard, pausing only to push open the gnarled oaken door on the far side.

It was like plunging into cool water, a tiny, simple chapel with no seating at all. Whitewashed walls, a wooden statue of St. Francis, the plainest of altars with an iron crucifix, a small rose-colored window through which the evening light sprayed color into the room.

"For me," Konrad said, "there is joy in simply being here, for in this place, I am aware of all my faults and weaknesses with utmost clarity. Here it is that I see myself as I truly am, and here also that I am most aware of God's infinite compassion and love. And that, Fräulein, gives me joy in life."

She sat, staring up at that rosy window, and made .her decision. "Have you ever heard of the League of the Resurrection?"

"Why do you ask?"

"Have you and your friends ever assisted with its work?"

"We are an enclosed order," he said gravely. "The contemplative life is what we seek."

"But you know of the work of Father Sean Conlin?"

"I do."

"And approve?"

"Yes."

She swung to face him. "He's up there now in Schloss Neustadt. Dachau all over again, and it's all my fault."

It was cold with the bedroom window open, but her face was hot, burning as from a fever again, and the evening breeze eased it a little. She stirred restlessly in the chair, and the door opened and Konrad entered with a glass.

"Cognac," he said. "Drink it down. It will make you feel better." He pulled a chair forward. "Now tell me more about this American professor Van Buren."

"I first met him in Dresden about eighteen months ago. I was just finishing my medical studies, and he was lecturing on parapsychology, a fringe interest of his. He made a point of visiting my father. Said he'd always admired his work. They became good friends. He even obtained a medical appointment for me in his own department at the Institute of Psychological Research. A wonderful opportunity—or so I thought at the time."

"You didn't like working there?"

"Not really. Harry Van Buren is a remarkable man—certainly the most brilliant intellect I've ever been exposed to. But it seems to me he has one fatal flaw. He's obsessed with his subject to such a degree that human beings become of secondary importance. At the institute, I saw him turn people around, change them completely. Oh, yes, there were the psychotics when it was a good thing—a miracle, if you like. But the others . . ."

Konrad said gently, "So—he betrayed you?"

"My father was ill—terminal cancer of the lung. They took him into hospital several weeks ago—I'm not certain of the exact date. They told me that the medical superintendent wanted to see me. When they took me to his office, I found Harry and a Colonel Klein from State Security."

"What happened then?"

"Colonel Klein told me that the radiotherapy treatment required to keep my father alive was costly and the equipment was needed elsewhere. It was usual medical policy to allow such cases to run their own course. If I did as I was told, they might be able to make an exception."

"Which was to entice Conlin over the border for them?"

She nodded. "Harry explained why it was necessary in the finest detail. It was as if he were trying to persuade me. How Father Conlin could be made to stand up before the world and say exactly what he had been told. Harry said it was necessary because Conlin was an enemy of the state. That he and his organization had been engaged in espionage."

"And you believed him?"

"My only thought was for my father."

"Honestly put."

She carried on. "Harry calls his technique thought reform. And it works. He'll have Father Conlin denying everything he'd ever believed in before he's through."

There was a long pause; then Konrad said, "And what is it you would have me do, Fräulein?"

"When they sent me across, they used a man called Schmidt in East Berlin who specializes in such matters. Klein said they allowed him to operate because it suited their purposes. Sometimes they put agents across to the other side in the guise of refugees. That sort of thing."

"Which makes sense. And they had you followed?"

"Oh, yes. An SSD operative, not that he lasted very long. The man who handled the actual crossing was an Englishman—a Major Vaughan. He and his partner have an undertaker's establishment in Rehden-strasse in the Western Zone. Julius Meyer and Company."

"You think he can help?"

"Perhaps. He was the only one who could see I was lying. Isn't that the strangest thing?"

She broke down then, harsh sobs racking her body. Konrad rested a hand on her shoulder briefly, turned, and went out. He paused for a moment, a slight frown on his face, then went to the far end of the corridor and opened a door which gave access to the farmyard at the rear of the main building. There was a monotonous jangle of cowbells as the small dairy herd was shepherded in from the water meadow by Brother Urban, a frail old man with white hair who wore a sack across his shoulders.

Brother Konrad opened the main door to the cow barn for him. "Tell me," he said, "what time does Franz deliver the milk to the inn in the morning?"

"Seven-thirty is the usual time, I believe, Brother," the old man replied.

"And Berg, from the schloss? What time does he collect his milk? Do you know?"

"He's usually waiting at the inn when Franz gets there."

"Good." Brother Konrad nodded. "When you see Franz, tell him that in the morning, I will take the milk."

Strange how cheerful he felt. He slapped the rear cow on its bony rump, and they all tried to squeeze through the entrance into the barn together, bells clanking.

In the bedroom, Margaret Campbell stood awkwardly at the open window, all her weight on one leg as she leaned across the sill to cool her burning face. It was almost dark, and yet it was still possible to discern the darker mass of Schloss Neustadt against the evening sky.

There was a light up there, gleaming faintly from one window after another as if someone were moving along a corridor. It was suddenly extinguished. She thought of Conlin alone up there in the darkness and was afraid.

The car which Klein had placed at Van Buren's disposal was a Mercedes staff car of the war years. It was in excellent condition, a pleasure to handle, and he enjoyed the hour and a half's run from Berlin in spite of the poor visibility toward evening.

It gave him time to think about the task ahead, and in any case, he liked being alone like this. But then, he always had. An onlooker instead of a participant. In that way one could see things more clearly. Sum up the strength of the opposition, which, in this case, meant Conlin.

It was almost completely dark when he reached Neustadt. There were lights at the windows in the village, but the schloss was in complete darkness. He drove up the narrow approach road, negotiating the sharp bends with care as it climbed the hill. There was a sentry standing in the mouth of the entrance tunnel out of the rain.

Van Buren held his identity card out the window. "Captain Süssmann is expecting me."

The Vopo examined the card by torchlight and

nodded. "Straight on to the main courtyard. I'll telephone through and tell them you're on your way."

Van Buren drove on, along the dark tunnel. There was a barrier at the far end, another sentry who examined his identity card again before raising the pole and allowing him through. Security was thorough enough, or so it seemed.

He drove across the inner courtyard and braked to a halt at the foot of a row of wide stone steps rising to a massive wooden door that stood open. A small group of Vopos waited to greet him: two privates holding lanterns, a sergeant, and a young man whose uniform carried a captain's tabs.

The captain saluted as Van Buren got out of the car. "A pleasure to meet you, Herr Professor. Hans Süssmann." He nodded to the sergeant, a large, brutal-looking man. "Becker."

Van Buren looked up at the dark bulk of the schloss. "What's going on here?"

"The place has its own power plant from the days when it was an army group headquarters. The dynamo is giving trouble. Nothing serious. There are a couple of electricians working on it now."

Van Buren took out a leather case and selected a cigarette. Süssmann offered him a light. The American said, "You've had your orders from Colonel Klein? You understand the situation here?"

"Perfectly."

"How many men have you got?"

"Twenty. All handpicked."

"Good. Let's go in."

The entrance hall was impressive, a marble staircase lifting into the darkness above. A silver candelabrum stood on the table in the center with a half-

dozen lighted candles in it. A short, stocky man
stood there. His dark beard was flecked with gray,
his hair tangled, and the elbows of his old tweed
jacket were crudely patched.

"This is Berg," Süssmann said. "The caretaker.
The place hasn't been occupied for any official purpose since the war."

Van Buren said to Berg, "We spoke on the telephone earlier. You've done as I said?"

"Yes, Herr Professor."

"Good—I'll see Conlin now."

Süssmann nodded to Berg, who picked up the
candelabrum and led the way up the marble stairs.
As they followed, Van Buren said, "What's the situation in the village?"

"Population, one hundred and fifty-three—agricultural workers in the main. The local innkeeper is
the mayor—Georg Ehrlich. He's Berg's brother-in-
law. There has never been any trouble here—not
from anyone. Oh, there are a handful of monks in
the old farm at the bottom of the hill by the river."

"Good God!" Van Buren said, genuinely astonished.

"Franciscans. Berg says they supply the village
with milk."

They were passing along an upper corridor now,
the light from the candelabrum in Berg's hand throwing shadows on the walls.

At the far end, two guards stood outside a door.
Süssmann unlocked it. Van Buren said, "I'll see him
alone first."

"As you wish, Herr Professor."

Süssmann opened the door for him. Van Buren
took the candelabrum from Berg and moved inside.

It was a fairly ornate bedroom with a painted

ceiling. Conlin was crouched at the end of the bed, his wrists handcuffed to one of the legs. He glanced up, blinking in the sudden light. Van Buren stood there, the candelabrum held high, looking down at him. He placed it carefully on the floor and squatted, taking out a cigarette and lighting it.

"I understand you smoke rather heavily."

"It's been said."

Van Buren placed the cigarette between the old priest's lips. "Enjoy it while you can. The last for a long time. My name is Harry Van Buren. Does that mean anything to you?"

"Oh, yes," the old man said calmly. "I think you could say that. Thought reform—an interesting concept."

"You know what to expect then."

"You're wasting your time, boy." Conlin smiled. "I've been worked on by experts."

"Not really," Van Buren said. "You only think you have." He took the cigarette from Conlin's mouth, turned to the door, and opened it. He handed the candelabrum to Berg and said to Süssmann, "We'll take him below now."

At the rear of the main staircase in the great hall, an oak door gave access to the lower reaches of the schloss.

As he unlocked it, Berg said, "There are three levels, as I explained to you on the telephone, Herr Professor, dating back to the fourteenth century."

They descended a long flight of stone steps and then a tunnel which sloped into darkness before them. Berg led the way, holding a lantern, and Van Buren and Süssmann followed, Becker bringing up the rear with Conlin between two Vopos.

Berg had to unlock two gates to reach the lowest

level. It was very cold now and damp. He paused finally at an ironbound door and unlocked it. The passageway stretched onward into darkness.

Van Buren said, "Where does that go?"

"More tunnels, Herr Professor. Dungeons, storage cellars. The place is a rabbit warren."

Berg opened the door. Van Buren followed him in, and the caretaker held up his lantern. The cell was very old, stone walls smoothed by time, shining with dampness. There was no window. The floor was stone-flagged, and the only furnishings were an enamel bucket in one corner and an iron cot with no mattress. The door had a small flap at the bottom for food to be passed through.

"Is this what the Herr Professor wanted?"

"Exactly." Van Buren turned to Süssmann. "Let's have him inside. No shoes, shirt and pants only, and leave the handcuffs on."

He moved out, ignoring Conlin as Becker and the two guards hustled him in. "Nothing to say, Professor?" the old man called.

"Why, yes, if you like." Van Buren turned to face him through the open doorway. "Frances Mary. Will that do?"

Conlin's face sagged; he turned white. Becker and the two guards came out; the sergeant closed the door and locked it.

"I'll take the key." Van Buren held out his hand for it. "And I want a sentry here at all times—understood?"

"Yes," Süssmann said.

"He stays in here for a week. Total darkness and no communication in any way. One meal a day. Bread and cheese, cold water, passed through the flap at the bottom of the door. Above all, no noise.

Better make your sentries wear socks over their boots or something like that."

"I'll see what can be done."

"Good. I'm returning to Berlin tonight. If anything comes up, contact Colonel Klein."

"And we shall see you again?"

"Exactly seven days from now. Then we really start to get down to it."

They moved away along the passage, leaving Becker with one of the guards. The sergeant gave him his instructions, then followed.

Inside the cell, Conlin stood listening, aware only of the muffled sounds of their going. *Frances Mary.* So long since he had thought of her. And if Van Buren knew about her, what else did he know? His heart raced, and the anguish at that moment was physical in its intensity.

He took a deep breath and shuffled cautiously through the darkness until he found the cot, then lay down on it carefully, the springs digging into his back. It was very quiet. *Phase One*, he thought. *Sensory deprivation leading to complete alienation of the subject.*

The darkness seemed to move in, and complete panic seized him as he remembered Dachau. To be alone, so alone, of course, was the worst thing of all —and then it occurred to him, as it had many times before, that he was not. He closed his eyes, folded his hands, awkwardly because of the handcuffs, and started to pray.

It was just before seven-thirty on the following morning when Brother Konrad and Franz pulled their handcart, loaded with milk churns, into the court-

yard of the local inn. Berg's old truck stood beside
the front door, and the innkeeper leaned against it,
smoking a pipe and talking to his brother-in-law.

Georg Ehrlich was a small dark man with an
expression of settled gravity on his face that never
altered. A widower, he left the running of the inn
mainly to his daughter, for he was not only mayor
but chairman of the farm cooperative and local
party secretary.

He managed a smile for the Franciscan. "Konrad,
we don't often see you."

"I wanted a word," Konrad said. "Official business, and besides, I thought the boy here might like
a little help for a change."

Franz, who at nineteen was the youngest member of the order and built like a young bull, grinned
and swung a full milk churn to the ground with ease.

Berg said, "I'm going to need at least one of
those a day from now on. Put it on the truck for
me, Franz, there's a good lad."

"A full churn?" Konrad said in surprise. "What
on earth for?"

"Vopos up at the schloss. Twenty of the bastards."

"Come on in," Ehrlich said. "Sigrid's just made
fresh coffee."

They moved along a whitewashed corridor and
entered an oak-beamed kitchen. Ehrlich's daughter,
Sigrid, a pretty fair-haired girl of seventeen in a blue
dress and white apron, fed logs into the stove. She
glanced up, and Ehrlich said, "Coffee and perhaps
a brandy to go with it? A cold morning."

"That's kind of you," Konrad said, "but a little
early in the day for me." He turned to Berg. "What's

all this about Vopos up at the schloss? I don't understand. What are they doing?"

"Guarding a prisoner they brought in the night before last. Twenty of them plus a sergeant and captain for one man. I ask you."

Konrad accepted the cup of coffee Sigrid passed him with a smile of thanks. "Someone important, obviously."

"That's not for me to say, is it?" Berg said. "I only follow orders, like we all have to these days." He leaned forward, the hoarse whisper of his voice dropping even lower. "I'll tell you one thing you'll never believe. You know where they're holding him? In a cell on the third level. Solitary confinement to start with. A full seven days before we even open the door on him again. That's what the man from Berlin said, and off he went with the key in his pocket. Van Buren, his name is. Professor Van Buren."

Konrad frowned. "Merciful heavens. I would have thought that even the rats might have difficulty surviving down there."

"Exactly." Berg emptied his glass. "I'd better be getting back with that milk now. They'll be wanting their breakfasts up there."

He went out. Ehrlich took down his pipe and started to fill it. Konrad said, "Some political prisoner or other, I imagine."

"I don't know and I don't care," Ehrlich said. "In times like these it pays to mind your own business. He talks too much, that one."

"He always did."

The innkeeper applied a match to his pipe. "What was it you wanted to see me about?"

"Ah, yes," Konrad said. "I'd like a travel permit, to go to Berlin to see my sister. I think I mentioned, when we last spoke, that she'd had a heart attack."

"Yes, I was sorry to hear that," Ehrlich said. "When do you want to go?"

"This morning, if possible. I'd like to stay a week. I'll remember, of course"—here, he smiled—"to wear civilian clothes."

Ehrlich said, "I'll make you out a permit now." He reached for the bottle. "But first, that brandy I mentioned, just to start the day right."

"If you insist," Konrad relented. "But just a small one." When he raised the glass to his lips, he was smiling.

Margaret Campbell had spent a restless night. Her leg ached, and she had fallen into a sleep of total exhaustion just before dawn. She was awakened at eight-fifteen by a knock at her door, and Konrad entered with a breakfast tray. She had a splitting headache, and her mouth was dry.

He took her temperature and shook his head. "Up again. How do you feel?"

"Terrible. It's the leg mainly. The pain makes it difficult to sleep. The pills you gave me last night didn't do much good."

He nodded. "I've something stronger in the dispensary, I think. I'll leave them out for Urban to give you while I'm away."

He placed the tray across her knees. She looked up in surprise. "You're going somewhere?"

"But of course," he said. "West Berlin, to see this Major Vaughan of yours. Isn't that what you wanted me to do?"

There was an expression of utter astonishment on her face. "But that's impossible."

"Not at all. The cooperative produce truck leaves the square at nine for Stendal, from where there are regular buses to Berlin. I'll be there by noon."

"But how will you get across?"

"The league will help me."

"The League of the Resurrection? But when I asked if you and your friends had ever assisted with its work, you said . . ."

"That we are an enclosed order. That the contemplative life is our aim."

She laughed suddenly, and for the first time since he had known her, so that for the moment, it was as if she had become a different person.

"You are a devious man, Brother Konrad. I can see that now."

"So I've been told," he said, smiling, and poured her coffee.

In Berlin, Bruno Teusen stood at the open window leading to the terrace of his apartment in one of the new blocks overlooking the Tiergarten and sipped black coffee. He was at that time fifty, a tall, handsome man with a pleasant, rather diffident manner that concealed an iron will and a razor-sharp mind.

At twenty-five he had been a lieutenant colonel of ski troops on the Russian front, where a serious leg wound had earned him a transfer to Abwehr headquarters at Tirpitz Ufer in Berlin where he had worked for the great Canaris himself.

His wife and infant son had been killed in an air raid in 1944, and he had never remarried. In 1950, when the Office for the Protection of the Constitution, popularly known as the BfV, was formed, he was one of the first recruits.

The function of the BfV was primarily to deal with any attempted undermining of the constitutional order, which, in practice, came down to a constant and daily battle of wits with the thousands of Communist agents operating in West Germany. Teusen was director of the Berlin office, a difficult task in a city whose inhabitants still tended to equate any kind of secret service with the Gestapo or SD.

It had been a hard day, and he was considering the merits of dining on his own and having an early night or phoning a young lady of his acquaintance, when his bell rang. He cursed softly, went to the door, and peered through the security bull's-eye.

Simon Vaughan was standing there, Brother Konrad behind him, wearing corduroy trousers, a reefer jacket, and tweed cap.

Teusen opened the door.

"Hello, Bruno."

"Simon." Teusen looked Konrad over briefly. "Business?"

"I'm afraid so."

"You'd better come in then."

He closed the door and turned to face them. Konrad took off his cap. Vaughan said, "This is Colonel Bruno Teusen, Bruno, Brother Konrad of the Franciscan Order of Jesus and Mary at Neustadt on the other side. I think you'll want to hear what he has to say."

He walked across to the drinks cabinet, poured himself a Scotch, and went out on the terrace. It was really very pretty, the lights of the city down there, but for some reason, all he could think of was

Margaret Campbell, trapped at Neustadt with her injured leg and probably frightened to death.

"Poor stupid little bitch," he said softly. "You shouldn't have joined, should you?"

It was perhaps fifteen minutes later that Teusen and Konrad came out on the terrace.

"Not so good," the colonel said.

"Can you do anything?"

"For Conlin?" Teusen shrugged. "I don't hold out much hope. I'll get in touch with the Federal Intelligence Service in Munich, but I don't see what they can do, other than inform interested parties."

"And who might they be?"

"The Vatican, for one. He is a priest, after all. Where was he born—Ireland?"

"Yes, but he's an American citizen."

"They might be interested then, but I wouldn't count on it. And we haven't got any proof that Conlin's over there. If anyone approaches the East German government officially, they'll simply deny any knowledge of him. In any case, from the sound of it, getting him out of Schloss Neustadt would take a company of paratroopers dropping in at dawn, and Skorzenys are thin on the ground these days."

Brother Konrad said, "And the girl?"

"We might be able to do something for her." Teusen turned to Vaughan. "Would you be willing to help there?"

For a moment, Vaughan saw again her pale face, the dark, weary eyes in the early-morning light on the bridge over the Spree. He smiled. "Julius won't like it."

"I know. Something for nothing again." Teusen glanced at Konrad. "When do you have to be back?"

"My permit allows me a seven-day stay in East Berlin."

"And where are you staying now?"

Konrad turned uncertainly to Vaughan, who said, "At our place in Rehdenstrasse. You might have to sleep in a coffin, but it's home."

Teusen said, "I'll be in touch. Possibly tomorrow —certainly by the day after. We should have the responses of all the interested parties by then."

He closed the door behind them and poured himself a Cognac. Then he went to the telephone, dialed a Munich number, and asked to speak to General Reinhard Gehlen, director of BND, the Federal Intelligence Service. Strange that he no longer felt tired.

FOUR

In Rome, on the following morning, in an upper room of the Vatican, His Holiness Pope John XXIII, close to death due to the effects of the stomach tumor from which he had been suffering for a year, held audience propped up by pillows in his bed.

A young monsignor sat by his side, reading from one letter after another in a low voice, His Holiness listening with closed eyes, opening them occasionally to sign a document when requested and again when his physician entered to administer a pain-killing injection.

The phone at the side of the bed buzzed, and the monsignor answered it. He said, "Father Pacelli is here."

The Pope nodded. "Admit him."

"This is not good," the doctor said. "Your Holiness knows . . ."

"That he has very little time and a great deal to do."

The doctor turned away, closing his bag, and the monsignor opened the door to admit a tall, gaunt old man with white hair and deepset eyes, a strangely medieval figure in the plainest of black habits.

"You look more like a bird of prey than usual this morning," the Pope said.

Father Pacelli smiled slightly, for this was an old game between them. He was almost seventy years of age, a Jesuit, second only in that illustrious order to the father general himself, director of historical research at the Collegio di San Roberto Bellarmino on the Via del Siminario, where he had been responsible for more than twenty-five years for the organization of the closest thing the Vatican had to a Secret Service department.

The Pope looked up from the document he was reading. "You Jesuits, Pacelli. The plain black habit, the lack of pomp. A kind of humility in reverse, don't you think?"

"I remind myself of the fact in my prayers each day, Holiness."

"Soldiers of Christ." The Pope waved the document at him. "Like Father Conlin. He reminds me strongly of a certain colonel of infantry I knew when I served as a military chaplain during the First World War. Whenever he went over the top to lead an attack, he never ordered his men to follow him. Simply took it for granted that they would."

"And did they, Holiness?"

"Invariably. There's a moral arrogance to that sort of action that I've never been too sure about. Still . . ." He handed the document to the young monsignor. "You're certain as to the accuracy of this information?"

"It comes from my valued contact in the West German Intelligence Service."

"And the Americans—have they been informed?"

"Naturally, Holiness. Father Conlin is an American citizen."

"For whom they can do nothing."

Pacelli nodded. "If the facts are as stated, the East Germans would certainly deny his presence."

"Even to us," the Pope pointed out.

There was a moment's silence. Pacelli said, "There would, of course, be the inevitable moment when they produce him for this show trial."

"Like Cardinal Mindszenty, saying all the right things? That the church, with the aid of the CIA, is engaged in some kind of underground struggle aimed at the destruction of the German Democratic Republic and everything Ulbricht and his friends stand for?"

"A suggestion not entirely without merit," Pacelli said. "But in my opinion, Holiness, it seems to me that on this occasion, it is not so much the church that is the target as the Americans. It would certainly cause President Kennedy considerable embarrassment if they succeeded in stage-managing the affair to coincide with his trip to Germany."

"Exactly, and the Berlin visit is of primary importance. When he stands at the wall, Pacelli, he places himself in the forward trench. He shows the Communist bloc that America is firm with the other Western powers."

The Pope closed his eyes, one hand gripping the edge of the damask coverlet of his bed. There was sweat on his face, and the doctor leaned over him and sponged it away.

Pacelli said, "So, Holiness, we do nothing?"

"To do anything official is not possible," Pope John said. "On the other hand, Father Conlin is a member of the Society of Jesus, who have always, or so it seems to me, proved singularly apt at looking after their own." He opened his eyes, a touch of the old humor there again in spite of the pain. "You will, I trust, find time to keep me informed, Pacelli."

"Holiness." Pacelli leaned down to kiss the ring on the extended hand and went out quickly.

The black limousine bearing the license plates of the Pope, which had brought Pacelli to his audience, returned him to the Collegio di San Roberto Bellarmino within twenty minutes of his leaving the Vatican City, in spite of the heavy traffic.

When he entered the small library which served as his office on the first floor overlooking the courtyard at the rear of the building, Father MacLeod, the young Scot who had been his secretary for two years now, rose to greet him.

"Neustadt," Pacelli said. "Have you come up with anything of interest?"

"I'm afraid not," MacLeod told him. "An agricultural village, typical of the region. These Franciscan Lutherans are the only remarkable thing about the place."

"And we have no church there?"

"Yes, Father. Holy Name. Founded in 1203. It's been closed for five years."

"Why?"

"Officially because there's no congregation."

"The old story. You can't be a good party member and go to church as well."

"I suppose so, Father. Is there anything further you would like me to do in this matter?"

"Father Hartmann, at the secretariat in East Berlin. Get a message to him by the usual means. I wish to see him in West Berlin at the Catholic Information Center the day after tomorrow. Get me a seat for the morning flight on that day. Inform him of Father Conlin's predicament, and tell him I will expect the fullest possible information."

"Very well, Father. The file on the American, Van Buren, is on your desk."

"Good." Pacelli picked it up. "Get me the Apostolic Delegate in Washington on the telephone. I'll be with the father general."

The young Scot looked bewildered. "But, Father. it's three o'clock in the morning in Washington. Archbishop Vagnozzi will be in bed."

"Then wake him," Pacelli said simply, and walked out.

The father general of the Jesuits, leader of the most influential order in the Catholic Church, wore a habit as plain as Pacelli's. He removed his glasses and closed the file on Van Buren.

"The devil and all his works."

"A genius in his own way," Pacelli said.

"And how will Father Conlin fare at his hands, would you say?"

"He survived Sachsenhausen and Dachau."

"A remarkable man." The father general nodded. "We all know that, but times have changed. New techniques of interrogation. The use of drugs, for example."

"I have known Sean Conlin for forty years," Pacelli said. "His is a faith so complete that in his presence I feel humble."

"And you think this will be enough to sustain his present situation?"

"With God's help."

The phone rang. The father general lifted the

receiver, listened, then handed it to Pacelli with a slight, ironic smile. "For you. Archbishop Vagnozzi —and he doesn't sound too pleased."

It was a surprisingly chilly evening in Washington for the last day in May, and in the White House, the Secretary of State, Dean Rusk, stood at a window in the Oval Office. The room was dark, the only light the table lamp on the massive desk, the array of service flags behind it. The door clicked open, and as he turned, the President entered.

John Fitzgerald Kennedy had celebrated his forty-sixth birthday only three days before and looked ten years younger. He wore dinner jacket and black tie, white shirtfront gleaming.

He smiled as he moved behind the desk. "We were just going in to dinner, and I've got the Russian ambassador down there. Is it important?"

"The Apostolic Delegate came to see me this evening, Mr. President. It occurred to me that it might be advisable for you to have a word with him."

"The Conlin affair?"

Rusk nodded. "You've read the file I prepared for you?"

"I've got it right here." The President sat down at his desk and opened a folder. "Tell me—did this come in through the German desk of the State Department?"

"No. A coded message to me personally from Gehlen himself." There was a pause while the President leafed through the file. Rusk said, "So what do we do?"

The President glanced up. "I'm not certain. It's

one hell of a mess, that's for sure. Let's see what the Vatican has to say."

The Apostolic Delegate, the Most Reverend Egidio Vagnozzi, wore a scarlet zapata on his head and the red cassock of an archbishop. He smiled warmly as he entered the room, and the Secretary of State brought a chair forward for him.

"It's good of you to see me on such short notice, Mr. President."

"A bad business," the President said.

"And one which could be a considerable personal embarrassment to you if Father Conlin is brought to trial, as is suggested. I refer, of course, to your Berlin visit."

"Does the Vatican intend to make any kind of official representation to the East German government?" Dean Rusk asked.

"What would be the point? At this stage in the game, they would certainly deny having him in their hands, and there are other considerations. The position of Roman Catholics, indeed of all declared Christians, is a difficult one in East Germany these days. We must tread very carefully."

"In other words, you'll do nothing," the President said.

"Nothing official," Vagnozzi said. "On the other hand, Father Pacelli of the Society of Jesus is going to Berlin as soon as possible to assess the situation."

The President smiled. "Pacelli himself, eh? So you're letting him off the leash? Now that is interesting."

"His Holiness, in spite of his unfortunate illness, is taking a personal interest in this matter. He would like to know, in view of the fact that Father Conlin is an American citizen, what your own views are."

The President stared down at the folder, a slight frown on his face, and it was the Secretary of State who answered. "There are various aspects which are far from pleasant. This man Van Buren, for example, has been a considerable embarrassment to us for years. Naturally, we've kept a very low profile on him, and so far that's worked."

"And then there's Conlin's own position," the President said. "They'll try to brainwash him into saying his Christian Underground has been a tool of the CIA for years. The point of the exercise. A total smear to ruin every good thing I'm hoping to achieve by the German trip. The improvement in relations between ourselves and Moscow since Cuba has been considerable. Together with the British, we're to resume three-power talks in Moscow aimed at a nuclear test-ban treaty. In a few days' time I'm making a speech here in Washington at the American University in which I intend to make clear our recognition of the postwar status quo in Eastern Europe."

"A move of profound significance," Vagnozzi said.

The President continued. "As far as East Germany is concerned, Ulbricht is a Stalinist. He hates Khrushchev, so my visit to Berlin is of profound importance in the general scheme of things because it shows Ulbricht that we mean business."

"Which helps Khrushchev to handle him."

"But more than that—it shows the Russians where we stand also. That trying to be reasonable doesn't mean we've gone soft. We stand by West Berlin."

Vagnozzi said, "So there is nothing we can do about Conlin?"

The President shook his head, and the steel that was always there just beneath the surface showed coldly in the eyes for a moment. "I didn't say that. What I'd like you to do is give me a little more time, that's all."

Vagnozzi stood up. "Very well, Mr. President. I will delay making my official reply until I hear from you."

"Before morning," the President assured him. "I think I can promise you that."

The archbishop went out. Dean Rusk said, "With the greatest respect, Mr. President, I must point out that to attempt an official move at this time, to involve the CIA for example, would be madness. If anything went wrong, it could only add substance to the kinds of charges they intend to bring against Conlin anyway."

"Exactly," the President said. "Which is why anything that is done will have to be on a completely unofficial basis." He reached for a copy of the *Washington Post*. "Did you know Charles Pascoe was in town?"

"No."

"There's an article here on page three. He's giving the Vanderbilt Memorial Lecture at the Smithsonian tonight."

"I thought he'd given up the academic life," the Secretary of State said. "I heard his brother died last year and left him a fortune."

"No, he's still a professor of modern literature at Balliol." The President folded the newspaper, stood up, and eased his back. "I'd like to see him—when he's finished his lecture, of course."

"As you say, Mr. President."

The Secretary of State started for the door, and President Kennedy called softly, "And, Dean?"

"Yes, Mr. President?"

"Let's make it the west basement entrance when you bring him in. No press on this one—by request."

Professor Charles Pascoe was bored, for the subject of his lecture at the Smithsonian, "Aspects of the Modern Novel," was one he found increasingly unrewarding, as he did the company of the academics who surrounded him at the reception afterward. The arrival of the polite young man from the State Department with a request that he visit the White House that very night had come as a happy release.

Charles Browning Pascoe was at that time sixty-six. The second son of a Birmingham cutler, he had chosen to go to the University of Heidelberg in 1914, an error of judgment which had cost him three years of internment. He had finally escaped to England by way of Holland and spent the last year of the war in Military Intelligence.

Afterward, a brilliant academic career that had included eight years as professor of modern literature at Harvard before a return to Oxford to his old college, Balliol. And then came Hitler's war, during which he was called back to Intelligence, first working with Masterman at M 15, helping smash the German spy network in England, then transferring to Special Operation Executive, where, more than anyone else, he had been responsible for the successful organization of the British and American Intelligence network in occupied France.

His wife died in 1943. There were no children. After the war he had returned to Oxford, to the academic life that was his first love. And then, in the summer of 1962, his elder brother, Robert, who had created one of the major electronics firms in

England, died, leaving him a fortune, which even after heavy death duties, was considerably in excess of one million pounds, a circumstance which had occasioned him little excitement. Certainly nothing like as much as he felt now, leaning back against the seat as the car moved along Constitution Avenue.

The limousine delivered him to the west basement entrance at the White House. The polite young man in the blue raincoat who had escorted him from the Smithsonian led the way past the Secret Service agents in the corridor and straight through to the Oval Office, where the Secretary of State was waiting.

He smiled and held out his hand. "Professor Pascoe. We have met, I think. A reception at the ambassador's house in London three years ago."

Pascoe was slightly built, with stooped shoulders, a shock of iron-gray hair falling across his forehead. He wore a dark evening coat over his dinner jacket, an old-fashioned wing collar and black tie.

"And just exactly what is all this about?"

The Secretary of State indicated the manila folder on the desk. "If you'd be kind enough to read that, I think it covers the situation more than adequately."

"And then?"

"The President himself will explain what comes after. I'll leave you now."

The door closed behind him. Pascoe sat down without removing his overcoat, took a pair of half-moon reading glasses from his breast pocket, put them on, and opened the file.

Twenty minutes later the door opened, and President Kennedy entered, followed by the Secretary of State. Pascoe glanced up.

"I couldn't resist trying the seat of power, if only for a time."

Kennedy grinned and turned to the Secretary of State. "You know, when *Why England Slept* was published, this man wrote me a letter twenty-two pages long, taking it apart word by word."

"A necessary stage in your education, Mr. President." Pascoe smile mildly and closed the file.

"Interesting?" Kennedy asked.

"Yes—I think you could say that. I've admired Conlin's work for many years. He's a remarkable man. I'm sorry to see him in such a plight." Pascoe removed his glasses. "A strange coincidence here, by the way. Colonel Teusen, the West German Intelligence officer who passed on the news from Berlin, is an old adversary."

The President frowned, and the Secretary of State said, "Teusen did serve under Canaris at Abwehr headquarters in Berlin during the war."

"Another remarkable man, the admiral." Pascoe stood up. "However . . ."

The President moved to the window, looked out, and said, "You spoke about the seat of power. You know what power is? Real power? It's not being able to do a damned thing because you're President and you've got to think of the country or the UN or what the Russians will do—or not do."

Pascoe said, "Yes, I can see how hard it must be to have to stand back and watch a good man go down the drain like this."

"Oh, no." The President shook his head gently. "I'm not prepared to do that," and in any event, I can't afford to. The Berlin trip is too crucial."

"The point is we can't do anything official—not at this stage," Rusk said.

"So where do I come in?" Pascoe asked.

"Donovan once expressed the opinion that you were the greatest mind at work in intelligence operations on either side during the war," the President told him.

"As Mark Twain said, I can live for two months on a good compliment."

"One is all you've got. My European schedule has me visiting West Berlin on June twenty-sixth."

Pascoe said, "You're serious? You really want me to try to do something about Conlin?"

"How many times did you handle similar operations during the war?"

"True." Pascoe nodded. "But that was eighteen years ago."

"No official help, of course. Not from anyone. The West German government can't afford any kind of involvement at this stage."

"And the Vatican?"

"Pacelli arrives in Berlin tomorrow," the Secretary of State said. "Again, entirely unofficially. Do you know him?"

"Worked with him at a distance during the war, but never met."

There was a pause. The President said, "There would be the question of the necessary funds."

"Hardly a problem," Pascoe told him. "My situation in that respect has changed considerably of late. I'm more concerned with my tutorials. My students are expecting me back next week. But I suppose something could be arranged."

The Secretary of State said, "If I might suggest, Mr. President, Archbishop Vagnozzi . . ."

"The Apostolic Delegate," the President said to Pascoe. "He's fully informed on the whole affair. It might be a good idea if you had words with him before leaving. He could arrange a meeting with Pacelli when you arrive in Berlin."

"And when exactly did you plan that to be, Mr. President?" Charles Pascoe inquired.

"I had a word with my appointments secretary while you were reading the file. There's a BOAC flight that leaves for London just before midnight, which would give you time to speak with Vagnozzi. You'd be in Berlin tomorrow afternoon."

"Presumably they have space available?"

"Already booked," the President said.

Pascoe nodded. "Very well. I have only one stipulation."

"Yes?"

"A meeting with Teusen and a request that he has ready, on my arrival, all possible information known to the West German Intelligence Service on the situation at Neustadt."

The President glanced at the Secretary of State, who nodded. "I don't think there will be any difficulty there."

"Good." Pascoe picked up the file. "I'm in your hands, it would seem. We don't have too much time if I'm to catch that plane."

They started toward the door. The President said, "I'd like to thank you, Professor."

Pascoe smiled. "Did I really have any choice? It is rather in the nature of a royal command, after all." And he turned and followed the Secretary of State out.

FIVE

Father Erich Hartmann, SJ, of the Catholic Secretariat in East Berlin, was an extraordinarily handsome
man, yet he seldom smiled, and there was a faintly
chilling quality in the blue eyes that made most people
who dealt with him proceed with considerable cau-
tion.

This included the Vopos at Checkpoint Charlie
who had grown used to the young priest in the battered little Volkswagen in which he passed through
to the Western Zone regularly on Vatican business.
A familiar sight after six months, as was the man in
the black leather raincoat who followed him at a
discreet distance on a light motorcycle.

Erich Hartmann was thirty-three, born in Dresden in 1930, the son of a butcher who was not only
a Communist, but also local party secretary. His
father had continued his activities after the rise to
power of the National Socialists, and on February
3, 1934, his wife had found him hanging from a meat
hook in his cold store. The official verdict was suicide.

Frau Hartmann sold the business and sent her son
to her brother in New York. She herself stayed

67

on, working actively against the Nazis with the Communist underground until she was arrested in October 1944 and sent to Dachau, where she was executed by firing squad just before Christmas of that year.

Her brother and his wife were devout Catholics, who raised the boy in the faith and spoke nothing but German in the home for the day when he could be reunited with his mother.

The news of her death, not confirmed until 1946, affected him deeply. He had always been something of an introvert. Now he withdrew completely into himself, even during his period at Notre Dame, where he was not only a brilliant scholar, but an all-American quarterback two years running.

No one had been particularly surprised when he declared his vocation for the priesthood. In the Society of Jesus he found an order of discipline and intellect that was perfectly in tune with his own rigid attitude toward the world around him.

Except for a brief curacy in Naples he had been employed mainly in the administrative section of the order, where Pacelli had discovered him and the curious fact that he was still officially a citizen of the German Democratic Republic.

His transfer to the Catholic Secretariat in East Berlin had been immediate, to duties ostensibly of an administrative nature, but in reality, to be his superior's eyes and ears in the capital.

It was just after two-thirty when Hartmann pulled into the curb in front of the Catholic Information Center in Budapesterstrasse. As he got out of the Volkswagen, the man in the black leather coat parked his motorcycle by a tree on the opposite side of

the road and dismounted. He started to light a cigarette, and Hartmann crossed over.

"If you get bored, there's the Zoological Gar-
dens behind you, Horst. I might be quite some time."

The man smiled genially. He had high cheekbones, a slightly flattened nose that gave him the look
of an ex-prizefighter.

"On the other hand, Father, you could be on
your way again before I know where I am, and
that would never do."

Hartmann shrugged, turned, and hurried across
the street. He ran up the steps of the old building
and moved straight through the reception hall, nod-
ding briefly to the young woman behind the desk as
he went up the stairs. He passed along an uncarpeted
corridor, opened a door marked PRIVATE without
knocking, and went in.

It was a small, untidy room, furnished as an
office and cluttered with filing cabinets. Pacelli sat
behind a desk by the window, reading a typed report.
He glanced up and smiled.

"You're looking well, Erich."

"I can't complain, Father."

Hartmann moved to the window and looked out
across the road at the man in the leather coat shelter-
ing under a tree. Pacelli joined him.

"SSD?"

"His name is Horst Schaefer. A Section Six man.
Surveillance of all important church leaders is their
specialty."

"You should be flattered." Pacelli sat down,
watching as Hartmann took off his coat. The old
man smiled. "But then, you couldn't allow such an
unworthy emotion."

"If you say so."

"You have the look, Erich, of some fanatical Roundhead in the England of Cromwell's time. The kind of man who could cry out on the Lord with fervor and in the same breath cheerfully burn young girls as witches."

"You sent for me, Father."

"Yes, you're quite right. I did."

He explained the situation quickly. When he was finished, Hartmann said, "I heard Van Buren lecture at the University of Dresden only three months ago."

Pacelli got up and walked to the window. "How regularly have you been making the crossing?"

"Twice a week—sometimes three times. I've even stayed the night on occasion."

"What about our friend with the motorcycle when you stay over? Don't tell me he stands out there all night. Or does someone else take over?"

"No," Hartmann said. "One agent per priest. That's bureaucracy for you. I usually warn him. A ridiculous situation, but no more than the world we live in. There's a small hotel with a bar just along the street. The sort of place streetwalkers use. He stays there. I always give him the keys to the car. It reassures him. He's a simple man."

"So?" Pacelli went back to the desk. He opened a black leather briefcase, took out a large envelope, and pushed it across.

"As, at the moment, your movements are restricted to East and West Berlin only, here's a present from the Vatican, signed by the Cardinal Secretary of State himself in the name of the Holy Father. A formal request that you be allowed to visit Neustadt without delay to consider the possibility of reopening the church there."

Hartmann opened the envelope and took out the letter. It was an imposing-looking document, stamped with a red seal. "This must be submitted to the Ministry of State Security, as you well know, Father, which means the information will automatically pass to Klein at Section Five."

"Who will be expecting something—some move or other from someone—or I miss my guess. You are correct. Father Conlin's presence at Neustadt and our official request for your visit are beyond coincidence, but my own feeling is that they will grant you leave to go. Under surveillance, of course."

"Why should they?"

"Why not? We have the right, under the constitution and under the Secret Treaty of Accord signed with the Vatican only last July." He smiled slightly. "And they can hardly use Conlin's presence as a reason for saying no, can they?'"

"But what is the purpose of all this?" Hartmann demanded. "What do we gain?"

"Submit your request to the Ministry of State Security immediately on your return this afternoon," Pacelli told him. "You should have a decision one way or the other tomorrow. I'll expect to see you back here the day after—and be prepared to stay overnight. It may be necessary."

Hartmann said, "Do I understand you to mean by all this that you contemplate an attempt to"—he hesitated—"to retrieve Father Conlin?"

"I'm not sure what I intend at this stage. I've a meeting with Colonel Teusen of West German Intelligence later today. He's expecting Charles Pascoe to arrive from America this afternoon, which could prove interesting."

"Pascoe?"

"Before your time. One of the great minds behind the British Intelligence system during the Second World War."

"So—you think something could be done?"

Pacelli said, "I'd formed the opinion that you did not approve of Father Conlin."

"Of his work—no. I've always doubted the usefulness of this League of the Resurrection of his."

"A little too dramatic for your taste?"

"Something like that. But the man himself . . ."

"I know exactly what you mean. Infuriating, isn't it? The people's saint, *Life* magazine called him. Vulgar, but apt." Pacelli got up and went to the window and peered down at Schaefer. "He's still there, waiting for you. Better be off."

Hartmann picked up his raincoat and moved to join him. "He isn't such a bad sort."

"As a Communist or a man?"

"Three daughters, and his wife is pregnant again."

He buttoned his coat. Pacelli looked out the window and sighed. "You know, Erich, I was just thinking how nice it would be to be a child again when life is full of innocent surprise."

"Interesting, Father, but hardly practical."

Hartmann went out. Pacelli stayed at the window, saw him emerge on the pavement below and get into the Volkswagen. As it moved away, Schaefer mounted his motorcycle and went after it.

It was evening again when Charles Pascoe moved onto the terrace of Teusen's apartment and looked out across the lights of the city. He should have been tired after his long journey, but instead he felt a sense of exhilaration. There was a step behind him, and the German emerged, a glass in each hand.

"You may find this difficult to believe," Pascoe said, "but this is my first visit, and yet twenty years ago, there wasn't a day in my life that wasn't focused completely on Berlin and Section Three of Abwehr headquarters on the Tirpitz Ufer, where a certain Oberstleutnant Bruno Teusen gave me considerable trouble."

"Who, in his turn, concentrated his attentions on SOE Headquarters at St. Michael's House, 82 Baker Street. It used to take you twenty minutes to walk there from your flat in Ardmore Court each morning—when you didn't stay overnight. Do you still like to ruin excellent Courvoisier with three large cubes of ice?"

Pascoe took the glass with a smile. "Do you still prefer those appalling Russian cigarettes you picked up a taste for in the Winter War?"

"You know, Pascoe, I learned so much about you, the most intimate of details, that in the end I actually grew to like you. Isn't that strange?"

"We could have met in June of '45," Pascoe told him. "I was offered the chance to handle your interrogation. I refused."

"May I ask why?"

"It would, I think, by then have been too personal. Like turning over one's own stone. Still . . . to business. You've had certain orders about this Coniin affair, I believe?"

"Not orders—just a phone call from General Gehlen."

"You know who I'm acting for?"

"Yes."

"Again, quite unofficially."

"Just like Pacelli from the Vatican, who's also here unofficially. I'm expecting him within the hour. They're all rather fond of that word, aren't they, as if we really had a choice? Afterwards, of course, win, lose, or draw, they'll say it never happened."

Pascoe said, "Can I count on your full cooperation as regards use of resources?"

"That's what I take my instructions to mean. There could be limits, of course. We'll just have to take each item on its merits. There is another factor of some importance also—Conlin himself."

"You knew him?"

"A marvelous man."

"Good." Pascoe emptied his glass and placed it down carefully. "I'd like to get started then."

In the study there were several files on the desk, and on the wall was a map of the general area from the border to Neustadt. There was also a large-scale plan of Schloss Neustadt, several photographs pinned beside it.

"Thorough as ever, I see." Pascoe put on his half-moon reading glasses and peered at the plan. "Where did you get it?"

"In the files," Teusen said. "No difficulty at all. It was an army group headquarters for most of the war, then a prison for *prominenti*."

Pascoe examined the photos. "It certainly looks formidable."

"During the First War it was used as a prison for French officers. There was not one single recorded instance of escape."

Pascoe nodded. "That I can believe."

"You'll find other maps and various drawings on the desk. Army engineers' stuff. New roads at various times during the war, drains. That sort of thing."

Pascoe turned to the desk. "And the rest?"

"Information on the various people involved. The Franciscans, for example, although I'll take you to meet this Brother Konrad later. The caretaker at Schloss Neustadt, Heinrich Berg, who served in entirely the wrong branch of the SS. And there's as much information there as we have on Van Buren, which is considerable."

"The Secretary of State provided me with a very comprehensive file on that gentleman before I left, courtesy of the CIA. No—I think this man Vaughan you were telling me about is the man I'm interested in at this stage."

"Then this is the one you need." Teusen pushed a manila folder across the desk. "Something of a cosmopolitan, our Simon, German grandmother, Irish mother."

"What was his father?"

"Captain of one of those sailing barges on the Thames for many years. He died just before the war."

"And what happened to Vaughan?"

"It seems that in 1917, when serving on the western front, the father carried in his colonel under fire. He was severely wounded during this exploit and awarded the Distinguished Conduct Medal. On hearing of his death, his old colonel insisted on making himself responsible for the boy's education. Sent him to Winchester, which I have always understood to be one of your most important public schools."

"My God," Pascoe said.

"Exactly." Teusen tapped the manila folder. "I think you'll find it makes interesting reading."

It was an hour later when Teusen came back to the study. Pascoe had turned the swivel chair behind the desk and sat, arms folded, looking up at the plan of Schloss Neustadt.

"You think there's a way?" Teusen said.

"Oh, yes." Pascoe removed his glasses and ran a hand over his face. "There's always a way, if only one looks close enough. You were right about Vaughan. A fascinating story. I've had a look at the rest of the stuff, only briefly. I'll work through it more thoroughly later."

"Father Pacelli is here."

"Excellent." Pascoe swung around in his chair. "Let's have him in."

Pacelli was wearing a collar and tie, a rather nondescript tweed suit under an old raincoat. Pascoe went around the desk to meet him.

"A real pleasure. How many years is it since we were last in touch?"

Pacelli took his hand. "Almost twenty. In 1943, when you warned us of the Führer's ridiculous scheme to kidnap the Pope."

"Don't look at me, either of you," Teusen said. "Even Skorzeny nearly had a heart attack over that one. Your coat, Father?"

"No need. I only have a few minutes, so I'd like to get down to business right away."

"Certainly." Pascoe waved him to a chair and sat down himself.

Pacelli said, "I had a call from Archbishop Vagnozzi in Washington, who explained to me that you would be acting in this affair, Professor."

"If I can see any way to act," Pascoe said mildly. "May I inquire as to your intentions?"

When Pacelli was finished, Pascoe said, "He sounds an interesting man, your Father Hartmann. How did you get the East German authorities to accept his appointment to your secretariat over there? I'm thinking particularly of his American background now."

"He's a citizen of the German Democratic Republic by birth. Even more important, both his father and mother were Communists who died for the cause. We can staff the secretariat as we choose. In their eyes, he would perhaps seem a better choice than most."

"If they have to have your people there at all?"

"Exactly. The position of the church, of all Christians over there, is an ambiguous one. Guaranteed by the constitution. The existence of these Franciscans at Neustadt, for example, is proof of this."

"But subject to continual harassment?"

"Exactly."

Pascoe nodded. "So, what do you think you gain, by sending Hartmann to Neustadt?"

"I haven't the slightest idea. We have the right that he be given permission to inspect the situation of the church there. A right which I happen to think, for rather delicate political reasons, vis-à-vis the Vatican, they will not deny."

"Under surveillance?"

"Naturally."

"And you accept that the request will indicate to Klein that you know they have Conlin there?"

"Of course."

Pascoe glanced up at Teusen. "An interesting situation."

"Which is putting it mildly," the German commented.

Pacelli said carefully, "Are your own plans in any way advanced in this matter?"

"Hardly," Pascoe said. "Why do you ask?"

"It occurs to me that Father Hartmann's presence in Neustadt could be useful."

"True," Pascoe said. "But in a way that might not prove acceptable to you."

"As a kind of tethered goat, you mean, to draw the tiger?"

"No, more of a Trojan horse."

"You have something in mind?"

"The glimmering of an idea only. Not far enough advanced to discuss at this point. It would mean Father Hartmann becoming the focus of their attentions."

"While something quite different was going on behind their backs?"

"That would be the point of the operation."

There was a long pause. The old Jesuit nodded calmly. "That would be perfectly acceptable."

"And Father Hartmann?" Teusen asked.

"Will comply with whatever is required of him." Pascoe started to speak, and Pacelli raised a hand. "Let me make something quite clear. I have known Sean Conlin for the best part of forty years. He is a stubborn and rebellious old Irishman, who loves his fellow creatures so much that he has proved totally incapable of following anything but the dictates of his own conscience all his life. He has been, on many occasions, a considerable source of embarrassment both to the church and the order he serves. In so doing, he has become a living symbol of faith in action to thousands of people. We, of the Society of Jesus, are not prepared to see him go under. Do I make myself plain?"

"I think so," Pascoe said.

"Good." Pacelli got up and buttoned his raincoat. "When may I hear from you?"

"You expect Father Hartmann to return the day after tomorrow?"

"Yes."

Pascoe glanced up at Teusen. "Perhaps you'll arrange a meeting then?"

Pacelli didn't offer to shake hands. "Let's hope, in the meantime, that you come up with something substantial."

He went out, followed by Teusen. When the German returned, Pascoe had swiveled in the chair again and was looking up at the plan of Schloss Neustadt. Teusen took out a cigarette and lit it.

Pascoe removed his glasses and ran a hand over his face as if weary. Teusen said, "You could do with some sleep."

Pascoe looked up at him. "Good God, no. At my age, my dear Bruno, there's time enough for that when you're dead." He got to his feet. "No, I think, if you'd be so good enough to take me, it's time I made the acquaintance of Major Vaughan."

The Mercedes turned into Rehdenstrasse and pulled up in front of the sign JULIUS MEYER AND COMPANY, UNDERTAKERS.

"Is this wholly a front or do they really offer a service?" Pascoe asked as they got out.

Teusen smiled. "Oh, yes. They'll bury you—if that's what you want."

He opened the judas gate and led the way through. The garage was in darkness, but there was a light in the glass-walled office.

The door opened, and Meyer looked out. "Who's there?"

There was a certain alarm in his voice. Teusen paused at the bottom of the rickety wooden steps. "It's me—Bruno. I've got a friend with me. Is Brother Konrad there?"

"Yes—come on up."

Pascoe followed Teusen up the stairs. There was a chessboard on the desk, and Konrad, who was sitting on the other side, got to his feet.

Meyer switched off the cassette player. "Where's Simon?" Teusen asked.

"He went to the bar at the end of the street for cigarettes. Who's this?"

"My name is Pascoe," the professor told him. "Charles Pascoe."

Meyer ignored him and addressed himself to Teusen again. "What's he want?"

"To offer you a great deal of money," Pascoe said. "In return for your help in retrieving Father Sean Conlin from his present predicament."

Meyer gazed at him in total astonishment. "What is this? Some kind of joke?"

"Ten thousand pounds, Mr. Meyer. Perhaps more," Pascoe said calmly.

Brother Konrad said carefully in halting English, "Is this true? You really intend to do something about Father Conlin?"

"That would depend," Pascoe said, "on many things. On you yourself, for example, and your friends at Neustadt."

The judas gate banged, and Vaughan appeared from the shadows below. He paused at the bottom of the steps, and it was Pascoe who moved out onto the small landing first and looked down at him.

"Good evening, Major Vaughan."

Vaughan glanced up and went very still.

"You know who I am?" Pascoe asked.

"You're on the syllabus at Sandhurst, didn't they ever tell you that?"

Pascoe started down the steps, and Vaughan sat on a coffin, unzipped his jacket, and took out a cigarette. Teusen and Brother Konrad stayed on the landing.

Meyer came down the steps. "Money can't buy a life, Simon. Tell him that."

"Money," said Pascoe, "always helps. One of the sadder facts of this gray little world, or so I've always found."

Vaughan lit his cigarette. "You've come for Conlin?"

"That is correct. Naturally, I'd like your assistance."

"Not interested."

"Ten thousand pounds." Pascoe glanced at Meyer. "Each."

"Money"—Vaughan said shrugging—"at the best of times is only a medium of exchange."

Meyer turned and went up the steps. He said to Teusen, "You want a drink, because I need one. Maybe even two. When he starts talking to himself, that devil down there, I know I'm in trouble again."

He vanished into the office. Pascoe said, "Do it for Conlin then. I understand you like him."

"He's been walking barefooted towards some kind of stake since the day he was born."

"All right," Pascoe said patiently. "Do it for yourself. Because there isn't really anything else left for you to do."

"Isn't there?"

"Let's look at the facts. Simon Vaughan, born July 27, 1926, not a stone's throw from the West India Docks."

"I'm a Sun-Leo," Vaughan said. "Most fortunate week of the zodiac. Did you know that?"

"A hell of a leap from the Isle of Dogs to Winchester. Did you make it?"

"Not really." Vaughan smiled without humor. "It's in the voice mainly. They got to me too late to make me word perfect."

"So you joined up in 1944, a year under age, and served with the Twenty-first Independent Parachute Squadron at Arnhem. Military Medal there. Afterwards, when someone discovered you spoke surprisingly good German, thanks to that grandmother of yours, they commissioned you into the Intelligence Corps. After the war, they kept you on. Even sent you to Sandhurst."

"See what a Labour government can do for you," Vaughan said.

"Captain with Field Intelligence in Korea, captured on the Hook, spent nearly two years in a Chinese prison camp. Afterwards back to Military Intelligence, where you specialized in handling subversives, revolutionary movements generally, and so on. The Communists in Malaya, six months chasing

Mau-Mau in Kenya, then Cyprus and EOKA. The DSO for that little lot and a bullet in the back that nearly put paid to things."

"I wonder how I managed to fit it all in."

"And then Borneo and the confrontation with the Indonesians. You commanded a company of native irregulars. The area around Kotabaru was rotten with terrorists. You were told to go in and clear them out."

"No one can say I failed to do that."

"You were certainly thorough. How many prisoners did you have shot? How many captives interrogated and tortured in custody? The newspapers made a lot out of that at the time. What did they call you? The Beast of Selangor. I suppose it was your medals that saved you. And the time in prison camp must have been useful. At least you weren't cashiered."

"Previous gallant conduct," Vaughan said. "Must do what we can. Pity the academy couldn't make a gentleman out of him."

"To sum up," Pascoe said. "You were told to clear the last terrorist out of Kotabaru and did just that. A little ruthlessly, perhaps, but you did it. Your superiors heaved a sigh of relief and threw you to the wolves."

"Leaving me with the satisfaction of having done my duty." Vaughan stuck another cigarette in the corner of his mouth. "Water under the bridge, Professor. Meyer knows Berlin. I speak fluent German. It isn't much, but it's a living."

There was a long pause. Pascoe said, "Well?"

"All right," Vaughan said. "I'll call your bluff. Twenty thousand—each," he added.

"You know, somehow I thought you might prove reasonable—in the end."

Teusen woke just after three o'clock in the morning with a bad headache. He found an aspirin and went to the kitchen to get a glass of water. To his astonishment, there was a light under the study door. He opened it to find Pascoe seated at the desk, working his way through the files.

"Good God," Teusen said, "haven't you been to bed?"

"Couldn't sleep." Pascoe removed his glasses. "Actually, I'm glad you're here. You can fill in a blank for me." He swiveled to the map. "Here, along the border, there must be dozens of crossing points, especially on the country back roads. Is there any where your intelligence people have a special arrangement to come and go where it suits them?"

"If you mean, are there border guards on the other side who are bribable, yes," Teusen said. "But it's getting tighter all the time."

"What about here, west of Neustadt? The direct route out?"

"Yes." Teusen moved closer, then found what he was looking for. "There's a crossing at Flossen. A hell of an area. Holstein Heath. I used to go shooting there when I was a youth. Wild boar."

"So—it could be arranged?"

"Yes, I think so. It would be difficult. Also expensive. If you want me to, I'll get in touch with my man in the area in the morning."

"It's morning now," Pascoe pointed out.

He put on his half-moon spectacles and returned to his files. Teusen stood looking down at him for a moment, feeling strangely helpless; then he turned and went out, closing the door behind him. He went back into his bedroom and sat on the edge of the bed.

"Now I know how we lost the war," he said to himself wearily, and reached for the telephone.

SIX

Pascoe, as a rule, did not enjoy flying in small air-craft. They were noisy, uncomfortable, and lacking in the more obvious amenities, but he could certainly find no fault with the plane Teusen had arranged to fly them from Tempelhof to West Germany at eleven o'clock that morning. It was a Hawker Sid-deley 125 and not long from the factory, a twin-jet executive aircraft of some luxury in which it was actually possible to conduct a conversation without shouting.

"We land here." Teusen ringed a spot on the map with pencil. "Bitterfeld. A Luftwaffe night fight-er base during the war. Not been used for years, but very convenient for the border. The field agent for the area will pick us up there."

"And how far to this crossing you mentioned at Flossen?"

"Seven or eight miles."

Pascoe examined the map in silence for a while, then opened his briefcase, took out a file, and started to make notes.

Teusen said, "When are you going to tell me what you have in mind?"

"When I know myself."

The German produced a case and extracted one of his Russian cigarettes. "But Vaughan provides an essential ingredient, I think."

"Oh, yes." Pascoe closed the file and replaced it in his briefcase. "Perfect for our purposes. A highly trained professional soldier. He speaks German as well as he does English—rather better, in fact. Also excellent Russian and passable Chinese. A legacy of nearly two years in that prison camp in Manchuria."

"A killer by trade and by instinct."

"But with brains. A combination not always to be found." Teusen shook his head. "A great tragedy, what happened to Vaughan. A brilliant career in ruins—and for what?"

"He did his duty as he saw it."

"You sympathize with him, I think?"

"Men like Vaughan are like the hangman," Pascoe said. "They carry the guilt for the rest of us. It takes a rather special brand of courage to do that."

"You think he was right to do what he did?"

"Not necessarily, but *he* did, and that's what's important."

"So did the SS."

Pascoe smiled slightly. "Point taken, but in this present situation, it's a purely academic one. Whether he was right or wrong to do what he did out there doesn't concern me. I need him now. That's all that matters."

They landed at Bitterfeld twenty minutes later. There were four hangars, and the watchtower was still intact, but the grass between the runways was waist-high, and there was an air of desolation to everything.

A black Mercedes was parked in front of the old

operations building, and a small, heavily built man in a hunting jacket and forester's hat got out quickly as the Hawker Siddeley taxied toward him.

Teusen was first out and shook hands. "This is Werner Böhmler, the field agent for the area."

"Herr Professor—a pleasure."

Pascoe had turned and was looking out across the runway. "This place is entirely unused, you say?"

"That's right."

"Good." Pascoe opened the rear door and got into the Mercedes. "Can we get started then?"

Father Conlin opened his eyes. Not that it mattered, for it was still dark. For a little while he lay there, his body so numb that he couldn't even feel the springs of the iron cot digging into his back, and then something clicked in his brain and he was filled with a sense of dreadful unease. Of some horror beyond understanding, crouched there on the far side of the cell.

He got to his feet, took a hesitant step forward, and blundered into a stone wall. He took two paces back, hand outstretched, and touched the other side. Three cautious paces brought him to the rear wall. From there to the door was four more. He was in a stone womb. Unbelievably cold. There was no beginning, no end. Only the fact of it.

I am a man. I exist, he thought. *I will not give in.* He lay down carefully on the bed and started to pray.

When Klein went to Van Buren's office at the University Medical Center in East Berlin, there was only a young medical secretary available, a pretty dark-haired girl in a white hospital coat.

"Colonel Klein," he said.

She jumped at once. "Oh, yes, Comrade. Professor Van Buren is expecting you. If you'd follow me, please."

She led the way along the corridor, knocked at a door at the far end, opened it, and motioned him through into a small room, neatly carpeted and furnished only with several easy chairs. Van Buren was sitting in one of them by what appeared to be a window looking into the next room. It was in semi-darkness, but as Klein approached, he saw that there was a man in there, strapped into what looked like a dentist's chair.

"What is this?" he demanded.

"General observation. I like to see how my patients are going on," Van Buren told him. "He can't see us, by the way."

In the other room, a picture appeared on a screen. A young girl—very young and extremely pretty. Suddenly the shadowy figure in the chair bucked, straining against the straps, and from the sound box above the window there issued a cry of agony. Van Buren reached up and turned it off and slid a panel across the window.

"What was that?" Klein demanded.

"One of the techniques we try here. The subject has a long history of rape, and he prefers them young. We show him suitable pictures, which naturally arouse him, then administer severe electric shock. If he's a bad boy, he gets hurt, you see. Childish, but extremely effective. The trouble is, it takes rather a long time."

"My God," Klein said.

"There are also several drugs which can be used in place of the electric shock to induce severe vomiting, but that becomes rather unpleasant for everyone. What did you want to see me about?"

"We're having trouble with the Vatican."

"To do with Neustadt?"

"Yes. It's still in the hands of the Ministry of State Security, so I can't give you full details yet. I'll see you this evening. Seven o'clock at my office."

"All right." Van Buren lit a cigarette. "I'm glad you looked in. I wanted a word with you about Conlin."

Klein sat down. "Nothing wrong, is there?"

"No, but I think there's something we should get straight. There isn't enough time for a thought reform program."

Klein paused in the act of lighting one of his cheroots. "But you told Ulbricht . . ."

"What he wanted to hear."

There was something close to horror on Klein's face. "Then what are you going to do?"

"To Conlin?" Van Buren said calmly. "Oh, break him, I think. It's all there's time for. Reduce him to a state where he'll simply do as he's told."

"You think you can do that?"

"I've done it before. In my early days in Peking I saw Ping Chow break a Catholic priest very effectively by putting him in a cell with ten other prisoners. Ordinary criminals. They had to take turns at keeping him awake; otherwise, they didn't get fed. Within a couple of weeks, he was so disorientated that he was agreeing to anything his interrogators told him."

"Then why aren't you down there at Neustadt now? Why are you here?"

"I've left Conlin to rot for a week in his own filth in total darkness," Van Buren said. "He comes out on the seventh day; then we start."

Klein stood up, walked nervously to the door, then turned. "I hope you know what you're doing, Harry, because if you don't . . ."

"Then both our heads will roll. I'll see you later."

Van Buren turned, slid back the screen, and peered into the other room, and Klein opened the door and left hurriedly.

Peter Bülow was a large, pleasant-looking man, in spite of the bad shrapnel wound on his right cheek. He was a sergeant in the people's police in command of the border post at Flossen, not because he was a good Communist, but because the small farm on which his parents had raised him had found itself a quarter of a mile on the wrong side of the line at the end of the war.

Flossen itself was half a mile into West Germany. Bülow had attended the village school as a boy. Half his relatives still lived there, which explained his frequent visits. And there was the village store, of course, where he could obtain delicacies not so readily to hand on his own side.

But that morning he had a special mission, for it was his daughter Lotte's birthday. He had ordered a dress for her a month previously. Something very special from Hamburg to surprise her with at her party that evening.

He hurried up the single street past the inn and crossed to the store. He went inside and unbuttoned his jacket.

Müller, the storekeeper, looked up and smiled.

"Ah, there you are, Peter. I was beginning to think you'd forgotten."

They were second cousins, and Bülow grinned as he shook hands across the counter. "Has it come?"

"Of course—I'll get it for you."

He went into the back. Bülow walked to the window and peered out into the street, taking out his pipe. He put a match to it and, turning, found Böhmler and Bruno Teusen standing behind the counter.

"Hello, Peter," Teusen said.

"Herr Oberst." Bülow was no longer smiling.

"I'd like a word with you."

"No." Bülow put a hand out as if to ward him off. "No more. You promised."

"I know, Peter, but this is special," Teusen said.

"How special?"

It was Pascoe who answered him, pushing back the curtain at the rear entrance to join them. "Fifty thousand marks."

Bülow gazed at him in astonishment, then turned back to Teusen, who said, "Plus asylum for you and your family in West Germany, a good job and housing guaranteed."

"Or the same in the USA if you prefer it," Pascoe added.

There was a moment's silence. Böhmler said, "You would do well to listen to the Herr Professor, Peter."

"No, thanks. For that kind of offer this has to be big—too big for me."

"Not at all," Böhmler said. "All you have to do is let a little traffic through on a few selected occasions during the next three or four weeks. For the next month you and young Hornstein will be on the night shift. I know that. Six P.M. till six in the morning. Is he still sneaking over twice a week to visit the mayor's daughter?"

"The same terms for him," Pascoe said.

Bülow shook his head violently. "I won't do it. We nearly got caught passing that agent of yours through in March, and there's Sergeant Hofer to consider. He's got a mind like a steel trap. A solid party member, too."

"He'll be on the day shift," Böhmler pointed out. "What he doesn't know won't hurt him."

"No," Bülow said.

Teusen sighed. "I could get very unpleasant, Peter. I could point out that a word in the ear of the right person in Berlin about your activities on our behalf in the past would have the SSD on your back before you knew it."

"You wouldn't," Bülow said.

"No, because there isn't any need—tell him, Werner."

Böhmler said, "The good times are coming to an end, Peter. We know of a secret meeting at highest government level last week in which Ulbricht ordered a crash program aimed at strengthening the border in rural areas, with the specific intention of keeping your lot firmly on your own side."

"No more visits to the store," Teusen said.

"It's also been decided as a matter of policy to transfer people like you, men with local connections, to duties in the east. By autumn, all men on frontier guard duty will be from other parts of the republic."

"You're lying," Bülow said, but there was no conviction in his voice.

"Don't be stupid," Böhmler told him. "You've been expecting something like this for a year now."

"And now it's come, and here we are throwing

you a lifeline," Teusen told him. "You should be grateful. Hornstein will be interested, would you say?"

Bülow sighed wearily and sat down in a chair by the counter, shoulders slumped. "Yes—I've been expecting him to defect for months now. He's crazy about the Conrad girl. He'll jump at a chance like this."

"Excellent."

"My wife, my daughter?"

"It will all be taken care of. When you come over for the last time, so do they—and Hornstein, of course."

"All right—what do you want me to do?"

"For the moment, nothing," Teusen said. "Werner will be in touch with you again during the next few days."

"Very well." Bülow got to his feet. He seemed to have aged ten years since entering the shop and looked very tired. "Can I go now?"

Müller moved forward from the back of the store hesitatingly, holding a large package, which he placed on the counter. His face was grave.

"The dress. And there's a ham and a bottle of wine with my compliments."

Bülow gazed at him blankly, and then something clicked. "Of course, how stupid of me. Thank you."

"I'm sorry, Peter," Müller said.

"For what?" Bülow replied bitterly. "Russia was worse, but only just."

He went out. Teusen moved to the window and watched him go. "We use people," he said. "Even when we think we're in the right, we use people as if they were paper coffee cups to serve our purpose and be tossed on one side."

"Yes," Pascoe said calmly. "War *is* hell, and make no mistake, my dear Bruno. That's exactly what we're engaged in." He glanced at his watch. "And now I think we'd better be getting back to Berlin. I've seen what I want to see here."

In East Berlin toward evening, storm clouds moved in across the city, and in Klein's office, Harry Van Buren, seated behind the massive desk, worked his way through Erich Hartmann's file. Klein was standing at the window peering out morosely and drinking coffee.

"My God," he said. "What weather. I've never known such a June." He turned. "What do you think?"

Van Buren held Hartmann's photo under the light. "Interesting face. He and Ulbricht would have a lot in common."

Klein frowned. "I don't understand."

"Religious obsession on the one hand, political on the other. Two sides of the same coin."

Klein, who had been raised a Catholic, was aware of a faint anger stirring somewhere deep inside. Strange how one could never quite erase the imprint of those early years.

"You would dismiss religion so lightly?"

"I don't see why not. Fear of the dark—a rage against dying. People have to have something, and if there's nothing there, they invent it. When was this application made?"

"Late yesterday, to the appropriate department. They passed it straight to me."

"I like the phraseology." Van Buren picked up

the typed letter. "Father Erich Hartmann, appointed Vatican inspector general to report on the state of the church at Neustadt to the Holy Father." He helped himself to a cigarette from the box on the desk. "Presumably you're going to tell them where to put their application?"

"No." Klein shook his head. "Not possible."

Van Buren glanced up sharply, a look of genuine astonishment on his face. "But this is nonsense. That church in Neustadt has been closed down tight for five years now, and they haven't done a thing about it. This application isn't just coincidence. It means they know we've got Conlin."

"Exactly."

"And Hartmann. Good God, you know what he is. A Vatican spy. It's here in your own file."

"Of course I do," Klein said calmly. "And Hartmann's superiors know that I do."

"Oh, I see," Van Buren said. "It has a certain ring to it, I must admit. A kind of lunatic logic."

"Politics, Harry," Klein said. "Let me explain. Last year we signed the Secret Treaty of Accord with the Vatican. A kind of blueprint for future relations."

"Which doesn't mean a thing. You're still screwing the Catholic church into the ground at every chance you get."

"But we have to continue some sort of dialogue at governmental level. A political decision on the part of the Council of Ministers."

"Under the inspired leadership of our esteemed comrade chairman."

Klein ignored the remark. "Relations with the Vatican have altered considerably. Unavoidable with a man like Pope John at the helm. His Peace on Earth encyclical in April was warmly received, I must remind you, not only in the West but as far east as Moscow."

"Beautiful," Van Buren said. "I hope you're all having a fine time. But underneath all that garbage, I presume what you're really trying to tell me is that Hartmann comes to Neustadt whether I like it or not. Do you actually expect some sort of rescue attempt?"

"Not really. I think he's going there to sniff out what he can, that's all. I'll hold him off for ten days."

"That's very kind of you."

"Naturally he'll have a Section Six operative tugging at the skirt of his cassock. A man called Schaefer. He'll have orders to report to you."

"That's it then." Van Buren got up belting his coat and crossed to the door.

Klein sat down behind the desk. "Cheer up, Harry. After all, what can Hartmann hope to accomplish? I would have thought you might find the situation quite amusing."

"Just what I'm looking for, something to lighten the more manic periods of my daily round."

He opened the door. Klein said, "I must say I'd like to be there at that first meeting. What will you say to him, Harry?"

"Oh, that's an easy one." Van Buren smiled. "Bless me, Father, for I have sinned."

When Vaughan opened the judas gate and went into the warehouse, everyone seemed to be there. Meyer, Teusen, Brother Konrad, and at the top of the steps in the glass-walled office he could see Charles Pascoe with Father Pacelli and a gray-haired man.

Meyer, who was pacing up and down, hurried forward. "You got my message?"

"I'm here, am I not?" Vaughan unzipped his jacket. "What is this, a board meeting?"

"Something like that," Teusen said without getting up from the coffin on which he was sitting with Konrad.

Vaughan nodded to the Franciscan. "Still here?"

Konrad smiled. "So it would seem."

"Who are the new arrivals?" Vaughan looked up to the office.

Teusen said, "The gray-haired one is Kurt Nordern, professor of forensic pathology at the university."

"Forensic pathology?" Vaughan said in astonishment. "Now what in the hell does he need him for?"

Teusen shrugged. "I presume that in his own good time he'll tell us."

Meyer smiled tightly. "More corpses."

"It comes to us all, Julius. It comes to us all," Vaughan told him cheerfully. "And the other one?" he asked. "Who's he?"

"Later, Simon," Teusen said.

Vaughan shrugged, lit a cigarette, and leaned against the side of the truck. There was silence, and then the office door opened and Pascoe appeared with Nordern.

"My thanks," he said in English. "I look forward to receiving your report, Herr Professor."

Nordern shook hands, then came down the steps, a tall, thin man with stooped shoulders in a tweed overcoat. He paused at the bottom, a slightly bemused look on his face, then pulled on a tweed hat that matched his overcoat, hurried to the gate, opened it, and disappeared into the night.

Pascoe looked down at them calmly. "Ah, there you are, Major. Good. We can get started then. If you'd kindly come up." And he turned and went back into the office.

On the wall were pinned a map of that section of the border stretching from Flossen to Neustadt and one of the large-scale military plans of the schloss and the village which Teusen had provided.

Pascoe said, "I'll take things step by step, gentlemen, and if you bear with me, I think you will see how several apparently disparate items join together to make a whole in the end."

No one said anything, and he carried on. "To start with, here just outside Flossen at Bitterfeld is a disused Luftwaffe fighter station which will serve as our base. The border post at Flossen itself is in our pocket. The Vopo sergeant and private who will form the night shift for the next twenty-eight days have agreed to come over. That gives us unrestricted access to the other side, within limits."

"And when you get there, what have you got?" Vaughan put in. "Around fifty miles to Neustadt, and most of that is Holstein Heath, one of the most sparsely populated areas in the country. A few woodcutters, a handful of farmers, and very little else."

Pascoe nodded. "I should imagine the traffic, such as there is, would tend to be Vopo military vehicles and prowler guards."

"Prowler guards?" Meyer said.

"Vopo motorcyclists with no set routine. Their brief is to roam the area at will, so that no one can ever be certain where they will be next."

Vaughan said, "In other words, anyone else passing through, even in an old potato truck, is going to stick out like a sore thumb."

"Oh, I don't know." It was Teusen who spoke. "We have a saying in the Harz Mountains. If you want to hide in a forest, you must pretend to be a tree."

"Exactly," Pascoe said. "I presume you are capable of riding a motorcycle, Major Vaughan?"

"I always did look better in uniform." Vaughan turned to Pascoe. "Nice one, Professor. Yes, I think I could manage that. What kind of machine? Cossack?"

"Yes," Teusen told him.

"Good," Pascoe said. "In principle, what I am saying is that any transport we use between Flossen and Neustadt will be of a military nature. Colonel Teusen assured me he can supply any kind of Vopo vehicle we need."

"No problem," Teusen said. "And the real thing, too. So many of them have come over to our side during the last couple of years."

"The map, of course, will have to be studied in detail, the roads committed to memory so that the chosen route and at least two alternatives to allow for unforeseen contingencies can be tackled by night at reasonable speed. Under most conditions, I see no reason why the trip from Flossen to the border should ever take longer than an hour and a half."

There was another of those pauses while everyone seemed to wait, and Vaughan said patiently, "All right, so now we're at Neustadt, where Conlin is being held . . ."

"By only twenty men."

". . . in a fortress so impregnable that when it

was used as a prison for officers, there wasn't a single recorded instance of escape, am I right, Bruno?" Teusen looked uncomfortable, and Vaughan carried on. "Look at it. That zigzag approach road, walls like cliffs, tunnel entrance, one guarded gate, then another. A panzer column would have difficulty getting in."

"But not a plumber or an electrician if they were needed," Pascoe said. "It isn't getting in that's the problem. It's doing it in such a way that you can come out with Conlin."

"All right, surprise me."

Pascoe indicated the plan of Schloss Neustadt again. "Three levels—and our information is that Conlin is kept on the lowest, which makes sense because conditions will be extremely bad down there. Now, look at this." He unrolled another plan. "During the war, when the schloss was an army group headquarters, there were considerable improvements made to the sewage system. Here, in the third level, not far from the cells, an inspection chamber gives access to a sewer pipe, concrete-lined and eight feet in diameter, dropping through several levels to the Elbe, which it never reached, by the way. According to the engineer's working report, work stopped a hundred and fifty yards from the river."

"Why?"

Teusen shrugged. "It was 1945, and the Russians were coming. No one needed army group headquarters anymore."

Vaughan looked down at the plan, a slight smile on his lips, for there was a certain black humor to the whole thing which rather appealed to him: the thought of those wretched army engineers laboring

away down there in the darkness while their whole
world collapsed above them.

"Which hardly helps Conlin."

"It does if you notice the interesting fact that
the tunnel passes close by the Home Farm, which
is the headquarters of the Franciscan Order of Jesus
and Mary at Neustadt," Pascoe pointed out. "There
is a large barn, as you can see, directly on the
boundary line. From there, sixty-five feet in a straight
line to break into the main sewer."

"Through a cemetery," Vaughan said to Meyer.
"Now you see why the forensic pathologist was
called in. I wonder just how many terminal diseases
can be caught digging through that kind of com-
post heap."

"Nothing that can't be handled with proper pre-
cautions and the right drugs," Pascoe said. "And as
Miss Campbell is at Neustadt, it does give us the
advantage of having a doctor on site."

"And who does the digging?" Vaughan turned
to Konrad. "Your people, is that the idea? All six
of you? And just how long do you expect it would
take?"

"A week," Pascoe said. "Ten feet down and easy
soil, so Brother Konrad informs me."

"Then what? So Conlin comes out through
this—this rabbit hole. How long before the blood-
hounds find their way to the farm?"

"By then the cupboard will be bare. Brother
Konrad and his friends come over, too."

Konrad smiled almost apologetically. "We were
nearing the end of things in any event. I do not think
we could survive another year with the kind of
political pressure mounted against us."

Vaughan nodded toward Pacelli. "Who's this?"

"My name is Pacelli," the old man said. "I represent the Society of Jesus in this affair. Of which Father Conlin is a member."

"What's he talking about?" Meyer looked bewildered.

"Jesuits, Julius," Vaughan told him. "Soldiers of Christ. They had such a fun time playing devious games with Elizabeth the First that they've never been able to stop since. And where does your little lot fit in, Father?"

"We will arrange for one of our representatives in East Berlin, Father Hartmann, to visit Neustadt to report on the state of the church there, which has been closed for five years."

"And what do you hope to gain from that?"

"Nothing," Pacelli said serenely.

"East German Intelligence would be justified in expecting someone," Pascoe said.

"So you give them Hartmann?"

"To keep them occupied."

"And he's happy about that?"

"Perfectly," Pacelli interjected.

"Good for him." Vaughan shrugged. "That's it then. What happens now?"

"Brother Konrad returns tomorrow the same way he came. You follow in two, perhaps three days, but we can discuss that later. There is one other point. It occurs to me that Conlin's state of health is likely to be such that once out, it might be advisable to get him west as fast as possible. I see here on the map, a quarter of a mile south of the farm, a meadow beside the river."

"Water Horse Meadow," Konrad said. "I don't know where it got the name. It is good, firm ground.

Three hundred yards of open space between trees."

"I understand it's not unknown for light aircraft to fly in by night on occasion under their radar screen to bring people out," Pascoe said. "Would you know anyone that foolhardy, Bruno?"

Teusen shook his head. "No, but they would."

Pascoe waited, and Vaughan sighed and looked at Meyer. "Any idea what Max is doing these days?"

"Max," Pascoe said, "is good, I presume."

"The Luftwaffe thought so."

"A long time ago."

"He did shoot down seventy-two Lancasters by night, and some things you never forget."

"Can you find him for me?"

"I can try."

"Good. As soon as possible, please." Pacelli stood up. "If there is nothing else, I'd like to get back. I've work to do."

"Of course," Pascoe said. "Major Vaughan, perhaps you could drive Father Pacelli back to the Catholic Information Center?"

The old man shook his head. "Not necessary. Just point me in the direction of the nearest underground station, Major. I need the exercise."

"I wanted a chance to talk to you, Major Vaughan," Pacelli said as they walked along the canal toward the bridge.

"So?" Vaughan said.

"You were a prisoner of war in Korea, I understand. The Chinese had you for two years, so you're something of an expert on Pavlovian and similar techniques. What will happen to Conlin?"

"I can only guess," Vaughan said. "Because this isn't a normal case."

"Explain."

"Our friend Van Buren doesn't have much time. And time is what you need for really good long-term results with thought reform. He's got to go for quick answers, possibly helping things along with drugs. But a lot can be done in two or three weeks if you can find the right soft spots."

"And Father Conlin is an old man and in ailing health."

"That could be in his favor. They don't want him dead, remember. Another thing—they'll have to go easy on the physical side of things and not just because the bruises would show. I wouldn't have thought his heart would take too much at his age."

"So—how will Van Buren begin?"

"Sensory deprivation, I'd say. A week or so in a dark room cut off from human contact. Can lead to a feeling of alienation so terrible that some subjects will grab the first hand that reaches out."

"This was done to you?"

"Several times."

"And you survived?"

"Let's say the cracks don't show." Vaughan smiled. "I've a vivid imagination, Father. The Irish bit of me. I used to make up stories to pass the time."

Pacelli smiled. "Father Conlin will survive."

"For a while. On the other hand, I don't know what his soft spots are. If Van Buren finds them, then he could be in trouble."

"And you think Father Conlin has these weaknesses? These soft spots you speak of?"

"He's a man, isn't he? What is it the Bible says? Conceived in wickedness? We're all touched by original sin, I thought that was what you lot preached." They had reached the bridge and went up the steps. "Follow your nose on the other side, and you'll find an underground station about a quarter of a mile along the road."

Pacelli turned to face him. "So you will see this thing through, Major Vaughan, but not for the money, I think."

Vaughan stopped smiling. "What then?"

"Nor the young lady. Oh, in part perhaps, but that would be too easy an answer. No, Major, you can be a hard man, your record proves it, but this is only surface stuff. The protecting shell. Underneath is the boy who crewed his father's barge that long, long summer on the Thames and never wanted it to end. The boy who found life more corrupt than he had hoped."

"You go to hell," Vaughan said harshly, and he turned and went back down the steps.

SEVEN

In Rome on the following day, His Holiness Pope John XXIII died at the age of eighty-one. In his bedchamber at the Vatican Palace, the circle of kneeling cardinals chorused the De Profundis, first of the millions who, throughout the world, would mourn the best-loved Pope of modern times.

In his office at the Collegio di San Roberto Bellarmino, the father general of the Jesuits was standing at the window when there was a light tap at the door and Father Macleod entered.

"You wanted me, Father?"

"Yes—Father Pacelli. Contact him in Berlin. He is to return with all possible speed."

"And Father Hartmann?"

"Is Father Pacelli's concern," the father general replied, without looking around.

The door closed softly, and he dropped to his knees and began to pray for the repose of the soul of the man who had started life as Angelo Giuseppe Roncalli.

Pacelli was standing impatiently at the window of his office at the Catholic Information Center in West Berlin when the battered little Volkswagen turned into Budapesterstrasse and pulled in at the curb below. The old priest gave an exclamation of relief, and Vaughan, who had been sitting in a chair in the corner reading a newspaper, got to his feet and joined him at the window.

"So that's him," he said as Hartmann got out and crossed the road to Schaefer, who was pulling his motorcycle up on its stand.

"And that's Schaefer, his Section Six man."

"They seem pretty chummy."

"You're sure you can handle him?"

Vaughan nodded. "I should think so."

"Good. I would offer you my blessing, but somehow I do not think it would be well received." The old priest smiled and held out his hand. "I can only wish you luck then, Major Vaughan."

"Which always helps," Vaughan said, and went out.

After a while there was a tap, the door opened again, and Hartmann entered.

"Ah, there you are, Erich."

"Father."

He was carrying a leather briefcase, which he placed on the desk. Pacelli said, "You've heard the news?"

Hartmann stared at him blankly. "News, Father?"

"The chair of Peter is vacant, Erich. The Pope is dead. I received word only an hour ago."

Hartmann was visibly shocked and crossed himself automatically. Pacelli sat down behind the desk. "You were successful?"

"Yes, Father." Hartmann opened the briefcase,

produced a large official-looking envelope, and passed it across.

Pacelli opened it and unfolded the document it contained. "Excellent," he said. "And countersigned by the minister himself."

"You will notice that I am not permitted to proceed to Neustadt for several days."

Pacelli shrugged. "So they delay things as long as possible. It was to be expected."

"And I am also to consider myself at the orders of the military governor for the district."

"Who will probably be Van Buren." Pacelli nodded, folded the permit, and handed it back. "I had hoped to stay to see you through this thing, Erich, but now I must return to Rome. You understand."

"Yes, Father." Hartmann hesitated, then said carefully, "The new situation in Rome. Does it change things?"

"Will the new Pope approve, do you mean?" Pacelli smiled coldly. "I think not, if the candidate who immediately springs to mind succeeds. He was once heard to say that he had little time for the Mafia, whether it was in or outside the church."

"And that is how he sees our order?"

"The Society of Jesus has always had its enemies, Erich, you know that. Those who object to our power, our influence."

"So, your orders in this matter could be countermanded?"

"Not if we move fast. There are eighty-two members of the Sacred College who should be present at the conclave in the Sistine Chapel when the new Pope is elected. Cardinal Mindszenty can't come, he's still trapped in the U.S. legation in Budapest, and the primate of Ecuador is too old to travel, but the rest will come, from every corner of the globe, and that will take time."

"How long?"

"A fortnight at the earliest, probably closer to three weeks before we see a Pope in Rome again."

"And the general plan concerning Father Conlin is well advanced now?"

Pacelli nodded. "At our last meeting I mentioned an Englishman to you—Professor Charles Pascoe."

"I remember."

"He is now in complete charge—*of everything*." Pacelli emphasized the phrase. "From now on you will take your orders from him. A meeting is arranged for you this afternoon, when the entire operation will be explained in detail. I think you'll find that Pascoe has an aptitude for this sort of thing."

"And Schaefer?" Hartmann walked to the window. "What about him?"

Pacelli joined him. "No problem. When you leave here, go down to the basement garage. You'll find an old truck there with Meyer and Company painted on the side. Just climb in the back, and you'll be taken to meet Pascoe." He smiled and placed a hand on the younger man's shoulder. "Are you frightened, Erich, at the prospect of Neustadt?"

"No, Father."

Pacelli sighed. "No, I didn't really think you would be, and in some ways, that's a pity."

"Father!" Hartmann hesitated, and Pacelli knew that he was debating whether to ask for a blessing.

Pacelli said gently, "You'd better go now, Erich. Professor Pascoe will be waiting."

Hartmann went out. Pacelli crossed to the window. Schaefer was pacing up and down under the trees, collar turned up, looking thoroughly miserable.

Pacelli felt sorry for him, but that would never do. He went back to his desk and started to pack his small case.

The basement garage was surprisingly large. It contained a half-dozen cars and the truck, as Pacelli had indicated. Hartmann approached the rear and started to climb over the tailboard as ordered. He hesitated, then walked around to the front and peered into the cab.

Vaughan leaned back in the driver's seat, cap over his eyes. He pushed it up and sighed. "In the back," the man said. "Rule number one in this game, always do as you're told."

Without a word, Hartmann turned, went around to the rear, and climbed over the tailboard. He sat down on the floor, his back against the cab, well out of view, and a moment later, the truck moved away.

In Teusen's study, Hartmann sat at the desk and worked his way through the last of the files Pascoe had given him—the one concerning Simon Vaughan. He closed it and leaned back with a sigh, running his hands over his eyes.

The door opened, and Pascoe entered. "Finished?"

"Yes."

"So—now you know as much as I do, Father. Our intentions in the matter. The background details of those you will be working with."

"Yes—most interesting. This Major Vaughan, for instance."

"You don't approve?"

"His motives worry me."

"I'm not interested in whether a man is a thief, Father. Only in whether he's a reliable thief. Vaughan works for wages. That makes him very reliable indeed."

There was a knock at the door, and Teusen looked in. "Konrad is here, Charles. He's ready to go."

"Good. Show him in."

Konrad entered. In his corduroy trousers, reefer coat, and tweed cap, he looked more like a workman than ever.

"Father Hartmann, this is Brother Konrad of the Franciscan Order of Jesus and Mary at Neustadt."

The two men shook hands. "You return to Neustadt today?" Hartmann inquired.

"No, only to East Berlin. I shall spend the night at my sister's house. Go on to Neustadt tomorrow."

"What situation will I find there?" Hartmann asked. "There are still good Catholics in the village, I presume?"

"Plenty, but it's the old story. You can't be a good party member and go to church at the same time. You know what happened at Holy Name, do you?"

"Yes, it was closed five years ago. Lack of support was the official excuse."

"The last priest was Father Honecker. A marvelous man and much loved. He was eighty and very frail, and the district commander was displeased because his congregation was so large. Honecker welcomed everyone, you see. It didn't matter to him if you were a party member or not."

"What happened?"

"There was a famous cross at Holy Name—

medieval, I think—named the Cross of St. Michael, in oak with a marvelous carving of Our Saviour on it. It stood in a stone socket by the altar. One night the district commander had it removed and taken down to the bottom of the hill and planted in a grove of trees by the Elbe. Honecker went to see him. He was told that the church stayed shut until the Cross of St. Michael was restored to its rightful place. The only stipulation was that Father Honecker had to carry it himself, which, as the thing weighed around a couple of hundred-weight, was hardly likely."

"He tried, of course."

"And died of a heart attack."

There was a silence, and beyond Konrad, Hartmann was aware of Vaughan in the doorway.

Pascoe said, "Yes, well, we mustn't detain you, Konrad." He picked up an envelope from the desk and handed it to the Franciscan. "That's for Dr. Campbell, Professor Nordern's report."

"Good." Konrad slipped it into his breast pocket and turned to Vaughan. "So—I will expect you when? The day after tomorrow?"

"I don't see why not," Vaughan said.

Konrad turned to face them all and bowed in a strangely old-fashioned way. "Gentlemen."

He went out. Pascoe said to Hartmann, "Right, Major Vaughan will take you back to the Catholic Information Center now, and this is what I want you to do."

Schaefer was out of cigarettes, cold, and thoroughly miserable when Hartmann came out of the Catholic

Information Center and crossed the road to join him.

Schaefer managed a smile. "There you are, Father. Can we go home now?"

"Sorry, Horst," Hartmann said. "I'm afraid I'm going to have to stay the night. I hope it won't inconvenience you too much."

"It won't have to, will it?"

Schaefer tried to sound injured, but women were his one great weakness, and his pulse had already quickened at the prospect of the streetwalkers who patronized the Astoria Hotel. He could see the entrance now, a hundred yards down on the other side of the road.

"I'll have to have your car keys, Father."

"Of course." Hartmann gave them to him. "There's one other thing I wanted to mention. Next Sunday . . ."

"You go down to Neustadt, some village or other that God forgot on the edge of Holstein Heath. Yes, I had heard, Father. The office does like to keep me informed about little things like that."

"How very efficient of them. I could be there for a couple of weeks, I'm afraid."

"The country air will be good for me. I smoke too much."

"And your wife?"

"She'll be fine. The baby isn't due for another three months, and besides, she has her mother living with us now. Another good reason to get away for a while. I'll see you in the morning, Father."

He kicked his BMW down off the stand and pushed it along the pavement toward the Astoria, and Hartmann hurried back across the road. When he went into the office on the first floor, Vaughan and Meyer were standing by the window.

"He took it quite well," Hartmann told them.

"Is that a fact?" Vaughan said. "Julius, take Father Hartmann to Bruno's place. Come back for me in an hour."

Hartmann looked puzzled. "You're staying here?"

"That's right."

Vaughan ignored him, intent on Schaefer down there, almost at the hotel. Hartmann hesitated, then followed Meyer out. Schaefer was at the Astoria now. He parked the BMW outside, locked the rear wheel with a chain and padlock, and went in. Vaughan brought a chair to the window, lit a cigarette, and settled himself down to wait.

When Schaefer went into the Astoria's tiny bar, he saw, to his disappointment, that it was quite empty except for the hotel's proprietor: Willi Scheel, a grossly fat man who was never seen anywhere else except perched on a stool behind the zinc cash register reading the sports papers.

He looked up. "Herr Schaefer. Nice to see you. You're staying, I hope?"

He reached for a bottle of Cognac, opened it, and poured some into a glass, which he pushed across.

"Just for tonight, Willi." Schaefer took the Cognac down in one swallow. "I'll have a pack of cigarettes. Trade a little slack?"

"Early yet," Scheel told him. "They'll be packed in here like sardines in another couple of hours with the weather like it is." He touched the lapel of Schaefer's coat with one podgy hand and shuddered. "You're wet through. What you need is a hot bath."

"Sounds good," Schaefer said.

Scheel raised his voice. "Jutta? Where are you? Get in here." He poured Schaefer another Cognac.

"Jutta?" Schaefer asked. "New, is she?"

Scheel nodded. "God knows, it's difficult enough to get decent help these days, but this one is the limit. An absolute slut. Around anything in trousers she's like a bitch in heat."

Schaefer drank a little of his Cognac. "Is that so?"

"You'll have to watch yourself with this one." Scheel smiled amicably.

"Yes, what do you want?"

The voice was hoarse, petulant. Schaefer turned and found a young woman standing in the entrance to the bar. She was small with high cheekbones and almond-shaped eyes and had the face of a corrupt child. Her black dress was far too short, crumpled, and soiled. The one incongruity was the shoes, which were black patent leather with immensely high heels.

Schaefer almost choked on the rest of the Cognac as Scheel said, "Take Herr Schaefer up to number nine and run him a bath. You can take your break then." He pushed the bottle of Cognac across the bar to Schaefer. "Better take this, do you good. Bring on a sweat when you're in the bath, eh?"

He started to laugh, and Schaefer took the bottle, throat dry, and hurried after the girl. She was already halfway up the stairs, the skirt straining at the seams across her buttocks, and there were runs in her black stockings. He stood close behind her as she fumbled with the key in the door and she pushed back against him and he felt the same old excitement surging inside him that never failed.

She turned to look at him calmly. "Better get that coat off quick. You'll catch your death. I'll turn the bed down for you."

Schaefer put down the bottle and unbuttoned his coat, and she leaned across the bed to turn back the coverlet, her skirt sliding back to expose bare flesh at the top of the dark stockings. It was more than he could stand, and he seized her from behind, his hands sliding over her breasts.

"Naughty," she said as he pushed against her. "You'll catch your death, I warned you. What you need is a good stiff drink to warm you up."

"And then?" he demanded.

"We'll see."

She went into the bathroom and came back with a glass, which she filled almost to the brim. He was already down to shirt and trousers.

She held out the glass. "There we are, sweetheart. A nice big one, just to slow you down. I mean, you'd like that, wouldn't you?"

He almost choked, getting it down, and then he dropped the glass and pulled her to the bed, sprawling across her thighs, his hands at the buttons of her dress. His fingers felt thick and clumsy, and the buttons refused to obey. She was talking to him, but he couldn't hear what she was saying, and then she just wasn't there at all.

The girl adjusted her dress, then went to the window, opened it, and leaned out. She came back to the bed, searched in the pocket of Schaefer's jacket, found his cigarettes, and lit one. Then she lay on the bed beside him, propped against a pillow, and waited.

After a while the door opened and Vaughan entered. "Oh, very nice," he said in German. "The

Blue Angel, slightly run-down version, if that's possible."

The girl smiled, and her voice, when she spoke, was now crisp and very upper-class. "I don't know what you put in the bottle, but it's certainly knocked him cold. Only just in time, too. The original randy bull, that one."

Vaughan lifted one of Schaefer's eyelids. "Good for ten or twelve hours, I'd say. Good stuff, but you need a strong heart to stand it. Hope he qualifies."

"You bastard," she said.

He went through Schaefer's jacket and found the wallet. It contained a few hundred marks, a photo of Margarete and the children, army discharge papers in the rank of sergeant, Schaefer's SSD identity card, and various social security papers.

He replaced them in the wallet. "I'll have this back to you in two hours. Put it back in his jacket; then you can go."

"Thanks very much."

"Are you working at the moment?"

"I've a television play next week and an audition in Munich the week after for a war picture."

"All go, isn't it?"

Vaughan went out, closing the door gently behind him. She lit another cigarette and leaned back, staring at the ceiling. Beside her Schaefer started to snore gently.

Teusen examined the identity papers in the light of his desk lamp and nodded in satisfaction.

"I told Jutta she could have the wallet back within a couple of hours," Vaughan said.

"No problem. I'll have one of my men deliver it."

"Good—I think she'd like to get out of there. She's a good actress, but playing the whore on a television stage is one thing—the reality is something else again."

"You haven't said anything to Hartmann about this?"

"Didn't think he'd like it."

Teusen nodded. "Yes, he could be a problem, that one."

"Where's Pascoe?"

"At the American embassy. They had a call booked for him on the scrambler to the Secretary of State. What are you going to do now?"

"Pascoe is still keen on the idea of using a lightplane to bring Conlin out?"

"Yes."

"Then I'd better find Max Kübel and quick."

"Do you anticipate any problems there?"

"Not really. You know how Max moves around, but Julius has put a few feelers out. Maybe he's come up with something."

They went into the other room. Hartmann was standing on the terrace, looking out across the city. Meyer was on the telephone. He replaced it and turned to Vaughan.

"That was Ziggy. He doesn't know where Max is playing this week, but it seems he's been using Madame Rosa as post office."

"Playing?" Teusen looked puzzled.

"Piano," Meyer said. "He makes his rent money playing jazz in some of the clubs."

Vaughan said, "We'll call on Rosa and drop you off on the way, Father."

Hartmann said, "Perhaps I could accompany you? It sounds as if it could be interesting."

"Possibly even rough. Too rough for that collar."

Teusen went into his bedroom and returned with a black silk evening scarf, which he handed to Father Hartmann. "Whose side are you on?" Vaughan demanded.

Hartmann adjusted the scarf to conceal his clerical collar. "Satisfied, Major?"

"Why not?" Vaughan said. "It could be an interesting evening." And he led the way out.

Vaughan drove, the three of them crammed into the cab of the truck. Over the Kurfürstendamm, West Berlin's smartest street, towered the floodlit Kaiser Wilhelm Memorial Church.

"Berlin," Meyer said. "What a place. Would you believe it, Father, but a third of it is green? There are more than a hundred working farms within the city limits, twenty theaters, the Berlin Philharmonic."

"And a considerable variety on more fleshly levels of entertainment for those inclined," Vaughan added dryly.

"Still the finest city in the world to eat in."

"You wouldn't think the Gestapo chased him out of the place in '39," Vaughan said.

But Meyer ignored him. "It's a terrible thing for an old Jew to confess, Father, but I adore Berlin food, and it's anything but kosher, believe me."

Vaughan turned into a street of old-fashioned apartment houses, pulled in at the curb, and got out. He went up the steps and checked the cards.

Hartmann said, "You've been together some time?"

"Not really," Meyer said. "Simon was in the army; then he had a little trouble in the Far East."

"Yes, I know about that."

"He was chief of police in a little Arab state in the Gulf when I met him. He saved my skin."

"You think a lot of him."

"He's a good boy."

Vaughan called, "This is it."

He pressed the bell push, then spoke into the wall mike. As they arrived, the door clicked open, and he led the way inside. It was decent enough, the walls painted in cream, and there was carpeting on the narrow stairs. The apartment was on the first floor, and the brass plate on the door said ROSA— CHINESE ASTROLOGER.

"My God," Meyer said. "The people we deal with."

"You don't approve?" Hartmann asked.

"Astrology, Chinese or otherwise, is nonsense."

The door opened. The woman who stood there was very old. She wore a long black dress, gold earrings, and white hair was drawn back tightly from the parchment face. Her eyes were darkly luminous.

"When were you born?" she said to Meyer in a voice that was little more than a whisper. "December twenty-eighty or ninth?"

He was genuinely shocked. "Twenty-seventh."

"Typical Capricorn," she said. "If he was dying and they brought him a doctor, he'd ask to see his diploma."

Vaughan grinned. "I'd say that was a pretty accurate reading, wouldn't you, Julius? I'm looking for Max, by the way. Max Kübel. Ziggy Schmidt thought you might be able to help."

"Max?" she said. "You're friends of his?"

"Definitely."

"All right, come in."

The sitting room was warm, a good fire in the stove, two white cats sleeping in front of it. Untidy, but comfortable, and there were books everywhere.

She sat down at a circular mahogany table and motioned them to join her. "I thought you might have come for a reading."

It was Hartmann who answered. "And why not? A little something for your time. How much?"

"Any gift is welcome." She was looking at him intently, and he took out his wallet and produced a hundred-mark note. "Which year were you born? With the Chinese it is the year which is important."

"In 1930."

"Year of the Horse." She nodded. "Late April, I think."

"That's right."

"Horse Taurus, then. You serve a hard master. The hardest in the world to follow, I think." She reached forward and pulled the scarf to one side. "See, I am right."

"So it would appear."

"Driven by fire and by fire consumed. You must take care."

"Thank you, I will," he replied gravely.

She turned to Meyer, who held his hands in front of his face. "No, not a word. I don't want to listen to such nonsense."

"Don't waste your time," Vaughan said. "Try me. July 27, 1926."

"The tiger and the lion," she said. "Both beasts of prey, and all men fear the tiger by night. You walk on corpses, Major." She stood up. "I'm tired. You'll find Max at a club called Tabu in Joseph-strasse."

She walked out. Hartmann said softly, "Madame

Sosostris, the wisest woman in Europe. You are familiar with the quotation, Major?"

"Particularly the line which comes later," Vaughan replied. "'I do not find the Hanged Man.' I've a feeling she just did. Eliot knew what he was talking about."

"Eliot?" Meyer demanded. "Eliot who?"

"Never mind, Julius."

"This club—the Tabu. You know it?" Hartmann asked.

"The Berliner, Father, likes to boast that he can offer you anything from the most elegant nightclubs in the world to seedy bars that can't supply much more than an odor of urine and petty crime."

"And the Tabu?"

"It could be worse, but not much. Maybe we'd better drop you off on the way."

"Nonsense," Erich Hartmann said. "A necessary stage in my education, wouldn't you say, Major?"

EIGHT

During the Second World War there was an almost incredible superiority of German fighter pilots in terms of confirmed victories. The Luftwaffe's leading ace was credited with almost nine times as many victories as his British and American adversaries, and no fewer than 35 Germans had scores in excess of 150, which charmed circle did not include Max Kübel, who had ended the war with a score of 149.

He was only twenty years old when he first saw combat flying with the Condor Legion in Spain. In Poland he was shot down and parachuted to safety, the first of eight such occasions.

The heady summer of the Battle of Britain, when victory had seemed so near, had been followed by the eastern front. Shot down near Kiev on June 12, 1943, and taken prisoner by the Russians, Kübel escaped, seized a Yak fighter, and flew back to German-held territory.

This exploit earned him the Oak Leaves to his Knight's Cross and made him something of a matinee idol to the German people for some considerable time after. Forbidden to fly in combat, he had endured a desk job with the Luftwaffe inspectorate for almost a year before securing an active posting with a night fighter unit in the spring of 1944.

In September 1944 he had joined a test unit operating the Me262, at that time the most advanced jet fighter plane in the world. On the morning of the second of October that year, he crashed in flames near Hamburg and, on Göring's personal instructions, was flown to a hospital, at Weissach in Bavaria, which had developed special techniques in the treatment of half-cooked human flesh. It was March 1946 before he had been judged fit enough to emerge into the outside world again.

Seated at the piano in the Tabu, he seemed considerably younger than his forty-five years, with his fair hair and the insolent blue eyes that women found so appealing.

He looked rather dashing in the old black leather Luftwaffe flying jacket, and he was surrounded by girls on the stand, above the small dance floor. As Vaughan, Hartmann, and Meyer leaned over the balcony rail, he moved into a solid driving arrangement of "St. Louis Blues."

"He's good," Hartmann said.

"He'd agree with you. Max is a great one for self-advertisement. He'd wear his Knight's Cross if he thought he could get away with it."

Meyer sat down at the table, called over a waiter. "You want something to eat, you two?"

Vaughan glanced at Hartmann and shook his head. "Bottle of wine, maybe. Niersteiner. Something like that."

Kübel glanced up and caught sight of them and waved. Hartmann said, "Such a flight by night would require great courage."

"At Innsbruck they have one of the oldest ski jumps in the world. When you take off, you can see one of the city's cemeteries by the church at the bottom. If you're genius standard, you may just land in one piece three hundred and sixteen meters below." Vaughan lit a cigarette. "Max still does that kind of thing for fun. He was wounded so many times during the war, I think they must have taken his nerves out while they were at it."

Max Kübel stopped playing, and an accordionist took over. The club was crowded, mostly middle-aged men or older, and the girls were, on the whole, past their prime.

"Love for sale," Vaughan said.

"A strange phenomenon," Hartmann observed. "We always assume we can give it, but we usually mean on our own terms. And why should you assume that sin should shock me, Major? The average priest listens to more evil and wickedness in the confessional in a week than the average man experiences in a lifetime."

Kübel appeared at the head of the stairs at that moment. He paused to light a cigarette, then pulled a chair forward and joined them at the table.

"Simon, Julius." He examined Hartmann coolly, and then his eyes widened. He reached out and pulled the scarf to one side. "Good God."

"Don't worry, he isn't after your soul."

"Not this time, at any rate." The priest smiled and held out his hand. "Erich Hartmann."

The waiter was unloading his tray, and Kübel

reached for the bottle of wine. Vaughan said casually, "Are you still flying the Black Bitch?"

"Wouldn't part with her."

"Where do you keep her?"

"Private club field near Celle." Kübel's voice was lazy, but there was an alert wariness in his eyes.

"Black Bitch?" Hartmann asked.

"An old Fiesler Storch spotter plane that Max owns. Painted black for camouflage on certain night flights he's in the habit of making."

"Not anymore," Kübel said. "They're getting too good over there these days. One of their MiGs intercepted Heini Braun in his Henschel in April and blew him out of the skies."

"A load of Russian rubbish," Vaughan said. "You could handle that, an old-timer like you."

Kübel smiled beautifully. "I've decided to settle for the simple things in my old age, Simon. A good piano, a glass of wine, an accommodating lady . . ."

"Nothing more?" Hartmann said. "Is there nothing more than this that you would like in the whole world?"

Kübel turned to him. "Not really, Father. All is vanity. Isn't that what the Bible says?"

Vaughan leaned forward. "One flight, Max, sometime during the next two weeks. Neustadt on the Elbe, fifty miles inside the line. Twenty minutes in, twenty out. Two passengers."

"I told you, you're wasting your time."

"One hundred thousand marks, or any other currency you prefer."

"My God, who do you want to bring out, Walter Ulbricht?"

"Not quite."

Kübel's fingers tapped restlessly on the table as he thought about it. "Who would I be working for?"

"I can take you to meet him now."

A buxom woman of forty or so had been hovering anxiously for some time. Her makeup had been applied a little too carefully, and her blonde hair was piled up in several layers in a style that would have suited a younger girl, but she did have a certain undeniable appeal.

Kübel smiled. "Good, then we go to see this friend of yours, but later, Simon." He reached for the woman's hand. "First, I must dance with Frau Zeigler because she is the owner of this disgusting establishment and one must always keep the boss happy."

Hartmann and Vaughan leaned on the rail and watched Kübel and the woman move onto the crowded dance floor.

"I thought he'd bite," Vaughan said.

"You consider yourself a man of sound judgment, Major?"

"I understand men like Max," Vaughan said calmly. "They're a breed of their own."

"Why?"

"His is a world of the senses. You think about it; he just does it."

"And what exactly do you mean by it?"

"Politics or conversation. Philosophy or sex." Vaughan glanced down to the center of the dance floor, where Kübel was massaging Frau Zeigler's buttocks with some feeling. "See what I mean?"

"And you, Major Vaughan?"

"When I was fifteen, my old grandma told me there were three things to avoid like the plague: drink, cards, and loose women."

"Have you followed her advice?"

"Well, I don't play poker, Father, because I've nothing to lose."

"On the contrary," Hartmann told him. "I would have said everything."

Vaughan laughed out loud and turned to Meyer, who had just finished eating. "Hear that, Julius? There's hope for me yet. For God's sake, let's pick up Max and get out before our friend here starts preaching from the balcony."

Outside, rain poured down relentlessly. The street was badly congested because one side of it had been excavated so that the old sewer pipe could be renewed. There was some sort of commotion going on at the far end. A small crowd made up of workmen and passersby. A police car drew up and then another.

"Where did you park?" Kübel asked, looking up at the rain with distaste.

"In the next street," Vaughan said. "I couldn't get any closer."

As they neared the crowd, he caught at the arm of one of the workmen hurrying past. "What's going on? Car accident?"

"One of the pipe layers is trapped in the storm drain, and the water level's rising by the minute with this rain."

He pulled himself free, and Hartmann strode forward. The ease with which he forced his way through the crowd was immediately apparent, and for the first time Vaughan was aware of the size of the man, the breadth of his shoulders.

"What's he playing at?" Meyer demanded as Hartmann paused to speak to a police sergeant.

In the sewer excavation below, water swirled three feet deep in a chaos of mud and broken planking.

A figure emerged from the dark mouth of the pipe, followed by three others. They reached wearily, and willing hands pulled them up.

"I've ordered everyone out," the first man said. "Had to. There's only a couple of feet of headroom left between the waterline and the roof, and the level's rising all the time."

Hartmann said, "Is he still alive, the man in there?"

"Not for long. There was nothing we could do. A half-ton block on his legs."

"What's his name?"

"Günter Braun."

"Good." Hartmann handed his raincoat to Vaughan. "Hold this, please, Major."

He leaped down into the excavation, ducked inside the dark mouth of the tunnel, and disappeared.

"Is he mad?" Meyer cried.

Vaughan didn't bother to answer, simply shoved the priest's coat into Meyer's hands, grabbed a hand lamp from an astonished policeman, jumped into the pit, and went after Hartmann.

The pipe was perhaps five feet in diameter, and the level of the water was now closer to four than three. He found Hartmann at once, the beam from the lamp picking him out of the darkness, and the white, desperate face of Günter Braun, the waters of the storm drain running with such force that they were already washing across his head.

As the light revealed Hartmann's clerical collar, Braun cried, "That's all I need, a priest. Come to hear my confession, Father?"

"Not at all, my friend." Hartmann leaned over him, feeling under the water.

Vaughan crouched beside them. "You're wasting your time. That block weighs half a ton. You heard what the foreman said."

"Just hold his head," Hartmann said calmly. "And pull him clear when he tells you to."

"Mad!" Braun cried. "Crazy!"

The Jesuit took a deep breath and plunged his head under the surface. The mighty shoulders heaved, and then, incredibly, his face came up out of the water, carved in stone, every muscle taut.

Braun screamed, and Vaughan lurched backward, dropping the lamp, plunging them into darkness, aware of the man's body floating free. A moment later he emerged into the excavation crater to the astonishment of the crowd. There were excited cries, and men dropped in to help.

Max Kübel reached down to pull him up. Vaughan said, "Half a ton, Max. The bastard lifted half a ton with his hands underwater."

Hartmann had appeared beside them, soaked to the skin, his face streaked with mud. Meyer helped him into his raincoat, an expression of awe on his face.

For the moment, the attention of the crowd was concentrated on Braun as he was lifted into a waiting ambulance. Hartmann said, "I think we'd better go now, gentlemen, while the going's good."

"He's right," Meyer said. "The last thing he needs is his picture on the front page of the *Berliner Zeitung*."

Hartmann moved away quickly, and they followed. Kübel said, "A remarkable man, this priest of yours."

"I know," Vaughan said. "Just what I needed. Another holy fool."

NINE

Emerging from the Berlin air corridor into West Germany, Max Kübel banked south and took the Storch down to a thousand feet.

Pascoe, sitting next to him, said, "I don't fly myself, but it seems a beautiful plane to handle. Wasn't it one of these Skorzenys used to airlift Mussolini off Gran Sasso in '43?"

"That's right, and during the last week of the war Hannah Reitsch landed one under Russian artillery shells on the east-west axis in the heart of Berlin."

Bitterfeld was below them now, and as Kübel turned into the wind and dropped the Storch down in a landing that was pure perfection, the black Mercedes drove to meet them, Werner Böhmler at the wheel. Kübel switched off the engine, and they sat there in the silence.

"You've never used this place, not even in the war?" Pascoe asked.

Kübel shook his head. "No. You say the landing lights still work?"

"So I'm informed. Also the radio communication system in the watchtower is regularly serviced by the Luftwaffe in case of need."

"What for?" Kübel said. "Do those bastards at HQ think we might get lucky third time around?" He looked angry. "I always did hate their guts. Big men behind desks."

"Like me?" Pascoe said.

"Exactly like you, Professor. Different uniform."

"Of course," Pascoe said. "But to the business in hand. Could you make the kind of flight I require to Neustadt under the conditions described?"

"No problem."

"And those MiG interceptors the East Germans are flying in the area, they don't worry you?"

"Of course they do," Kübel said. "On the other hand, their radar can't reliably discriminate between low-altitude targets and ground clutter, which means that if I take this old bitch in under six hundred feet all the way, they won't even know I'm there. And those kids they have flying those things—all they have is flight training. No combat experience at all."

"So you'll do it?"

"I suppose so," he said morosely. "Deserted airfields always did bring out the worst in me. This is a bad place. Good men died here. Not that it matters. The same for all of us in the end." He shivered and opened the door. "Come on. You'd better introduce me to this man of yours."

In Washington, it was still very early in the morning, and President Kennedy, unable to sleep because of the pain in his back, sat at his desk in the Oval Office and worked on one of his speeches for the coming visit to Germany.

There was a light tap on the door, and Dean Rusk looked in. "I heard you were up."

The President put down his pen. "Anything important?"

"The Conlin affair. I've heard from Pascoe."

"Fine. Help yourself to coffee and bring me up to date."

Dean Rusk did so. When he was finished, the President said, "I suppose Pascoe knows what he's doing. God help them, that's all I can say."

Rusk stood up. "Oh, and General Gehlen has briefed Chancellor Adenauer on this one, as you requested. I think that just about covers everything for the moment."

"Good," the President said. "Keep me informed."

Rusk went out, and the President moved to the window, pulled a curtain, and peered outside. It was still dark—no sign of light at all—and for some unaccountable reason, he felt depressed. But that, as always, was something to be fought against. He went back to his desk, picked up his pen, and started to write again—*for unless liberty flourishes in all lands it cannot flourish in one.*

It was just before three o'clock in the afternoon when the cooperative produce truck pulled up in front of the inn at Neustadt and Konrad climbed down. Georg Ehrlich and Berg were standing in the porch talking, and the mayor smiled and waved.

"So, you're back, Konrad."

A Mercedes staff car crossed the square and drove past. Harry Van Buren was at the wheel, and a young woman in a Volkspolizei uniform sat beside him.

"My God," Berg said. "That's him—the new boss. Back a day early. I'd better get up there." He jumped into his pickup truck and drove away at once.

"Poor Heinrich," the mayor said. "For him, life is just one damn thing after another. How was Berlin?"

"As Berlin always is."

"And your sister?"

"About the same, thank you. How about here? Have the changes up at the schloss made any difference to things?"

"Not really. Some of the Vopos come in for a drink. The commander is a Captain Süssmann, and there's a sergeant major called Becker who's the original bastard. Still, it takes all sorts. Have you time for a coffee?"

"Not just now, thank you. Later perhaps. I'd like to see how things have been getting on at the farm," Konrad told him, and he went back down the steps.

Margaret Campbell was sitting by the window in her wheelchair, reading, when entered her room. She glanced up, and her delight was immediate.

"Brother Konrad. How marvelous to see you." She dropped her book to the floor and held out her hands.

Konrad said, "You're looking well. Are you walking yet?"

"A little. But never mind that. What happened?"

He walked to the window and looked up at Schloss Neustadt. "He's back."

"Who is?"

"Van Buren. He just drove through the village in his car. He had a Vopo lieutenant with him. A woman." He turned to face her. "I saw him, this Major Vaughan of yours."

"My Major Vaughan?" She was blushing now.

"Oh, yes, I think so. A remarkable man."

"But can he *do* anything?"

"You could ask him yourself. If everything goes according to plan, he should be here tomorrow night."

She went very pale and held out her hands again. "Tell me—tell me everything."

The room which Berg had shown Van Buren into was at the top of the main stairway leading up from the hall. It was comfortable enough, furnished as an office with a large, empty stone fireplace.

"Yes, this should do very well," Van Buren said. "Especially when you get a fire in here."

"This was always the general officer commanding's office both for our own people and the Russians when they were here."

Van Buren had been going through the desk drawers and smiled, holding up a Russian pineapple grenade. "Evidently. There's at least a dozen of these things in here. The last man in charge must have been the kind of paranoid who expected the paratroopers to drop in at dawn."

"Another advantage . . ." The caretaker moved to a door in the corner and opened it.

Van Buren joined him and peered down a dark stone spiral stairway. "Where does that go?"

"The rear courtyard. It makes a convenient private entrance in case of need."

He glanced nervously at the lieutenant standing by the window, a military overcoat, with fur collar, slung from her shoulders.

"Lieutenant Leber will require a room," Van Buren said coldly.

"Certainly, Herr Professor."

Süssmann hurried in, buttoning his tunic. "My apologies, Comrade. I was only just informed of your arrival."

"Lieutenant Ruth Leber. She'll be with us for a while."

"Comrade."

Van Buren said, "All right, Berg. See that she gets the best."

Berg picked up her suitcase and she followed him, and Süssmann watched her go, frank admiration in his eyes.

Van Buren said, "Let me make one thing clear. She isn't here to supply comforts for the troops. She's important to my plans for Conlin."

"As you say, Comrade."

"How is he?"

"I have no idea. As you ordered, he has been left in total isolation."

"Take me to him now."

On the third level it was cold and very damp, and the sentry outside the cell wore a winter great-coat and woolen scarf.

"Anything to report?" Süssmann demanded.

"No, Comrade. Not a sound."

"Open the trap," Van Buren ordered.

The sentry did so, and the American crouched. The stench from inside the cell was immediately apparent.

"Perhaps he's dead," Süssmann suggested.

"No, he's fine." Van Buren kicked the trap shut. "I have an instinct for these things. He's just as I want him, and tomorrow we get to work."

Margaret Campbell sat by the window in her wheelchair, reading Professor Nordern's report. It was succinct and to the point and quite fascinating.

She read it once, sat thinking about it for a while, then worked her way through it again.

Working in a cemetery in the manner indicated should not pose too many difficulties. The area, being close to the river, must be fairly damp. Most of the occupants will be poor to middle class in simple wooden coffins rather than lead.

If the working party were to come across a recent body—that is, one buried within, say, twelve months—things could be very nasty.

The coffin will have dropped to pieces owing to gas pressure. The body will have distended, cavities will have ruptured, and copious putrid gas and fluid will be permeating the soil. There will be streptococci present of a virulent kind. If any of the working party were to cut themselves, the result would be disastrous with the possibility of the kind of infection leading to gas gangrene very quickly.

Most of the bodies will have been there for some time. They will have become partly converted to adipocere, a fatty substance with an all-pervading stench. This is not dangerous, but the stench is appalling. There is a remote chance of infection by anthrax and TB but so remote as to be hardly worth considering.

Although the usually accepted depth for a grave is six feet, this is not always so. In this part of East Germany, nine feet is common, and in any case, changes in subsoil and compacting mean that human remains may be found up to twelve feet deep.

The sewer could be the dangerous place, depending on how it has been used. There are often pockets of CO_2 and methane—chokedamp and fire-damp. The first will suffocate. The second not only will suffocate, but will explode from a spark if conditions are right. The immediate risk is to fall in the effluent. Nausea, vomiting, and rapid death within hours can occur due to a gutful of human pathogens.

There is also the possibility of viral hepatitis. No obvious scratch is needed for this. It may be transmitted orally and manually. There is a 10 percent morbidity rate.

It cannot be stressed too strongly that any kind of scratch or abrasion contracted during any phase of this operation MUST receive immediate drug therapy. If this procedure is not followed, septicemia will be contracted within twelve hours, if not something worse.

So, there it was. She sat there with the notes on her lap, thinking about it. After a while the door opened, and Konrad came in.

"Ready?" he asked.

"As I ever will be."

He wheeled her out.

They were all seated around the wooden dining

table in the kitchen when Konrad wheeled her in.

God, but they are all so old, she thought as she looked from one serene face to another. *It just isn't possible.*

There was Franz, of course, who was only nineteen and built like a young bull, but Florian, Gregor, and Augustin were all in late middle age, and Brother Urban was just a frail old man with not long to go under any circumstances.

They were waiting. She said, "Brother Konrad has told me of your decision, and I think it's marvelous, but do you really think it's possible?"

"Oh, yes," Konrad said. "Gregor was an officer of engineers during the war. He considers it entirely practical."

"The soil in question is extremely light," Gregor said. "Easy enough to work. We have plenty of wood for props and a considerable amount of corrugated iron sheeting in the barn, which we can utilize as lining."

"Won't there be a problem with air supply?" Margaret asked.

"No, not at that depth. And the length of the tunnel will be quite short, remember. Naturally one will need to see how work progresses for the first day or two, but I think it could be managed in a fortnight at the outside, possibly sooner."

"All right," she said. "Fine, but there is one unusual aspect here: the fact that we'll be digging through a cemetery. This will involve certain fatal health risks. Brother Konrad has brought me a detailed report on what to expect, from a very eminent Berlin pathologist. I'd like to go through it with you now."

The trap at the bottom of Conlin's door was pushed open. Light gleamed as a plate was pushed through. The trap was closed again. He waited, listening, and heard the rustle in the darkness of the solitary rat which had taken to appearing each day exactly at mealtime.

The fear left him then, as quickly as it had come, and he chuckled and said softly, "Conditioned reflex, my friend. Pavlov would have approved of you."

Then he lay down on the cot again, folded his hands, and started to say his office from memory.

At Flossen, as darkness was descending, the heavy farm truck passed through the guard post on the West German side, through the neutral zone, and paused at the barrier pole, where Private Gerald Hornstein stood waiting, rifle slung from his shoulder. The door of the guard hut opened; Peter Bülow emerged and approached the truck.

Werner Böhmler was at the wheel. He wore an old army field cap, and filthy overalls and badly needed a shave. He held out his papers without a word. Bülow inspected them, then handed them back. He nodded to Hornstein, who raised the barrier, and Böhmler drove through.

Ten minutes later, he rolled to a halt at the side of the narrow road in thick forest, went around to the rear of the truck, and unfastened the high tailgate, lowering it so that it formed a sloping ramp to the road.

There was the roar of an engine firing inside, and Vaughan ran a Cossack motorcycle and sidecar down the ramp and braked to a halt. He wore a full Vopo uniform, heavy dispatch rider's raincoat, ankle-length, helmet, and heavy goggles, which just now were pulled up. Across his chest was suspended on a sling a Russian AK assault rifle with folding stock, a thirty-round magazine in place, ready for instant action.

"Well, you look the part anyway," Böhmler said.

Vaughan grinned. "Let's hope the opposition thinks so. See you tomorrow night. Eleven-thirty as arranged. I'll try not to keep you hanging about."

Böhmler listened until the sound of the Cossack had faded into the distance; then he got into the truck and drove back toward Flossen.

Vaughan rode on, the yellow beam of his headlight cutting through the darkness, pine trees crowding in on either side. He had burned the map into his brain, reducing the journey to a kind of formula beforehand. Right at the first crossing. Then left. Right at the crossroads. Then came the first village. Ploden. A half-dozen houses and an inn.

There was a Vopo field car parked outside, a uniformed driver lounging beside it as if waiting for somebody. He raised a hand in salute as the Cossack went by. Vaughan waved back. It was as easy as that.

Filled with a sudden fierce exhilaration, he opened the throttle wide and roared on into the night.

Margaret Campbell was sitting in her wheelchair in the chapel. Ever since that first occasion on which Konrad had taken her there, the place had held a peculiar fascination. It was not that in any sense she had experienced a religious conversion, she was honest enough to admit that, but there was peace here of a kind she had never known before, with the wooden statue of St. Francis smiling down at her in the candlelight. She didn't know what it meant yet, but that didn't matter.

The door creaked open behind her, and Konrad peered in. "Ah, there you are," he said. "I was looking for you. Someone to see you."

He stood back, and a Vopo in ankle-length rain-coat, helmet, and goggles, a submachine gun across his chest, moved into the room. She felt a moment of complete panic, and then he pushed up the goggles.

Brother Konrad left them. Vaughan put a can-vas pack he was holding in her lap.

"Present for you from Professor Nordern."

She found difficulty in speaking, so great was her emotion. "What is it?"

"Medical supplies. Various drugs he thought you might find useful."

She gazed up at him, eyes burning. "You were right, weren't you? You saw through me like clear glass. The only one."

He took off his helmet and put it down. "You've had a hard time. It shows."

"I'm so glad to see you. So glad."

He smiled, lit a cigarette, and sat down beside her. "That's all right then."

It was just after ten when Heinrich Berg stumbled out of the inn and headed for his truck. He wasn't exactly drunk, but he did have a weakness for apricot brandy, and that last glass had definitely been one too many.

He clambered up behind the wheel and fumbled for the key, and the barrel of a pistol nudged his right ear. A cold voice said softly, "Up the road towards the schloss, there's a disused barn on the left-hand side on the edge of the wood."

"What is this?" Berg said. "What do you want?"

"Do it!"

The pistol barrel screwed into his ear painfully, and he hurriedly switched on the lights, aware that the other man was a Vopo, no more than that. The pistol nudged him again.

"Come on! Move it! I haven't got all night."

In total panic now, Berg pressed the starter button and drove away rapidly.

It was cold and damp in the barn, but quiet as Berg moved uncertainly around into the light of the headlamps where Vaughan stood.

"Look, what is this?" Berg tried to sound firm. "What do you want?"

"It's really quite simple," Vaughan said. "You've got a man called Conlin up there in the schloss in a cell on what you call the third level. Am I right?"

Berg moistened dry lips. "But that is a state security matter. The SSD are in charge."

"Exactly," Vaughan said cheerfully. "Anyway, some friends of mine would like to get him out, and we thought you might give us a hand."

Berg gazed at him in total horror. "You must be insane. Why should I do such a thing?"

"Because you've been a naughty boy, old chum. Staff Sergeant Heinrich Berg, or should I say Hauptscharführer? Isn't that what they called the rank in the SS?"

Berg tried hard. "This is nonsense. I don't know what you're talking about. I was an army man. Infantry for the whole of my service."

"SS," Vaughan said softly, and took a bundle of papers from his pocket and laid them on the hood of the truck. "Not Waffen SS. At least they were fighting men. You were Einsatzgruppen. Extermination squads, recruited from the jails of Germany. You never faced a soldier in battle in your life. All you did was execute people. Lots of people. Anyone they told you to."

"It's a lie!"

"See for yourself. Those are photostats of your military career, although as an ex-professional soldier myself, I must say it sticks in my throat having to use a phrase like that in connection with you."

"If I was SS, I would have my blood group tattooed under my left armpit," Berg whispered.

"Normally, but in your case, you didn't finish training at Dachau until the autumn of '44, and by then your superiors knew the game was up. The tattooing was stopped. I mean, they didn't want to make it too difficult for you after the war. It's all there, read it."

With trembling hands, Berg opened the papers, and Vaughan carried on relentlessly. "Amazing how detailed these SS records are. They certainly had a mania for putting things on paper."

"Go to hell!" Berg launched himself forward, and Vaughan kicked him casually under the right kneecap, dodging out of the way as Berg fell to the ground.

"Which method did you favor? The gas chamber, a phenol injection, or just a bullet in the back of the neck?"

On his knees now, Berg crumpled the papers in his hands. "I'll tell. I'll confess. Why shouldn't I? There are SS at every level of government. The police, the SSD are full of them." He was momentarily beside himself, almost unaware of what he was saying. "And when I tell them about you, they'll be grateful."

"You'll still lose your head one way or the other," Vaughan said. "Here, let me show you. See here on the last sheet. Mauthausen, April 8, 1945. You executed a man called Willi Stein, a man who'd been operating with the Communist underground against the Nazis right through the war."

"I don't recall."

"You should. It's right here in the records. You hung him on a meat hook."

And Berg remembered. It showed in his face. "So?"

"I don't know how hot you are on political history, but back in 1933, when the Nazis came to power, one of the first things they did was to crush the old KPD, the German Communist Party, of whom a prominent member was one Walter Ulbricht. Present chairman of the Council of State. You have heard of him?"

"Yes," Berg whispered, waiting for the ax to fall.

"Ulbricht escaped arrest because one of his closest friends in the movement risked everything to get him out. And you know who that man was?"

"God, no!" Berg cried.

Vaughan said, "I wonder what Walter Ulbricht would do to the man who butchered Willi Stein."

Berg crouched beside the truck, head in hands. Vaughan went to the door and peered out. As he turned, Berg stood up.

"What alternative do you offer?"

"Much as we object to helping a pig like you, asylum in the West with a guarantee of no criminal proceedings. You'll be transported out of here with everyone else involved at the appropriate time. No problems."

"All right. What do you want me to do?"

"Van Buren came back today, didn't he?"

"Yes."

"What's he like?"

"What can I tell you?" Berg shrugged. "He's a cold fish."

"Why do you say that?"

"Well, he's taken over the suite of rooms that's always been used by the commandant. It has a private entrance. A spiral staircase going down to a door in the rear courtyard. I thought I was doing him a favor when I mentioned it to him, especially with this woman he's brought with him. The Vopo lieutenant."

"But he didn't think you were?"

"No."

"Maybe he just doesn't like women." Berg stirred uncomfortably, and Vaughan lit a cigarette. "All right, now you tell me about the setup at the schloss —everything. And then I'll tell you what you're going to do."

TEN

*I will bless the Lord who gives me counsel,
who even at night directs my heart. I keep the
Lord ever in my sight. Since he is at my right
hand I shall stand firm.*

The words, whispered aloud, comforted Conlin,
and it was necessary to hear a voice occasionally,
even if it was only his own. It was an old story
this. He had experienced solitary confinement before
at both Sachsenhausen and Dachau concentration
camps under the Nazis in company with that great
and good man Pastor Niemöller.

Niemöller had taught him how to fight using
every resource of brain and intellect. To be especially
strong at those darkest moments that sometimes
struck on waking when the fear was for some name-
less horror that would end all things.

The technique was a simple one. There was
the missal to remember page by page, the correct
order of services, and so on. Then poetry which
could be recited out loud. It was amazing how much
came back, particularly the Irish of his youth which
he'd not used for so long. "The Midnight Court," for
instance. As a boy, he had been able to recite the

whole of it. Had received his own leather-bound
Bible from his grandfather for doing so.

> *Ba ghanth me ag siubhail le chiumhais na na*
>   *habhann,*
> *Ar bhainseach ur's an drucht go trom* . . .

> I used to walk the morning stream,
> The meadows fresh with the dew's wet gleam.

And then there were the books. *David Copperfield*,
for one. He'd read that many times anyway. It had
all the reassurance of an old friendship.

He was reliving again the death of Steerforth
in that terrible storm off Yarmouth when the door
opened with total unexpectedness and light poured in.

Harry Van Buren was standing there, Süssmann
and Becker behind him. The cell stank like a sewer,
and Süssmann stepped back hurriedly.

Van Buren held a handkerchief to his face. "How
are you, Father? Fighting fit?"

The rat streaked from under the bed and disappeared into the darkness of the far corner, and
Van Buren's eyes followed it.

"You really are being rather stupid if you do
intend me to make my appearance in court whole
and unblemished," Conlin said. "As an old concentra-
tion-camp hand, I can assure you that six to twelve
days after a rat bite in conditions like these, with
human excrement present, it's usual for the victim to
develop Weil's disease."

"Is that so?" Van Buren said.

"Death follows due to liver failure in up to
thirty percent of cases."

Van Buren turned to Süssmann. "Bring him up; then have this place cleaned out."

He turned and walked away along the passage, and Süssmann and Becker followed, holding Conlin gingerly between them.

When Vaughan pushed Margaret Campbell into the old barn at the Home Farm, they found Konrad and Franz already waist-deep in a large hole over in the far corner. Brother Gregor pushed an empty wheelbarrow in through the open doorway to the next room. He started to fill it again from the growing pile of loose soil.

"How's it going?" Vaughan asked.

Konrad climbed up out of the excavation, wiping sweat from his brow with the back of one hand. "So far so good."

"How are you getting rid of your soil?"

"The least of our problems. Come, I'll show you."

Brother Gregor had just filled his barrow again, and Konrad took it into the next room, and Vaughan followed, pushing the girl in front of him. The room had a stone floor, and there was a jumble of rusting agricultural machinery. There was a well in the far corner, its wooden cover pulled back, into which Konrad tipped the contents of the barrow. It seemed a long time before they heard a splash.

"Seventeenth century," he explained. "We haven't used it in years. I should think it will accommodate our tunnel refuse adequately."

They moved back to the other room. Margaret said, "Where are the rest?"

Konrad picked up his shovel. "There is work to

be done, Fräulein. The farm to run, milk and eggs
for the villagers. We must keep up appearances. Brother Urban is too old for such work as this. He sees
to the cows and chickens. Florian handles our milking
and deliveries in place of Franz, and Augustin sees
to the cooking and other household chores."

"I could do that," she said. "It's time I got up
on this leg more, and I can operate from the wheelchair when I feel tired." He looked uncertain, and
she pulled at Vaughan's arm. "Tell him, Simon! Make
him see! The courtyard gate is always barred. To
gain admittance, outsiders have to ring the bell. That
means I can't be caught out."

"She's right," Vaughan said. "Which would free
Augustin to do what he can here. And while we're
at it, if you can give me something to wear instead
of the pretty uniform, I've got the rest of the day
to kill."

The bath was very old with brass taps, and the
water, when it came, spouted from the mouth of
a cherub. None of which mattered, for the only
important thing was that when Süssmann and Becker
lowered him into it, it was blissfully warm. Conlin
sighed and closed his eyes.

Van Buren nodded to the two Vopos, who
went out. Lieutenant Leber came in. She wore a
white overall and carried towels over her arm.

"Wash him thoroughly and disinfect the water."

"Have I got you worried then?" The old priest
smiled and opened his eyes. And then he saw the
woman. His smile faded; his hands moved down to
cover himself defensively.

"You're ashamed to be seen naked by a trained nurse?" Van Buren said. "Now there's an unhealthy attitude. There's nothing obscene in the human form, or did they teach you differently at the seminary when you were a boy? I've often wondered about those places. Celibate priests and adolescent boys."

"I find it even stranger that a man of your training should find the notion of celibacy so difficult to take." She was soaping his body now, and Conlin winced. "What is this supposed to be? A study in conscious humiliation?"

"You know, I really do find it interesting," Van Buren said. "That you should find the situation so disturbing. So shameful?"

For the first time, the old man lost his temper. "God forgive me for saying it, but why don't you go to hell?"

"Ah, but I see now," Van Buren said, as if suddenly gaining insight. "Not shameful, but frightening. You're afraid in such a situation. That is interesting." He turned to the woman and said in German, "Have him out now and dress him. I'll see him when he's eaten."

He left, and Ruth Leber helped Conlin out of the bath and toweled his body without a word, handling him gently as if he were a child. Then she brought clean underwear, corduroy pants, a shirt and warm sweater, socks, slippers and waited for him to dress, still without speaking.

When he was ready, she opened the door and led the way into the next room. Van Buren was not at his desk, but a great fire of logs blazed on the stone hearth, and a meal was waiting on a small card table in front of it.

She held the chair for him to sit, then walked to the door. As she opened it, he said in German, "Thank you, my child."

She didn't even pause but kept right on going, closing the door softly behind her. Conlin sighed, reached for his fork, and raised a piece of beef to his mouth. It was really excellent, and the wine was Chablis, his favorite and beautifully chilled. He was under no illusions as to the purpose of all this, none at all, but his body needed all the strength it could get to sustain it in the days to come.

When Berg went down to the third level, he found the Vopo sentry swilling out Conlin's cell with buckets of water carried from a tap in the passageway.

"He's still up above then?" Berg asked.

"That's right. What have you got there?"

Berg carried a spot lamp in one hand, a bucket in the other, and he lifted it up. "Rat poison. Like some?"

The boy shuddered. "No, thanks. Will you lay it in here?"

"No. Lower down. That's where the bastards breed," Berg said. "I'll see you later."

He moved along the passageway and turned the corner, his spot lamp cutting into the total darkness ahead. A hundred yards, descending all the way, and he entered a vaulted chamber. What he was seeking was in the center, a heavy metal plate, bolted and padlocked. He knelt down, took a bunch of keys from his pocket, and got to work.

He had never had occasion to open the plate

before and had to try six keys before he found the right one. The plate was heavy and took both hands and all his strength to lift.

He probed the darkness below. There was an iron ladder perhaps ten feet deep, and he descended it quickly. The tunnel stretched before him, ten feet in diameter, sloping downward and perfectly dry.

It was twenty minutes later when he emerged. He snapped the padlock back into place, then reached for the bucket and laid down some of the rat poison, thinking of Vaughan as he did so. He'd like to have had him back at Mauthausen in the old days. By God, he'd have made him dance. But the bastard did have the whiphand. The prospect of what would happen to him if Ulbricht ever got a sight of his SS service record was too terrible to contemplate.

On the other hand, there were certain advantages to this situation. It meant he could go west and in safety, relieved at last of the nagging fear which had plagued him for years that his past would catch up with him. As he retraced his steps along the passageway, he began to whistle softly.

Conlin rationed himself to one glass of wine and was just finishing the last of the food when Van Buren came in.

"You look like a different article." He settled himself into the wing-back chair on the other side of the fire and lit a cigarette.

"What now?" Conlin asked.

"What do you think?"

"First you were nasty; then you offer me comfort. Nothing very extraordinary in that. The Ges-

tapo were just the same when I first found myself in
the cellars at Prinz Albrechtstrasse. There was the
brute who beat me half to death with a whip, then
the clean-cut boy who begged me to confess to save
myself."

"And in the end, he turned out to be worse than
the other guy. Right?"

"What is it you want of me?"

"Not me," Van Buren said. "I only work here.
Klein wants the Christian Underground. Names,
places. The works. Plus details of your connection
with the CIA. That's the general idea."

"But there isn't one."

"Does it matter? What's truth? What's reality?
It's all a question of perspective. It's a chain reaction
in a way. Klein wants to please Ulbricht by giving
him what *he* wants, and I want to please Klein." He
smiled beautifully. "And that means, old buddy, that
you've got to please me."

"I'm afraid I'd find that very difficult."

"I thought you might."

"So, what happens now?"

"You tell me."

"Phase Two, the object of which will be to
drive me to the edge of insanity. To take me to
pieces, then put me together again in your image.
Good Marxian psychology, which believes that each
man has his thesis, his positive side, and his antithesis, the dark side of his being. If you can find out
what that is and encourage its growth, then the guilt
will be too much for me to bear. Isn't that what
you would tell your students?"

"Very good," Van Buren said. "And where
would you say I should probe for your antithesis? In
the sexual area? You certainly did seem a little dis-

turbed over that slight incident in the bathroom with Lieutenant Leber."

"Why is it you people find the notion of celibacy so bewildering?" Conlin asked. "You really should pull yourself together, boy. Read a different class of book."

Van Buren wasn't in the slightest put out. He pressed a button on the desk, and Süssmann came in. "Take him back now."

Conlin stood up. "Is that all?"

"Should there be any more?" Van Buren selected another cigarette. "Good night, Father. Sleep well."

Süssmann didn't say a word on the way back to the third level until they reached the cell where the sentry stood guard.

Conlin paused at the door, and Süssmann said, "No, the next one, if you please."

The cell was exactly the same as the other except that it was clean and fresh. There was a chemical toilet, a mattress on the bed, blankets.

"You will be more comfortable here, I think, Father. Good night to you." The door closed; the key turned in the lock.

A moment later, the light was switched off. Conlin unfolded the blankets. At least he had a breathing space. Why, he didn't know, but he at once relaxed, tension draining out of him, and knelt down beside the bed to say his prayers.

The cell was filled with a hideous, frightening clamor. He scrambled to his feet and saw that a large bell was fixed just above the door that rang continually while a red light flickered on and off rapidly.

What a fool he'd been. The key rattled in the

lock, the door was flung open, and Süssmann and Becker appeared to drag him away along the passageway between them.

Vaughan climbed up out of the excavation wearily, and young Franz dropped in beside Gregor to take his place. They were about seven feet down, and the going was harder now.

Florian came in from the other room, pushing the empty barrow. "Had enough?"

"Just about. Not used to hard labor." Vaughan glanced at his watch. "In any case, I'm going to have to get moving."

Margaret Campbell swung in through the door on a pair of old wooden crutches, followed by Konrad carrying a jug of coffee and several mugs on a tray.

"What's all this?" Vaughan demanded.

"Konrad found them for me." She laughed. "It makes me feel halfway like a human being again."

The gate bell rang. In the pit Franz paused, his pick raised above his head to swing. Everyone waited. Konrad said, "I'll get it," and went out.

Vaughan peered through the crack of the half-open door out through the rain. Margaret Campbell moved beside him and whispered, "What do you think?"

Konrad had the gate light on and was unbarring the postern. He opened it, and Henrich Berg stepped through. He muttered something to Konrad and peered around the courtyard nervously. Konrad shut the gate and came back to the barn.

"He wants you, Major."

Berg paused inside the door, cap in hand, his dark, watchful eyes taking in everything. The excavation in the corner, the girl. Everyone waited. He managed an ingratiating smile. "Major? I didn't realize."

"Did you find it?" Vaughan asked impatiently.

"Oh, yes, Herr Major, just like you said. A heavy manhole cover in the lower chamber. Padlocked and bolted."

"And you went in?"

"Yes."

"Tell me."

"There was a ladder—a steel ladder, maybe twelve or fifteen feet down. The tunnel was around ten feet in diameter and sloped down all the way. At other stages there were two further ladders to descend. Ten foot each—no more."

"You went all the way?"

"Yes. It's all concreted except for the last thirty or forty feet. That's still rough. You can see where they were digging when they finished, and there's a certain amount of rubble."

"And you were able to breathe—no foul air?"

"Fresh and clean. There was some water—perhaps a foot deep in places. Not sewage—springwater, I think."

Konrad said, "If the air is fresh, it means the tunnel must be vented to ground level and in more than one place."

"Exactly." Vaughan said to Berg, "You've done well. I won't be seeing you for a while. A week at least."

"Is there anything else you want me to do in the meantime?"

"Find out as much as you can about the day-to-day treatment of Father Conlin. Keep Brother Konrad informed—say, every two days."

"As you say."

"All right, you can go now."

Konrad saw him out and bolted the postern again. When he came back, he said, "You think we can trust him?"

"He doesn't have any other choice. He'd sell us out if he could, but he can't. For people like Berg life is just a series of accommodations." He glanced at his watch. "I'd better get changed. I don't want to keep my friend hanging around at the border."

When he stepped out into the porch, he was once more in the heavy dispatch rider's coat and helmet, the AK assault rifle across his chest.

Margaret Campbell said, "I don't like you in that."

"You're not meant to." Behind her Konrad pushed the Cossack and sidecar out of a shed into the courtyard, then went to open the gate.

Vaughan touched her cheek briefly with the back of a gloved hand. "You look too good to leave standing there in the lamplight, Maggie, my love, and nicely helpless on those crutches."

"And what would you do with me?"

"I'll think of something." He mounted the Cossack. "See you at the weekend."

He drove out through the gate. Konrad closed it. The girl stood there, listening to the sound of the engine fade into the night; then she turned and went back inside.

In the old operation room at Bitterfeld, Pascoe sat at the controller's desk, examining the plan of Schloss Neustadt in the light of a reading lamp. Bruno Teusen was asleep in a chair in the far corner. It was very quiet—almost midnight—and Pascoe wondered what had happened. What had gone wrong. And then there was a knock on the door, and Vaughan stepped into the room, followed by Böhmler.

Pascoe leaned back in his chair and smiled. "You know, for a while there I was beginning to worry. I must be getting old. Everything went all right at the border?"

Vaughan removed his helmet. "Like a charm. I didn't see a soul between Neustadt and Flossen, until I made contact with Böhmler here."

"That was just after eleven," Böhmler said. "We put the bike in the back of the truck and proceeded to Flossen, where Bülow passed us straight through—no fuss."

"Excellent," Pascoe said. "Now, tell me what happened out there. Everything."

Böhmler and Vaughan crossed the airstrip at Bitterfeld to what had been the officers' mess in the old days.

"It's not bad," Böhmler said. "Army cots, I'm afraid, but there are plenty of blankets, and the caretaker got the boiler working again today. There should be plenty of hot water by tomorrow."

One of the hangar doors stood partially open, light seeped through, and there was the sound of an electric drill. "What's going on?" Vaughan asked.

"That crazy friend of yours, Kübel. He seems to work on that plane of his every hour of the day or night."

"I'll catch up with you," Vaughan told him.

When he went into the hangar, he found the

Storch standing all alone in the immensity of it. Max Kübel was working on one of the wings with an electric drill, whistling cheerfully. He wore a pair of black mechanics' overalls that had certainly seen better days.

He switched off the drill and grinned. "So, return of the hero. What was it like?"

"Interesting. I see you still love planes more than women."

"Much more reliable. Tell me, my friend, the girl you mentioned. You found her well?"

"About the only thing I'm sure of anymore is that I did find her." Vaughan paced restlessly to the partly opened door.

"And how do you feel?"

"Uneasy."

"For whom? Yourself or this young woman of yours?" He laughed out loud. "My poor Simon."

"You go to hell," Vaughan said, and made for the door.

"Undoubtedly," Max Kübel shouted cheerfully, and he picked up his electric drill and switched it on again.

Father Conlin crouched in the corner of a cell on the first level. It was painted white, contained no furniture at all, and seemed filled with a hard white light that hurt his eyes.

He was aware of a dull, solid, slapping sound, a continuous rhythm that never ceased. It seemed to be very near and yet far away. It made no sense.

The door opened, and Van Buren appeared with a young Vopo guard. "Bring him," the American ordered.

When the Vopo got Conlin into the corridor, the old priest found Van Buren standing at the next cell, peering in through a barred window. The slapping sounds continued, and when the guard hustled Conlin close enough, he saw, inside the cell, a man in tattered shirt and pants, spread-eagled across a bench. Süssmann and Becker, stripped to the waist, were systematically beating him with rubber hoses.

The man on the bench moaned, turning his head, and Conlin saw to his horror that it was Karl, the driver who had delivered him by truck to Margaret Campbell's cottage that first night.

"What does this prove?" he asked Van Buren. "He knows nothing about the Underground. He can't tell you a thing—that's the way I organized the system."

"Oh, I believe you," Van Buren said. "But without a penitent, reform is not possible, isn't that what your church teaches? Shouldn't we take an interest in his soul? And pain is a purgative. I mean, take the cross. What a way to go. Squalid, filthy, and degrading and yet three days later . . ."

ELEVEN

It was just after eight o'clock on Saturday when Bülow waved the truck through at Flossen. About a mile up the road, Böhmler forked left into a forest track and, a couple of hundred yards later, emerged into a clearing in which stood the ruins of an old sawmill beside a fast-flowing stream. The wheel that had once provided its source of power had not turned in years, and the doors at the front of the building sagged on their hinges.

He drove inside, took a hand lamp, went around to the rear, and dropped the tailboard. The Cossack and sidecar were inside, together with various other items and Vaughan, once more a Vopo. He passed down a foot pump with a long hose attached and a couple of plastic buckets. Böhmler took them without a word and went and filled them at a tap in the corner.

Rain started to drum against the roof, and he grinned. "Twenty minutes earlier and it would have saved us some work."

"And exposed us to the chance that some nosy parker might have seen a piece of Volkspolizei hard-

169

ware entering East Germany from the West and wondered what was going on," Vaughan pointed out.

He put the end of the foot pump in one of the buckets and started to operate it vigorously as Böhmler sprayed the truck. Very quickly, the dirty-gray water paint with which it had been painted dissolved away, and the truck now stood revealed for what it was, a Volkspolizei field truck painted in the dark green and brown camouflage colors of the forest sector and bearing divisional and group signs.

Ten minutes was all it took, and Böhmler went and threw the pump and buckets into the millrace. He came back, wiping his hands on a rag. "All yours, Major."

Vaughan clambered up behind the wheel. "One hour after midnight. Okay?"

The engine roared into life, and he drove out across the clearing. Böhmler went after him, and by the time he reached the main road the sound of the field truck had faded into the night. He turned and started to jog back toward the border post.

Vaughan should have known that it was too good to last. No matter how good your organization it was always the unexpected that fouled things up. The stupid little things you hadn't planned for.

The first ten or fifteen miles passed uneventfully enough. Nothing but trees and darkness, and then, as he passed through Ploden, he noticed a Cossack and sidecar that were twin to his own parked outside the inn. Obviously a regular stopping-off point for Vopo patrols. On the other hand, it was probably the only pub for miles.

The truck slewed violently as one of the rear

tires burst. He fought to control the wheel, stamping hard on the brake, and managed to come to a halt in one piece in the grass verge.

Cursing softly, he got out, took the jack from the toolbox, and unbolted one of the two spare wheels. It was dark, too dark to see what he was doing, so he got the hand lamp from the cab, placed it on the ground, and started to unfasten the wheel bolts. They were apparently immovable, and it struck him suddenly that they had probably been tightened automatically in the garage. It took all his strength, as he concentrated fiercely. Perhaps because of that, he was unaware of the sound of the approaching engine until it was too late to do anything about it.

The Cossack pulled onto the verge, and the Vopo came forward and stood over him. In other circumstances it might have been funny, for he could have been Vaughan's twin: helmet, goggles, coat, even the AK across the chest.

"Trouble, Comrade?"

"What do you think?" Vaughan demanded sourly. His hand slid into his right pocket, found the butt of the Walther he carried there, and he slipped off the safety catch.

"I'll give you a hand."

The Vopo started to pump up the jack vigorously. "Where are you heading?"

"Stendal," Vaughan told him. "Divisional machine stores."

An establishment which existed, he knew that. His newfound friend wrestled the old tire off. "What, on a Saturday night?"

Vaughan rolled the spare forward. "An emergency. One of our recovery trucks ran off the road near Flossen and broke an axle. It's needed for Monday, so that means getting the part tonight and working through tomorrow." He started to tighten the wheel bolts. "There goes my weekend."

He released the jack, and air hissed. The Vopo chuckled. "Had something good lined up, did you? Not Dirty Gerty at the inn at Ploden. Is that who you mean? I heard she was a certain turn."

Vaughan slung the jack into the tool locker. "Beggars can't be choosers, not in a dump like this." He scrambled up behind the wheel. "Anyway, thanks, Comrade. Got to get moving."

The Vopo said, "Hang on, you've forgotten the wheel you took off. I'll sling it in the back for you."

Vaughan heard the footsteps go around to the rear and didn't wait for the reaction, simply stamped on the accelerator and drove away.

He didn't stand a chance, not in any kind of race with a machine as powerful as the Cossack. In his mirror he was aware of its headlight coming up fast, and he swerved across the road as it tried to overtake him.

This maneuver served him well for a while, but then he ran out of forest and emerged onto a causeway three miles long that ran across a wilderness of mud flats and great pale barriers of reeds higher than a man's head. An alien world inhabited only by birds.

And here it was no longer possible to weave because the slightest miscalculation would have the field truck over the causeway and into the marsh. Very sad for Sean Conlin and Margaret Campbell, not to mention Simon Vaughan.

Perhaps if he kept in close, inviting the Vopo to overtake, there would be a chance to crowd the

Cossack over the edge. Vaughan tried it, but the Vopo showed no intention of accepting the invitation, staying right on his tail.

There was a shot, then another as he fired his AK one-handed, and Vaughan, doing the only possible thing, braked hard, skidding to a halt. He left his engine ticking over, slid across the passenger seat, went under the far door, and crouched beneath the field truck.

The Cossack had stopped, and footsteps approached. The boots, the tail of the coat passed close to his face. The driving door was wrenched open.

There was silence, and Vaughan came up from beneath the field truck behind the Vopo. Vaughan's knee went into the small of the back, his left arm around the throat, bending the Vopo's body back in an agonizing bow. His right hand jerked the helmet back hard against the nape of the neck. It broke cleanly as the Vopo gave one frantic choked cry and died.

Vaughan held him in his arms for a few moments, breathing heavily, then dragged him back to the motorcycle and eased him into the sidecar, which wasn't easy because he was a large man. Then he mounted the machine. When the engine was ticking over nicely, he jumped off and twisted the accelerator. The Cossack surged forward under its own power, over the edge of the causeway.

He got the hand lamp from the field truck. The Vopo had been pitched forward, the machine falling on top of him. It didn't take long to disappear, but Vaughan waited anyway, not satisfied until the surface mud was calm again.

So—one Vopo missing from patrol, plus his machine, which with luck would indicate to security that he had defected to the West. And even if the marsh did decide to reveal its secret, there was nothing to indicate anything more than an unfortunate accident.

He got behind the wheel and lit a cigarette. It tasted foul. He threw it out the window and drove away, gripping the wheel too tightly.

Vaughan walked down the sloping ramp of planks into the excavation with Brother Gregor and peered along the length of the tunnel.

"How far?" he asked.

"About twenty feet. It's really gone very well."

It was well lit with electric light bulbs strung from a long cord at regular intervals. The roof and sides were lined with rusting corrugated iron sheets and propped up with balks of timber.

"You can't exactly swing a pick in there," Vaughan observed.

"No, admittedly only one man can actually work at the face itself with a laborer at his shoulder to help fill the cart. Four feet wide, three feet six high."

"Couldn't you advance faster if two men could actually work on the face at the same time?"

"By widening the tunnel? Not really because the volume of soil to be brought out would increase dramatically. I spent some considerable time on the mathematics of it." Gregor smiled apologetically. "The engineer in me still comes out occasionally."

"You're in charge," Vaughan said. "After all, as long as that tunnel is wide enough for a man to get through, that's all that's needed."

"Exactly. I had the same problem during the final days in Stalingrad with trench communication."

"I can imagine."

There were three sharp raps from up ahead, and Gregor looked up at Konrad and the others standing above. "Haul away."

Someone pulled on a rope, and as Vaughan watched, a wooden cart mounted on a set of old pram wheels appeared, loaded with earth. It came straight out on crude rails, continued on up the ramp, where Konrad started to shovel it into a wheelbarrow.

Vaughan ducked into the tunnel and crawled along the centerpiece of wooden planks until he came to Franz, crouched at the soil face, hacking away with an old trenching shovel, Florian crouched at his shoulder. They were both stripped to the waist, their bodies streaked with sweat and dirt.

Franz grinned. "Back again, Major? Do you want a shovel?"

"No, thanks," Vaughan said. "You seem to be enjoying yourself."

"A nice, safe, enclosed feeling. Like being back in the womb. And interesting souvenirs." He searched in the loose soil with his hand and came up with a finger bone. "There you are. A present from Neustadt."

Vaughan crawled back, out into the pit, and went up the ramp. "Nothing unpleasant so far?"

Gregor shook his head. "Only old bones. I've inspected the cemetery, and this side is mainly seventeenth and eighteenth century."

"And what comes after?"

Konrad paused, leaning on his shovel. "Considerably later, I'm afraid. Some graves as recent as last year."

There was a nasty silence. No one seemed to

know what to say, and then the barn door opened and Margaret Campbell limped in, no crutches now. Just a heavy walking stick to lean on.

"Supper everyone," she said, and when she smiled at Vaughan, it was as if a lamp had turned on inside.

It was toward the end of the meal that the gate bell sounded.

"That should be Berg," Konrad said. "I was expecting him tonight."

He went out and came back presently with the caretaker. Berg was obviously surprised to see Vaughan and stood just inside the room, nervously twisting his cap in his hands.

"You're back, Major."

"So it would appear. What's happening up there?"

"They don't exactly take me into their confidence. I only get to see some things."

"Get on with it, man," Vaughan told him.

"Well, Conlin is in good condition. I mean he can walk under his own power. I saw him leaving Van Buren's office this afternoon under guard."

"Is he still on the third level?"

"Yes." Berg hesitated. "They've been concentrating on another man."

"Who?"

"I overheard Captain Süssmann talking to Becker. It seems this man drove the truck Father Conlin was in when he first came here."

"And what have they done to him?"

"Everything," Berg said simply. "They had him in the yard for hours tied to a pole. I'd say he hasn't got long myself."

Margaret Campbell's distress was apparent to everyone. Vaughan took her hand under the table and held it tight.

"The Vopo officer—the woman he brought with him? What's her story?"

"Lieutenant Leber. A nurse from the Medical Corps." He shrugged. "Frankly, I hardly ever see her. She's up there with Van Buren most of the time."

There was a pause while Vaughan thought about it; then he nodded. "All right, you'd better stay and hear what I have to say as you'll be a part of it." He stood up. "Tonight I drove here in a Vopo field truck, a troop carrier. It's in one of the sheds in the courtyard."

"And that's our way out when the time comes?" Konrad asked.

"Exactly. There are Vopo uniforms and rifles in the back for everyone, including you, Berg. Even if the whole countryside is roused, in such a vehicle, you'd never be questioned."

Berg cleared his throat. "But surely all border posts would be notified by phone to allow no traffic through."

"Exactly," Vaughan said. "By happy chance, the one we shall use is in the hands of friends."

"And what about a timetable?" Margaret Campbell asked. "How can you possibly arrange that?"

"No need for one." He went to the sideboard and picked up a leather army knapsack. He brought it back to the table, opened it, and took out a small black wireless transmitter.

"You intend radio communications?" Konrad said. "But such a thing is madness. The security forces have dozens of units whose sole task is to monitor all radio frequencies. They would track you down in a matter of hours."

"Exactly," Vaughan said. "But bear with me and you'll understand. At Bitterfeld, from next Wednesday on, my friends will be on constant standby. A Storch spotter plane is waiting with a pilot who has made this sort of flight many times. The day I decide to go in for Conlin, this transmitter is switched on. It sends out an ultra-high-frequency signal, specially coded, and switches itself off automatically after two minutes. That alerts them at Bitterfeld. That procedure will be repeated the moment I bring Conlin out, and when that signal is received at Bitterfeld, the Storch will take off."

"And how long will the flight take?" Margaret asked.

"Twenty minutes at the outside. The pilot will land at a spot called Water Horse Meadow by the Elbe about half a mile from here."

"But can he land in such a place at night?"

"This pilot can, and I have all the help he needs right here in this knapsack. Konrad will deliver me to the landing site with Conlin. The old man and I will return to Bitterfeld in the Storch."

"And the rest of us?" Berg demanded.

"Konrad drives back here to pick you all up, in uniform, of course." He smiled at the girl. "There's even one for you."

"I didn't know they made them that small."

"Neither did I. You'll have to pull your cap down over your eyes. There's a map in the truck with the fastest route to Flossen clearly marked. You'd better find time to memorize that, Konrad."

"Of course."

"And one more thing, and burn this into your brains. On the night in question, whenever it is, it's absolutely essential that everyone does what he has to exactly on time. If anyone is missing at the final stage, then he's on his own." He turned to Konrad. "You don't hang about for anyone."

Berg shook his head. "Crazy," he said. "Absolutely crazy."

"No, it isn't," Konrad told him. "It's really very simple, if you think about it. One part fitting neatly into another like a good Swiss watch."

"And you know what happens to those when something goes wrong with one of the parts," Berg said morosely. He pulled on his cap. "Anyway, I'd better be off. I'll see you again the day after tomorrow."

Konrad took him out, and the others got up. "Back to the salt mines," Franz said cheerfully, and they all went out.

The girl turned to Vaughan, and there was concern in her eyes. "You look tired."

For a moment he almost told her of the incident on the causeway, that he had recently killed a man, but it was better left unsaid. She was not someone who would ever be able to accept such things lightly, however good the cause.

"I must be getting old," he said, and smiled.

Konrad came back in. "What time do you leave?"

Vaughan glanced at his watch. "In about an hour. My contact man expects me at one o'clock on the dot."

The girl put a hand on his arm. "You're going back tonight?"

"Yes, it's necessary. I've got things to do. But I'll be back next Wednesday. You know about that."

Konrad said, "You think it will work, this scheme of yours?"

"I don't see why not."

"And Father Hartmann? You haven't told him?"

"I'd rather present him with the situation as a fact. He might argue about it."

"You know best." Konrad hesitated, glancing from one to the other. "I'll leave you for a while, if I may, and see how things are progressing in the barn."

He went out. Vaughan lit a cigarette. Margaret Campbell folded her arms and leaned back in her chair, watching him.

"How long have I known you? A year? A hundred?"

"It never pays to be specific."

"Have you any idea how I felt on the bridge that morning? How much I wanted to tell you everything?"

He leaned across and touched her face. "More water under the bridge."

"And you believe in all this?" she said. "Believe in what you're doing? You must. You couldn't go to such lengths."

"If you mean do I dislike what goes on over here, then you'd be right," he said. "There are thirty thousand troops guarding the wall, did you know that? Any soldier who prevents the escape of a fellow guard gets promotion two ranks, the Merit Badge of the National People's Army, five hundred marks, and a vacation in Moscow for two. I don't suppose they told you that at the university."

"No, they didn't."

"Not that it's doing the bastards much good. More than two thousand guards have defected already. You see, they'd rather experience the fleshpots of Western capitalism than the purity of Marxist ideology."

"You're angry," she said.

"Am I?"

"Tell me about Borneo."

"What would be the point?"

"I'd like to know, from your point of view. Please."

She laid a hand on his arm very lightly.

"Last year, in Borneo, there was an area around Kotabaru that was absolutely controlled by terrorists, and most of them weren't Indonesians. They were Chinese Communist infiltrators. They burned villages wholesale, coerced the Dyaks into helping them by butchering every second man or woman in some of the villages they took, just to encourage the others."

"And they put you in to do something about it?"

"I was supposed to be an expert in that sort of thing, so they gave me command of a company of irregulars, Dyak scouts, and told me to clean things up. I didn't have much luck until they burned the mission at Kotabaru, raped and murdered four nuns and eighteen girls. That was it as far as I was concerned."

"What did you do?"

"An informer tipped me off that a Chinese merchant in Selangor named Hui Lui was a Communist agent. I arrested him and, when he refused to talk, handed him over to the Dyaks."

"To torture him?"

"He lasted only a couple of hours; then he told me where the group I'd been chasing was holed up."

"And did you get them?"

"Eventually. They split into two groups, which didn't help, but we managed it."

"They said you shot your prisoners."

"Only during the final pursuit, when I was hard on the heels of the second group. Prisoners would have delayed me."

"I see. And Mr. Hui Lui?"

"Shot trying to escape. Absolutely true, and that's the most ironic part of it. I was quite prepared to take him down to the coast and let him stand trial, but he tried to make a break for it the night before we left."

"And do you regret any of this now?"

"What I did to him he'd have done to me. The purpose of terrorism is to terrorize. Lenin said it first, and it's on page one of every Communist handbook on revolutionary warfare. You can only fight that kind of fire with fire. I did what had to be done. Malaya, Kenya, Cyprus, Aden. I'd seen it all, and I was tired of people justifying the murder of the innocent by pleading it was all in the name of the cause. When I finished, there was no more terror by night in Kotabaru. No more butchering of little girls. That should count for something, God knows."

Her face was very calm, her eyes hooded, brooding, arms folded beneath her breasts as she leaned on the table. "So you ruined yourself. Career, reputation—everything."

"I'd better go now."

He got up, took his long dispatch rider's raincoat from behind the door, and buttoned it up. He slung the AK assault rifle across his chest and put on his helmet, adjusting the strap.

"Will I do?"

"I should think so."

He had the door open when she said softly, "I see now what it was I saw in you from that first moment—sensed and never understood. There is always in your heart, I think, a sense of justice outraged."

There was silence between them. The door closed softly, and he was gone.

It was just after 2:00 A.M., and Meyer was lying in one of the narrow military cots of Bitterfeld, blankets piled thickly about him, for he felt the cold easily. He was reading one of Vaughan's books, a critical appreciation of the philosophy of Heidegger.

The door opened, and Vaughan came in. "Simon, you're back!" Meyer said.

"You sound surprised." Vaughan stripped off his helmet and raincoat, sat wearily on the edge of the bed, and lit a cigarette.

"Everything go all right?"

"I had to kill a Vopo prowler guard who tried to stop me on the road."

"My God."

"Don't worry. I dumped him and his motorcycle in a marsh on Holstein Heath. With any luck, his superiors will think he's defected."

"There are times when all you can do is close the windows and wait for darkness to pass," Meyer said gravely.

"A century or so ago when I was seventeen, I used to go dancing, Julius, at the old Trocadero. Your kind of music. You'd have loved it."

"So what's the point?"

"That seventeen is an age of infinite promise.

Seventeen is walking girls home five miles from a dance in the rain for not much more than a kiss. Seventeen is being filled with a restless excitement, the knowledge that something is waiting just around the next corner. Seventeen is standing under a street-lamp with a girl in your arms and rain drifting down like silver spray."

Meyer said, "That was then, this is now, Simon. You're thirty-seven years of age, and you've been a professional soldier for twenty of them. Let's face it, business is business and killing is your trade. You can't stop. Malaya, Kenya, Cyprus—all those little wars you served in. Now this. For you, there'll always be another little war because you can't stop it, this game you play. In the end it has you by the balls, my friend, and one day, no matter how good you are, how smart, a sniper is waiting on a rooftop somewhere to put a bullet in your back. No honor there."

"I spent two years in a Chinese prison camp," Vaughan said wearily. "That's honor enough for one lifetime."

"You're damaged goods, Simon. Let her go, there's a good boy. Get her out safe for a mitzvah, a good deed, then let her go. She's entitled to a life."

Vaughan got undressed and climbed into the other bed. Meyer said, "Do you mind if I keep on reading? Does the light bother you?"

"No."

"Interesting fellow, this Heidegger. He says that for authentic living what is necessary is the resolute confrontation of death. Do you agree?"

Vaughan's voice was muffled when he replied, "A good man in his day, Heidegger. Just like me."

Walter Ulbricht's office was furnished with spartan simplicity. A framed photograph of Stalin with a dedication occupied a prominent position on one wall, and the generally chilly atmosphere was not solely the product of the comrade chairman's well-known dislike of central heating.

Early-morning sunlight streamed into the room through one of the narrow windows but did little to lighten the somber atmosphere as he sat there at the desk, methodically working his way through a pile of papers presented to him by a male secretary, signing the occasional letter where requested.

There was a tap at the door, and Helmut Klein entered. He made a distinguished-enough-looking figure in the heavy overcoat with the fur collar, and yet in the presence of the older man he seemed to shrink. Ulbricht ignored him for a while, continuing to sign letters. Finally, he paused, removed his glasses, and ran a hand over his eyes.

"Leave us," he said softly, and the secretary went to the door at once, opened it, and left without a word.

Ulbricht looked up at the other man for a full minute before speaking. "Well, Klein, I'm waiting. I've been back from Moscow two days and no word from you."

"Comrade Chairman," Klein began, "these things take time."

"You told me that this American, Van Buren, was the best. I wasn't happy about his lack of political commitment, but you assured me that didn't matter. You promised me results. In fact, it wouldn't be exaggerating the position to say that you actually guaranteed me results."

Klein's mouth was bone-dry. He moistened his lips and managed to whisper, "Yes, Comrade Chairman."

"Good. Failure in this affair will not be tolerated. I hold you personally responsible. I look forward to hearing from you soon with favorable news."

He picked up his pen and returned to his documents, and Klein got out as fast as he could.

He had his driver take him to the Ministry of State Security at Normannenstrasse at once. When he entered the outer office of Section Five, Frau Apel rose to greet him. "Good morning, Colonel. The Leipzig office has been on the line."

"Never mind that now," Klein told her. "Get me Captain Süssmann at Schloss Neustadt."

He went back into his office and sat behind his desk without taking off his coat. He saw now that he stood on the brink of a precipice. He had placed his life, his career, entirely in Harry Van Buren's hands.

The phone rang, and when he picked it up, the voice said, "Süssmann here."

"What's happening there, Süssmann? Is he getting anywhere? The truth now."

"Not in my opinion. Too much conversation. Now if Sergeant Major Becker and I could have a free hand . . ."

"No," Klein said. "Another week, and then we review the situation. Naturally, I expect you to report to me on Van Buren's activities in minutest detail."

"Of course, Comrade."

"This affair could mean considerable advancement for you, Süssmann, if we can reach a successful conclusion."

"I'll do my best."

"Another thing. This priest, Hartmann, will be turning up the day after tomorrow. I want to know what he gets up to as well. Telephone me at any hour. You have the private number where you can reach me at night if I'm not at the office. Now transfer me to Van Buren."

Van Buren was alone in his office with Ruth Leber, going over his notes on the last session with Conlin, when the phone rang.

He picked it up, and Klein said cheerfully, "Hello, Harry. I haven't heard from you for a few days, so I thought I'd see how things were going."

"Fine," Van Buren said. "I'm making real progress."

"Good. It's just that I had to see Chairman Ulbricht on other matters this morning, and he did mention the Conlin affair. He told me he expects to see some really positive results quite soon now. If Conlin's trial is to coincide with Kennedy's visit, then preparations must be put in hand as soon as possible."

"I see."

"Would it help if I came down?"

"No, that wouldn't do at all," Van Buren said hastily. "The whole technique of this thing depends on the closeness of my personal contact with him. The fact that no one else is allowed to enter the private area of our relationship."

"A week, Harry, that's all I can give you."

"But that's ridiculous."

"No, it isn't. It's Ulbricht."

The line went dead. Van Buren replaced his receiver and sat there frowning.

"Trouble?" Ruth Leber asked.

"No, I don't think so. We're just going to have to move a little faster, that's all." He stood up. "I think I'll have another word with Conlin."

When he opened the cell door, Conlin was sitting on the bed, staring at the wall. He looked very frail, the flesh on his face reduced so that every bone showed clearly.

"You don't look too good," Van Buren said.

"I'm getting old, that's all."

Van Buren lit a cigarette, and the smoke was pungent on the cold air. Conlin smiled dryly. "A waste of time. I've gone through my nicotine withdrawal symptoms. I haven't breathed so well in years. You've done me a favor there, Harry."

It was totally unexpected, the use of his name, and Van Buren was aware of a spurt of anger—or was he trying to rationalize a fear syndrome? Perhaps deep inside he felt the old man's familiarity as a personal threat.

He said to Becker, "Bring him along," went out and along the passage, and unbolted the door to another cell.

The truck driver, Karl, lay in the corner. Blood oozed from his nostrils, the corner of his mouth; his eyes were fixed as if on some spot in the middle distance.

"We pride ourselves on a sense of logic and order," Van Buren said, "but inside, we are savages. A predisposition to violence is man's most enduring attribute."

Conlin got down on his knees painfully and leaned over the broken body. There was a flicker of recognition; the lips moved. Karl said, "Save me, Father. Help me."

He tried to clutch at the old man's shirtfront, but he hadn't the strength and slumped back again.

"For pity's sake, Harry," Conlin said. "Get him a doctor."

"Too late," Van Buren told him. "But I've done the next best thing. I've brought him a priest."

He went out; the door closed; the bolts rammed home. Conlin put an arm around Karl and leaned the broken head against his shoulder.

"Karl," he whispered, "I want you to make an act of contrition. Say after me, 'O my God, who art infinitely good in thyself.'"

TWELVE

L'Osservatore Romano is one of the world's oldest newspapers, but its distribution is not confined to the Vatican alone, and there are special weekly versions in English, French, Spanish, and Portuguese.

Although the members of the editorial staff pride themselves on their coverage of general world news, there is little doubt that anything of significance to the position of the Roman Catholic church has special importance for them. The report from one of their German correspondents was received on Wednesday morning, and a reporter took it straight into Manzini, the managing editor.

"Where did this come from?" he asked.

"West Berlin. You think there could be any truth in it?"

"I don't know. If there is, it could be a hot one. Leave it with me, and I don't want it discussed. Not with anyone."

The reporter went out. Manzini sat there thinking about it for a while, then reached for his phone and told his secretary to get him the father general of the Jesuits at Collegio di San Roberto Bellarmino.

191

Over 600,000 people, the greatest number ever assembled to honor a Roman pontiff, had filed past the embalmed body of Pope John as it lay in state for three days in St. Peter's Basilica. In addition to the Italian president and his entire Cabinet, diplomatic representatives of fifty-five countries had been among the mourners. And finally, he was buried in the Crypt of St. Peter in private in accordance with his dying wish.

For Pacelli, it had been a busy time: so many church dignitaries arriving in Rome from all over the world; conferences to attend with various departments of the Italian security services; new policies to be hammered out.

When he knocked on the door and went in, the father general was standing by the window. He turned. "Ah, there you are. I've just had Manzini on the phone, from *L'Osservatore Romano*. They've got wind of the Conlin affair."

"To what extent?"

"A minor report from one of their Berlin correspondents, totally unconfirmed, that Conlin has disappeared and that the East Germans have him."

"What did you tell Manzini?"

"I asked him not to use the story, naturally. I told him that matters of the gravest security were concerned. He agreed at once. He is a man of the utmost dependability. He did point out that if the rumor exists, then sooner or later, it must come to the attention of other news agencies, and there is nothing we can do about that."

"An unfortunate situation," Pacelli said. "It's amazing how minor leaks of this nature can take place, no matter how strict one's security system. I'll see about the other news agencies. We do have a certain influence in these areas."

"Do what you can."

"May I remind you that it is today that Father Hartmann proceeds to Neustadt?"

The father general, who had sat down behind his desk, looked up. "Then we must pray for him."

"Indeed we must," Pacelli said. "For he will need all our prayers, I think."

In the basement garage of the Catholic Secretariat in East Berlin, Erich Hartmann was loading his suitcase into the back of the Volkswagen. The garage was dimly lit. There were only two other cars to be seen, and a State Medical service ambulance. He wondered what it was doing there, and then there was the rattle of a motorcycle engine and Schaefer came down the ramp in his BMW.

He wore his trench coat, a cap, and goggles, and there was a canvas suitcase strapped to the luggage carrier of the BMW. He pulled the machine up on its stand and walked across, pushing up his goggles.

"Why couldn't we have gone down this afternoon, Father, in daylight? I hate biking after dark."

"I had a considerable amount of paperwork to clear up this afternoon," Hartmann said, which was not strictly true. He had left his departure until eight o'clock at night because Pascoe had asked him to, although there had been no explanation as to why.

"All right, Father, we might as well get started."

"This is nonsense," Hartmann said. "Why can't you drive down with me in comfort?"

"Regulations," Schaefer replied. "Where you go, I follow."

"Which seems to me to be stretching bureaucracy to the limits."

"That's democratic socialism for you, Father."

Hartmann smiled. "How's your wife?"

"Glad to get rid of me for a week." Schaefer grinned. "I'll tell you what, Father. Halfway there on the far side of Rathenow there's a roadside café called the Astor. Pull up there, and I'll let you buy me a coffee."

"Done," Hartmann said, and he got into the Volkswagen and drove out of the garage.

Schaefer paused to pull on his gloves, and a voice called softly from behind, "Excuse me."

He turned and found a tall man advancing toward him, hands in pockets. There was something strange about him, something Schaefer couldn't put his finger on, and then he realized what it was. The other man was wearing a trench coat that was twin to his own, tweed cap, navy blue polo-neck sweater, gray tweed trousers. All the same.

"Horst Schaefer?"

Schaefer, sensing that something was very badly wrong here, reached for the holstered Walther under his left armpit, too late, for already he found himself staring down the muzzle of its twin.

"So am I." Vaughan smiled.

The ambulance rolled forward and braked to a halt, and two men in white uniforms got out. One of them jerked Schaefer's arms behind and handcuffed him, and Vaughan removed his wallet. He took out only the identity papers and slipped them into one of Schaefer's pockets. He kept the more personal items, a letter from Schaefer's father, a couple of snapshots of his wife and children.

He produced identical identity papers, which he

slipped into the wallet, then put it in his own inside breast pocket. He removed Schaefer's goggles and put them on.

"What is this?" Schaefer was frightened now. "Who are you?"

"I'm Horst Schaefer," Vaughan told him amicably. "These two gentlemen are members of what you would call an illegal organization—the Christian Underground. I wouldn't advise you to give them any trouble. They're not too good at turning the other cheek."

One of them led Schaefer to the rear of the ambulance, the other opened the door, and they pushed him inside and down on one of the bunks. Before he knew what was happening, a hypodermic appeared and the needle was jammed into his arm, right through the leather sleeve.

On the opposite bunk there was a body totally covered by a red blanket. Vaughan pulled it back to disclose the waxen features of a young girl, eyes closed in death.

"We always try to make it a young girl. It makes the Vopos feel bad at the checkpoint."

"I don't understand." Schaefer could hardly keep his eyes open now, and his limbs felt as heavy as lead.

"Into the Western Zone. All quite legitimate. These gentlemen have got the papers."

A concealed trap was lifted in the floor, a space revealed about the size of a coffin. Schaefer was lowered into it, his senses already slipping away from him as the lid was lowered.

It was a quiet night at the Astor café. There were only four people in the place, the girl behind the counter, two truck drivers having their evening meal, and Erich Hartmann, who sat with a cup of coffee in front of him at a corner table.

He made a conspicuous enough figure in his broad-brimmed shovel hat and black cassock, and the others watched him curiously. He wondered what could be keeping Schaefer, for traffic on the road had been light. He became aware of the sound of a motorcycle engine outside and looked out and saw the BMW turn into the car park and pull up beside the Volkswagen.

"Fräulein?" he called to the girl. "Another coffee, if you please."

A moment later, the door opened. He turned with a smile, and then the smile faded as, to his total astonishment, Simon Vaughan entered the café.

Vaughan spooned sugar into his coffee. Hartmann waited for the girl to go back behind the counter before whispering, "What on earth is going on here?"

Vaughan took out his wallet, extracted his card, and passed it over. "Horst Schaefer, your friendly local SSD man."

The card was a perfect facsimile of Schaefer's own, except that the thumbprint, the physical characteristics, where appropriate, and the photo were Vaughan's.

Hartmann passed the card back. "Where's Schaefer? What have you done to him?"

"Should be in West Berlin right about now," Vaughan told him. "Sleeping soundly, and when he wakes up, he'll find Bruno Teusen at his bedside."

Hartmann's face was calm, but there was anger in the eyes, and his right fist had clenched. "Why wasn't this discussed with me?"

"Because it was felt you might argue about it. Now you can't."

"Damn you, Vaughan."

"Strong words for a man of the cloth, Father," Vaughan said. "And while we're on the subject, why the fancy dress? Conspicuous consumption by any standards, I should have thought."

"I want them to know who I am when I get to Neustadt. I thought that was the idea. To pull all attention onto me."

"Something like that," Vaughan said. "Well, is it war or peace between us?"

Hartmann smiled ruefully. "Do I have a choice?"

He got up and moved out, and Vaughan followed him.

It was shortly after ten when Hartmann pulled up in front of the inn at Neustadt. A Vopo field car was parked a few yards away. Hartmann sat there for a while, then reached for his suitcase and got out. He went up the steps to the entrance, paused, then opened the door.

Georg Ehrlich was behind the bar with Sigrid. Heinrich Berg and a half-dozen of the village men sat in a circle together drinking beer; Süssmann and Becker were at a table by the fire, plates of stew before them.

It was Sigrid who saw Hartmann first and sucked in her breath sharply. And then the whole room went silent. Hartmann put down his suitcase and moved to the bar.

"Are you Herr Ehrlich, the mayor here?"

"That's right."

"My name is Hartmann. I believe you've been

warned to expect me. I'm here to consider the question of the church."

Ehrlich's eyes flickered nervously to the two Vopos by the fire. "Yes," he said slowly. "I received word from the Ministry of State Security some days ago. You're wasting your time here, Father, you must know that."

The door opened, and Vaughan entered carrying his canvas holdall. He dropped it beside Hartmann's suitcase and came forward. "So, you made it, Father?" Heinrich Berg stared at him, his mouth gaping in astonishment, a kind of horror in his eyes, and Vaughan nodded cheerfully.

Süssmann got up, wiping his mouth on a napkin, and walked across the room. He stood for a moment, looking them both over. "Papers," he said curtly.

Hartmann handed him his Ministry of State Security permit. Süssmann examined it, handed it back to him without a word, then turned to Vaughan.

"And you?"

"Schaefer—Section Six."

Vaughan proffered his SSD card, and Süssmann checked it. "So, where he goes, you follow?"

"Something like that."

He returned Vaughan's card, and Hartmann said, "Would you be the military commander of this area?"

"No," Süssmann said. "Why do you ask?"

"I was told to report my presence to him on arrival."

Süssmann hesitated. "The person you seek is busy tonight. You must try tomorrow. In the morning at Schloss Neustadt."

He walked back to the table and sat down, saying something to Becker, who laughed coarsely. Hartmann said, "Have you room for us to stay, Herr Ehrlich?"

Ehrlich shook his head. "That is not possible."

"I see," Hartmann said calmly. "Is there a priest's house still?"

"Yes," Ehrlich said reluctantly. "But it has not been used for some time. I have the key."

"Perhaps if you could spare a few blankets," Hartmann said. "I'm sure Herr Schaefer and I could manage, unless, of course, you can find him room here."

Ehrlich looked hunted, and Vaughan said cheerfully, "Can't let you out of my sight, now can I, Father? I think we'd better stick together."

"All right," Ehrlich said. "I'll find you some blankets and get the key."

"And the church?" Hartmann said. "Have you the key to the church?"

"The church stays locked." It was Süssmann who had spoken.

Hartmann turned to look at him, and Ehrlich said hurriedly, "I'll get the blankets," and fled.

The villagers were discussing the situation among themselves in low tones, and Hartmann and Vaughan sat down at a table to wait. Sigrid brought two beers without a word. She was a pretty girl in traditional costume, her flaxen hair plaited around her head. She gazed at Hartmann in fascination, unable to take her eyes off him.

He toasted her. "Thank you, that's very kind."

Becker got up and swaggered forward, a stein of beer in his left hand. He emptied it, put it down on the table, and stood over Hartmann, looking down at him contemptuously.

"Skirts on men. What next?" He made a kissing sound with his lips and patted Hartmann's cheek.

Hartmann's hand fastened around his wrist, and the smile was wiped from Becker's face, and he staggered, then fell to one knee, forced down by the relentless pressure of all that enormous strength. Hartmann released him suddenly so that Becker lost his balance and fell back. His rage was terrible to see, and he pulled at the flap of his pistol holster.

"Becker!" Süssmann called. "Enough!"

The sergeant major got to his feet, his hand on the butt of his Walther now. This time, when Süssmann spoke there was iron in his voice. "Becker! For the last time!"

The sergeant major went back to the table, and Ehrlich returned with the blankets and an oil lamp. "All right, gentlemen, if you'll follow me."

The house was next to the church, a small, two-storied building with wooden shutters, which were closed.

"I'm surprised you haven't let someone move in," Hartmann said.

"There is no shortage of housing in this village, Father. Agriculture is declining in these parts, and most young people move to Berlin if they can to get work in the factories there. I'm afraid the electricity is not connected, which is why I've brought the oil lamp, but there's water on tap and a lavatory. You should be all right."

The front door opened onto a stone-flagged passage. There was a wooden staircase going up to the second floor, and Ehrlich led the way along to the kitchen. There was a wooden table, chairs, and an old iron stove.

"Plenty of wood out at the back if you want

to light a fire. Two bedrooms upstairs. I don't know what condition the mattresses will be in."

"We'll manage," Hartmann said. "You've been very kind."

"That's all right, Father," Ehrlich told him gruffly. For a moment, it seemed as if he might say something more and then thought better of it and went out.

"Now what?" Hartmann said.

"Make a fire. Fill in a little time. Then I'd like to see how the Franciscans have been getting on."

"May I come with you?"

"If you like. One thing is definite. We stay as far away from that place as possible during the day. Not even a hint of a connection."

"As you say."

Vaughan lit a cigarette. "I like what you did to that big ox back at the inn. I didn't know your lot went in for things like that."

"Soldiers for Christ, Major Vaughan. Didn't you know?" Hartmann picked up the lamp. "And now, I'll see if I can find some wood in the yard."

The gate bell made a lonely sound, rather eerie, and there was no response for some considerable time, then footsteps. The shutter was opened, and frail old Brother Urban peered out. The bolt was withdrawn; he opened the gate.

"Major," he said in his dry old voice, "they're in the barn."

"How are things?"

"Not good."

It was the smell which was most noticeable the moment Vaughan opened the door. Konrad and

Florian were loading on the edge of the excavation, and both of them were wearing bandages wrapped about their faces to cover mouth and nose. The half-light of the barn enhanced the effect, strange and disturbing.

When Konrad paused to speak, leaning wearily on his shovel, his voice was thick, muffled. "Good, you made it. Did everything go all right?"

"Perfectly. This is Father Hartmann."

"I won't shake hands," Konrad said. "For obvious reasons."

Hartmann moved to the edge of the excavation, his face pale. "Is it bad in there?"

"I'm afraid so. We've made excellent progress, but we've started to hit more recent graves, and it isn't nice."

"That smell is terrible."

There was a movement down below, and some-one emerged on hands and knees. When he stood, Vaughan saw that it was Gregor, in spite of the fact that the head, as well as the mouth and nose, was swathed in bandages. He carried a piece of sacking in two hands, holding it out in front of him, and from the bulge it was obvious that it contained something.

"An arm, or what's left of one," he said to Konrad. "It's not going to be pleasant getting the rest out."

He went through into the other room. "The well?" Vaughan asked.

Konrad nodded. "Then lime and more soil. Nothing else we can do."

"Where's Dr. Campbell?"

"In the house attending to Franz. He cut himself, and she's most insistent that every injury, even the slightest scratch, is treated at once."

"We'll have a word with her."

They found her in the kitchen with Franz, who was stripped to the waist. There was a large zinc bath of heavily disinfected water on the table and an assortment of drugs. She was giving him an injection as they went in, and Vaughan at once saw the dressing on the boy's left arm, fastened into place by surgical tape.

"Simon." She smiled, but her cheeks were sunken.

"How goes it?"

"Fine. Have you seen Konrad?"

"Yes, we took a look. Nasty."

Franz said, "I'll get back now."

"And don't forget," she told him. "The slightest thing—any kind of ache or pain or headache—come and see me at once."

"Fräulein," he said grinning, "I ache all over already."

He went out, and she said, "So this is Father Hartmann."

Hartmann took her hand and smiled warmly. "A pleasure, Fräulein. I've heard a great deal about you."

"Can I get you coffee?"

He hesitated, glancing at Vaughan. "No, thanks. I think I'd like to go back to the barn. There may be something I could do."

"Tea and sympathy," Vaughan said with brutal directness. "No more than that. They've got their job to do—you have yours. I don't want you getting your cassock dirty. Spend too much time in there, and the villagers will smell you coming as you cross the square."

"All right," Hartmann said angrily, "I take your point."

When he'd gone, Vaughan turned to the girl. She was putting the kettle on the stove and turned to face him, looking tired and somehow past everything that ever was and totally vulnerable.

"You've no idea how glad I am to see you," she said, and came into his arms.

Every resolve he had made faded away. He held her close. "Bad, is it?"

When she looked up at him, her eyes were filled with a deep disgust. "Horrible, Simon. Like something out of a nightmare, and the trouble is, I think it's going to get worse."

It was cold in the early dawn and still dark when the two Vopos dragged Conlin into the courtyard. He stood between them, shivering, wondering what was to come. The headlamps of a field car parked close by were switched on, and their twin shafts picked Karl out of the darkness, strapped to a post in the center of the courtyard.

Süssmann and Becker appeared, and the captain said, "Bring him," and went forward with the sergeant major, the two Vopos dragging Conlin behind.

Karl hung in the straps, his head lolling to one side. Becker peered closely at him. "I think he's dead," he announced.

"Make sure," Süssmann said coldly.

Becker took out his Walther, cocked it, and fired into the skull at point-blank range. Pieces of bone and blood sprayed; the body sagged. Conlin cried out sharply. Süssmann and Becker walked away, the two

Vopos released their grip, and Conlin sank to the ground at Karl's feet, all strength going out of him.

Footsteps approached; the damp air was scented with cigarette smoke. Harry Van Buren squatted beside him.

"You could have prevented this if you'd been sensible. He'd have still been alive if it hadn't been for that incredible self-righteousness of yours. The insistence that you must be right in all things, even when it kills people."

"Go away," Father Conlin said in a low voice.

"Like poor Karl here," Van Buren told him. "Or your sister."

He stood up and walked away quite quickly, his steps echoing on the cobbles. Conlin crouched there, his head against Karl's knee.

"Oh, dear God, Frances Mary," he said. "I never wanted it, you know that."

For the first time in years he started to cry.

Vaughan and Hartmann sat on two chairs on the landing outside Van Buren's office and waited. After a while, Vaughan got up, went to the balustrade, and looked down at the imposing sweep of the great staircase, the hall below.

"Perfect for a remake of *The Prisoner of Zenda*, but not exactly comfortable," Hartmann remarked.

The door opened, and Süssmann looked out. "He'll see you now—together."

Hartmann led the way into the room, Vaughan at his heels, and Süssmann closed the door behind them and stood against it. Van Buren waited, seated at his desk. Hartmann produced his permit.

Van Buren ignored it and looked him over, an amused, slightly contemptuous smile on his face. "Are you going to a costume ball?"

"I think you know why I am here," Hartmann said carefully. "I was ordered to report to the area commander on arrival, and I have now done so. Am I permitted to leave?"

"Very good." Van Buren clapped his hands solemnly. "Nothing like a religious education for teaching a man how to behave."

"I heard you lecture at Dresden three months ago. 'The Psychological Basis of Religious Persuasion." You were very eloquent."

"But failed to make my case?"

Hartmann said, "I happen to believe that in every human being, there is something profound and mysterious that can never answer to your more rational explanation."

Van Buren held up a hand to cut him off. "No, thanks. I'm not interested in philosophical argument, not at this time of day. Let's stick to the facts. Just what do you intend to do while you're here?"

"Examine the state of the church. Meet the people. Discuss their religious needs."

"With a view to reopening the church itself?"

"If that is what people want. The right of each and every citizen to follow the religion of his choice is part of the constitution."

"So is censorship of the papers. And the fact that trade unions are forbidden the right to strike. Which is right, which is wrong?"

"I thought you said you'd no time for philosophical discussion at the moment."

Van Buren smiled. "Your point, Father." He lit a cigarette and leaned back. "All right. Play your little games if you must, but don't get underfoot. Any incident of the most minor nature, and I'll have you back to Berlin within the hour."

"As you say. There is one thing. I understand you have the keys to the church."

Van Buren sat staring up at him for a while, then opened a drawer, took out three large keys on a ring, and threw them across the desk. "There you are, but no public services."

"Which means you think I'd actually get a congregation. Thank you. That's most encouraging. And thank you for your time."

Hartmann moved to the door. As Süssmann opened it for him, Van Buren said in English, "They tell me you were at Notre Dame. All-American quarterback two years running."

"That's right."

Van Buren laughed. "A jock," he said. "In a black frock. That I should live to see the day."

Hartmann refused to be drawn and went out without a word. Van Buren laughed, got up, and moved to the fire, not a bit put out. He threw on another log and turned to Vaughan. "So, you're Schaefer?" he said in German.

"That's right, Comrade."

"I hear you've moved into the priest's house with him."

"There was little choice. The mayor said he couldn't accommodate us at the inn, and besides, I like to stick close to him. That's my job."

"And that's exactly what you will do," Van Buren said. "Stick like glue. Anything he does that's the slightest bit out of the ordinary, I want to know about it."

"You're in charge, Comrade."

Van Buren nodded. "All right. On your way and stay in touch."

Vaughan went out, and Süssmann closed the door.

"Are you going to let him get away with it, this priest?"

"His permit is signed by the minister of state security himself. All a question of politics, Süssmann. Tell Lieutenant Leber I want her, will you?"

The captain went out, and Van Buren sat down at his desk and, opening a drawer in search of blank paper, again discovered the Russian grenades. He took one out and saw that it was very similar in design to the American version: a ring pin to pull with finger or teeth; the safety lever to hold until the final second before throwing.

He was handling one when Süssmann came back. "Nasty little item," Van Buren said.

"A fragmentation grenade."

"Yes, we used babies like this in Korea, and they suffer from the defects of their kind. If you ever want to throw one, make sure you're under cover. They can scatter fragments for a two-hundred-meter radius."

Süssmann, who had never seen action and secretly envied Van Buren his war experience, nodded. "I'll remember that, Comrade. Lieutenant Leber will be along in a moment."

"Good."

"Is there anything else, Comrade?"

"Yes, you'd better bring Conlin up here again and we'll see how he's getting on."

THIRTEEN

The church was cold and smelled of damp, which was only to be expected. It was rather dark, the glass of its narrow windows stained in somber hues that were not particularly pleasing.

"Nineteenth century," Hartmann said. "But these pillars are medieval."

It took Vaughan straight back to his boyhood and the forced attendance at church each Sunday evening with his grandmother. There had been a church smell then; there was a church smell now. Nothing changed.

There was a row of oak pews on either side of the aisle, a small dark chapel to the left with an image of the Virgin floating there in the half-light. Hartmann walked along the aisle and genuflected in front of the altar.

Vaughan followed him, and Hartmann said, "See, here beside the altar rail?"

There was a square hole set into the floor and lined with brass.

"What is it?" Vaughan asked.

"The socket for St. Michael's Cross, I should imagine." He stared across the church, a slight frown on his face. "There's something unusual here. Have you noticed how clean everything is?" He ran a finger along the altar rail. "Not only is there no dust, but it smells of polish."

He crossed to the sacristy and opened the door. There wasn't much in there. A table, chairs, a cupboard, which, when he opened it, contained the church registers and also a plentiful supply of candles.

It was Vaughan who made the most interesting discovery of all, for when he tried the side door, it proved to be unlocked and opened to his touch.

"Now, what do you make of that?" he asked. "At least we now know how the cleaning staff get in."

"I wonder if our friend the mayor knows about this." Hartmann tried the light switch, which proved to work. "See," he said. "Even the electricity is still connected, which is more than you can say for the house. I wonder why."

Vaughan lit a cigarette. "Probably there are hordes of lovable peasants out there just aching to come back to the arms of Mother Church."

"Perhaps," Hartmann said. "Tell me, do you think it at all possible that Brother Konrad and his friends might manage what he was talking about last night?"

"What, break through within the next three days? I don't see why not. Is it important?" And then Vaughan saw the way things were going. "You'd like more time here, is that it? You'd like to really get your teeth into the situation. Well, forget it, Father. We're not here to save souls. We're here to save Conlin."

Hartmann didn't reply but got up and went back into the church. Vaughan sat there, finishing his cigarette, and suddenly, to his complete astonishment, heard organ music.

When he went in, he couldn't see Hartmann at first, then discovered him seated at the organ masked by a curtain above the choir stalls. As Vaughan went up the steps to join him, Hartmann was experimenting, pulling out one stop after another, his hands running over the keys.

"Something else you managed to pick up in the football squad at Notre Dame?"

"Not good," Hartmann said. "But not bad. One could hardly expect an outstanding instrument in a village like this, and the reed stops have suffered in all this damp."

He moved into the opening of the Bach Prelude and Fugue in D Major, and he was good. Vaughan sat down in one of the choir stalls, hands in pockets, head back, and simply listened, and one didn't have to be a music lover to enjoy it. The music filled the church, echoing into the rafters as Hartmann played on, lost in some private world of his own.

Finally, he stopped. Vaughan said quietly, "You should have made all-American for that, too."

Hartmann turned on the seat, smiling hugely for the first time since Vaughan had known him, obviously genuinely pleased, and then he paused, looking out over Vaughan's shoulder.

When Vaughan turned, he found Sigrid Ehrlich sitting in the front pew.

A scarf was bound around her head, and her tweed coat was simply slung from her shoulders as if put on in a hurry. She sat there, clutching it about her, her eyes never leaving Hartmann, a kind of awe in them.

He came down the steps from the choir stalls,

smiling. "Fräulein Ehrlich, isn't it? It's good to see you here."

"Father." Her voice was almost a whisper.

"And what brings you?" He sat down in the pew beside her.

"I could hear the organ."

"In the inn?"

"Yes."

"You must forgive me. I was obviously forgetting myself."

She leaned forward eagerly. "No, not at all. It was wonderful. It's a long time since I heard anything like it. Father Honecker used to play, but I was only a child then and didn't really appreciate such things."

"You knew Father Honecker?"

"Oh, yes."

"I see," Hartmann said carefully. "Tell me, are you a Catholic, Fräulein?"

She flushed. "I—I am baptized, Father, but there has been no priest here since Father Honecker's death."

"Yes, I know that." There was a slight pause. She stared down at her hands, folded now in her lap. Hartmann said gently, "The church is obviously well looked after. Clean, sweet. Do you do that?" She glanced at Vaughan, her face troubled. "Come on, you can speak freely. Herr Schaefer won't tell."

"All right. Several of the older women come in regularly each week."

"I see." He was not smiling, but there was a light in his eyes that somehow illuminated his entire face. "I will pray for you, my child. All of you."

He started to get up, and she caught hold of his sleeve, her face strained and anxious. "Father, hear my confession." He seemed transfixed, staring down at her, his face pale.

And suddenly she was on her knees, clutching at his hand, tears running uncontrollably down her cheeks. "Oh, Father, it's been so long."

"Of course, my child." He raised her up and sat her down. "Stay there. I shan't be long."

He went out into the sacristy, and Vaughan followed, but when he got there, there was no sign of Hartmann. He opened the side door and saw the priest going into the house.

Vaughan sat on the table and lit a cigarette. "Oh, my God," he whispered, "that's all I need. A truly good man."

A few moments later, the door opened, and Hartmann entered, holding a black velvet bag. "Don't tell me," Vaughan said. "Let me guess. Your vestments and other assorted goodies."

Hartmann opened the bag and started to take things out. "You surely didn't think I came unprepared, Major." He put on his alb and threw a violet stole over his shoulder.

"Would it be too much to ask you to remember why we're here?"

Hartmann paused, a hand on the door. "Major Vaughan, there is one thing I have that I share with the Pope himself. Whatever else I am, whatever my background, however high I rise, I am still priest, first and foremost. That is something I can never escape. It is my reason for being."

"So we're back in the drainpipe again?"

"If you like."

Hartmann went into the church, and Vaughan followed him to the door, watched him speak to Sigrid Ehrlich. She stood up, and they walked together to the confessional box and entered their separate compartments.

There was a murmur of voices, and then the sound of passionate weeping from the girl. Vaughan shivered as if suddenly aware that he had no right to be there. He closed the door softly, let himself out into the garden, and walked up and down aimlessly under the plane trees, smoking.

It was a good half hour before Hartmann and the girl appeared. He had taken off his alb and stole and was once more attired in black cassock and dark hat. The girl gazed up at him intently as he talked to her.

As they approached, Hartmann said cheerfully, "Ah, there you are, Horst. Kind of you to wait." He smiled down at Sigrid. "Herr Schaefer is in some respects my keeper." She glanced up at Vaughan, a certain alarm in her eyes, and Hartmann laughed. "Don't worry. He won't bite. We have what you might call a working relationship."

He was in excellent spirits, more animated than at any time since Vaughan had known him. "You've finished in there, I presume."

"For the moment, yes. Sigrid's going to show us the Cross of St. Michael, down by the river."

"That should be nice," Vaughan said.

The irony in his voice seemed totally lost on Hartmann. "How far did you say it was, Sigrid? A mile? Then we'll walk, I think."

It was a nonsense, of course, the whole affair, but in a sense Vaughan was trapped, a fact of which, he decided, Hartmann was only too well aware. He trailed along behind the priest and the girl, across the square, and along the main street, attracting curious glances from the few villagers whom they passed. Beyond the last house, the road sloped down to the Elbe between a double row of pine trees, and the view was rather beautiful.

At one point, the girl laughed, and he heard Hartmann say, "But there is no law forbidding priests to visit you. Surely one or two must have visited you here during the past five years, from neighboring villages perhaps?"

"With party cards in their pockets," she said contemptuously. "They only seem like priests."

The road turned to the right to follow the course of the river. To the left, a rough track led to a grove of trees, and the cross stood there, plain to see, black, heavy oak, as was the figure of Christ nailed to it. It was obviously the work of a peasant hand and had no great artistic merit, but it possessed a certain dignity for all that. It had been set into the earth, and grass grew thickly about the base.

Hartmann stood looking up at the figure of Christ intently. "And Father Honecker tried to lift this on his own?"

"He must have been mad," Vaughan said.

"No. Desperate, I think."

"He died here," Sigrid said. "Died trying, here on this very spot."

Hartmann bowed his head in prayer.

Vaughan took the girl by the elbow and led her some little distance away.

The Elbe rushed by, brown and swollen, and he took out his cigarettes. "Do you use these things?"

"No," she said.

"Good for you." He put one in his mouth and lit it.

"My father says you're a policeman."

"You could put it that way."

"Why are you always with Father Hartmann?"

"Oh, he needs looking after, wouldn't you say?"

"He's a good man," she said, "a wonderful man," and turned to where Hartmann stood at the foot of the cross.

His voice was blown to them by the wind, strong and firm. "*Requiem aeternam dona eis, Domine, et lux perpetuas luceat eis.*"

He was saying the Mass for the Dead.

On the way back, Vaughan expressed interest in the Catholic cemetery, and the girl took them in. It was surprisingly well looked after, the grass cut, some of the newer graves decorated with flowers. The tunnel line stretched from the wall of the barn to the northeast corner of the cemetery, Vaughan knew that, but above-ground things looked perfectly normal. A fall down there, of course, and that would be something else again. The consequences would be disastrous.

He turned away and followed Hartmann and the girl out of the entrance and across the street to the church. The mayor was standing in the porch of the inn and came down the steps and moved a few paces toward them.

"Sigrid, go in at once, you're needed."

She glanced uncertainly at Hartmann. He nodded gently, and she hurried past her father and went inside.

"Don't be angry with your daughter, Herr Ehrlich," Hartmann said. "She was kind enough to show me one or two places I wanted to see."

Ehrlich moved close, and his voice was low and full of passion. "She was in the church, do you think I don't know that? I don't want her in there again. I don't want her mixed up in this sort of thing, you understand? In the world we live in today, Father, it's too dangerous."

"It's always been dangerous, my friend," Hartmann said. "But surely as mayor and local party secretary, you'd be the last person to deny the constitution under which each individual has the right to exercise free will in the matter of religion?"

"Oh, go to the devil!" Ehrlich turned and hurried back toward the inn.

"What are you after?" Vaughan demanded as they went up the steps to the entrance of the church. "What are you trying to prove?"

"I'm supposed to provide a diversion, am I not? I should have thought I was succeeding admirably." Hartmann opened the door and moved inside, and then he stopped with an intake of breath.

There were flowers everywhere, or so it seemed. In the Lady Chapel and on the altar. And more. There was a ruby glow to the sanctuary lamp. Hartmann walked slowly down the aisle and stood at the bottom of the steps. There were even fresh candles, neatly stacked beside the offertory box.

"So, Sigrid is not alone, it would seem." He picked up a candle and placed it in one of the holders and said to Vaughan, "Light it, please."

Vaughan struck a match and touched it to the wick. As the candle flared, Hartmann turned to him and smiled. "To Saint Jude, patron saint of the impossible."

Conlin was tired and listless, eyes sore from lack of sleep. When he closed them, all he could see was the back of Karl's skull dissolving as the bullet fragmented bone endlessly, and occasionally, he seemed to hear the voice in his ear, begging him to confess.

Which was all perfectly understandable, of course. Such hallucinations were common under conditions of extreme stress, and his physical state was not good now. Experience and logic told him as much, but it didn't help him sleep. It didn't enable him to close his burning eyes.

He vomited into the bucket, and the guard looked in to see what was happening. Conlin sat on the bed, feeling very ill indeed. Finally, he heard steps approaching, the door was opened, and Van Buren appeared. Lieutenant Leber was with him in her white coat, carrying her medical bag. It occurred to Conlin, and for no particular reason, that he had never heard her talk.

Van Buren said, "Are you ill?"

"It's nothing," Conlin told him wearily. "I was sick a couple of times, that's all, and I can't sleep."

"We can do something about that at any rate," Van Buren said solicitously, and turned to the woman. "Give him a shot."

Conlin didn't argue. There would have been no point. She produced a hypodermic and gave him an injection in his right arm. It hurt rather a lot because there wasn't too much flesh on his bones now, but he was really past caring. When she rubbed it afterward, her fingers were particularly light and soothing.

Van Buren said, "We'll leave you. Try to get a good night's sleep. I need you fresh for the morning."

"What was it she gave me?" Conlin asked, already aware of the languor that seeped through his veins.

"Something good, I promise you." The door

clanged shut. The echo seemed to go on for a very long time, and then there was silence.

He was lying on a bed and it was not dark and there was a pale, diffused light to things which he found rather pleasant. It was warm, which was an improvement, for he seemed to have been cold for so long now.

He was aware of a slight movement and turned his head and saw Lieutenant Leber standing on the other side of the room. She was wearing her Vopo uniform—tunic, skirt, and leather boots. Her face was very calm as she started to unbutton the tunic.

Underneath, she wore a white cotton blouse, and when she molded her hands to her waist, the blouse tightened, a nipple blossoming at the tip of each breast.

She came across to the bed, leaned down, and put a hand on him. He tried to push her away, but there was no strength in him at all, his arms moving in a kind of slow motion.

She spoke in a distorted and remote voice. "There's nothing to fear. Nothing to be ashamed of."

She unfastened the zipper at the side of her skirt and slipped out of it. And then she sat on the edge of the bed and unfastened the blouse. Her breasts were round and full and very beautiful, and then, as she leaned over and put a hand on him, he started to laugh uncontrollably, his entire body shaking with helpless mirth, eyes tightly shut.

And after a while, when he opened them again, she had gone.

Van Buren was standing, staring down into the heart of the fire, a glass of Cognac in one hand, when there was a knock on the door and Ruth Leber entered. She was in full uniform, including her great-coat, which was unbuttoned at the front. The one incongruous feature was the small vanity case she carried in one hand.

"I left one or two things in the bathroom," she said. "Can I get them?"

"Help yourself."

He lit a cigarette, and she returned and stood looking at him, as if waiting for something. "Are you sure you want me to go?"

"Nothing for you to stay for, is there?"

"I don't suppose there is."

"You can take the Mercedes."

She paused, a hand on the door. "Is there any way you can get out of this thing, Harry?"

He turned to look at her, surprise on his face. "Why should I want to?"

"How many times have I worked with you? How many cases? Fifteen, twenty?"

"So?"

"He's different, this old man. He isn't like the others."

"Why, because he's got God on his side?"

"Perhaps."

He smiled coldly. "Careful, angel. If Klein heard you talking like that . . ."

"Good-bye, Harry."

The door closed softly behind her.

He sat, slightly dazed, in front of Van Buren's desk, a blanket around his shoulders. His mouth was dry, obviously the aftereffect of the drug, and he sipped eagerly at the coffee provided. After a while, the door opened and Van Buren came in. He sat down on the other side of the desk.

"How do you feel?"

"Terrible. Sorry about that drug of yours, whatever it was."

"We'll have to go back to the lab and try again."

"That poor girl." Conlin shook his head. "What was she supposed to do? Prove I'm a sinner like anyone else? I already know that. Arouse my dormant sexuality? Induce an erection?" He shook his head. "There are times, Harry, when I despair of you. Didn't it ever occur to you that the Almighty might consider that a perfectly reasonable chemical reaction?"

Van Buren smiled in spite of himself. "You could have a point there."

"I could indeed. Man is a creature of instinct as well as reason. Even that old fraud Sigmund Freud admitted that sometimes a cigar is only a cigar."

"You'll have to be careful," Van Buren said. "Much more of this and you'll leave me only one choice."

"The same as you gave Karl? But I'm not afraid to die, Harry. Maybe that's the difference between you and me. One loses consciousness—sleeps. The corruption of the body afterwards is something else. One isn't involved. We die from the day we're born."

"Only some of us go rather sooner than others," Van Buren said. "Frances Mary, for instance."

It was just after eight when Vaughan went across the square to the inn. When he went in, Van Buren was sitting at the best table, the one beside the fire, with Süssmann. They were deep in conversation.

Becker sat at a smaller table on his own, obviously
excluded and not liking it. He scowled at Vaughan,
who ignored him and went to the bar.

Ehrlich nodded formally. "What can I get you?"

"A beer would be fine, and what about something to eat?"

"Potato soup, cold sausage, sauerkraut. I can do
nothing more."

"That would be fine."

Ehrlich gave him his beer, and Van Buren called,
"And where's the Holy Father tonight?"

If he'd expected to draw a laugh from the locals,
it failed miserably, and the silence which followed
was one of disapproval.

Vaughan moved across. "Seeking out the faithful.
He's like a traveling salesman, going round knocking
on doors, hoping someone will buy."

Süssmann said, "Shouldn't you be with him?"

Schaefer's position in the SSD gave him the
equivalent rank of a lieutenant in the Volkspolizei,
so Vaughan didn't see any pressing need to be polite
to Süssmann. He said, "My official brief is to keep him
under observation and know where he is at all
times. As far as I'm concerned, I do."

He nodded to Van Buren, walked across to
another table, and sat down. Becker was scowling at
him harder than ever. Sigrid came in from the kitchen
with a tray. There was soup and black bread, a bottle
of hock with the cork already drawn.

"Where's your father?" Vaughan asked.

"In the kitchen. He thinks he's a better cook
than I am."

She was really very pretty in her peasant skirt.

As she went back to the bar, Becker grabbed her
hand and pulled her on to his knee. He acted as if

two-thirds drunk, but Vaughan suspected otherwise. There was too much of the brute to Becker for liking. A suggestion of the animal.

As the girl struggled, Becker laughed, one hand fondling her left breast, the other sliding up under the skirt. She writhed, tears of humiliation in her eyes, and he laughed again coarsely.

"You like that, eh?"

Vaughan glanced across at the villagers. No one made a move. *They're frightened to death,* he thought, and turned to Van Buren and Süssmann. The Vopo captain seemed totally unconcerned, and Van Buren poured a glass of wine and threw another log on the fire. But now, it was beyond enduring. There was only lust on Becker's face, and the girl moaned in pain. Vaughan said, "Let her go!"

Becker turned his head sharply. "What was that?"

"I said, let her go. I mean, she doesn't know where you've been, does she?"

Van Buren was interested now, his eyes watchful over the rim of his glass as Becker pushed Sigrid to one side and got up. He crossed the room with exaggerated slowness and leaned on the table with both hands.

"You know what I'm going to do with you?"

Vaughan was in the act of pouring a glass of hock. In an almost casual gesture, he reversed his grip and smashed the bottle across the side of the Vopo's head. As Sigrid cried out, Becker staggered and fell to one knee.

Vaughan picked up a chair and brought it down across the great shoulders. Becker grunted and started to heel over, and Vaughan smashed the broken chair down again. He threw the pieces to one side and backed away.

- - -

Slowly, painfully, Becker reached for the edge of the table and pulled himself up. He hung there for a moment, then turned to Vaughan, wiping blood from his face casually.

And then, incredibly, he charged, head down, hands reaching out to destroy. Vaughan judged his moment exactly, swerved to one side, and punched him in the kidneys. Becker cried out and fell to the floor. He tried to get up again, but there was nothing left, and he rolled onto his back, moaning.

Sigrid's face was very white, and she was trembling. Her father, who had appeared from the kitchen, drew her behind the bar. Süssmann came forward, his face angry, and knelt down beside Becker.

He looked up at Vaughan. "This is a serious matter."

Van Buren pulled on his coat, smiling cheerfully. "Nonsense. He asked for it—he got it. You'd better see if you can wire him together again while I have words with our good comrade here."

Vaughan followed him outside. Van Buren paused at the top of the steps to light a cigarette. "Very good for a Section Six man. I didn't think your training took you quite that far."

"We do our best," Vaughan said warily.

"And Father Hartmann? Has he been behaving himself? He's not trying to pack them in there or anything, is he?"

"Not as far as I know."

Van Buren was already on his way across the square, and Vaughan followed. The American pushed upon the main door, and they went in. Candles flickered in many places now, and a half-dozen women and three men sat in a row beside the confessional box, waiting their turn.

"Now what do you make of that?" Van Buren said. "Very naughty indeed, I'd call it."

"I know," Vaughan said. "Karl Marx was right. Opiate of the people. Just like cigarettes. One taste and you're hooked again."

"That's good. I'll remember that one." Van Buren pulled up his collar. "So far and no farther. Tell him that from me." He turned and went out.

Vaughan waited for a while, but it was obvious that Hartmann was going to be some little while yet, and it was time he checked on how things were going at the farm. He went out, hurried across the square, and disappeared into the darkness of the side street opposite.

His pull on the gate bell was answered by old Brother Urban, and as he crossed the yard, Konrad opened the barn door and peered out.

"Oh, it's you. What about Hartmann?"

"About God's holy work," Vaughan said. "I think he's decided Neustadt needs him."

"He could be right, Major. Stranger things have happened."

There was a mild reproof in Konrad's voice, no more than that, and they went into the barn. Gregor was doing some measurements on a plan opened out on a small table. Margaret Campbell stood beside him, pouring coffee into several mugs, and Berg was there also, peering over Gregor's shoulder, a cigarette in his mouth.

Augustin, stripped to the waist, came in from the other room, pushing a barrow. He wore no bandaging about his face, and Vaughan suddenly realized that the dreadful all-pervading smell had gone.

"Considerably fresher than when I was last in here."

Konrad nodded. "In that respect, things have improved tremendously. We have made real progress. Far, far better than any of us could have hoped."

"Where are the others?"

"Franz and Florian are working at the coal face, which is what we call it now."

As he talked, Vaughan was watching the girl. She had not looked at him directly. She had a scarf tied around her hair and seemed absurdly young with great, sunken eyes.

He pulled himself together and turned to Berg. "Well, how are things up at the schloss?"

"Not so good. The truck driver, Karl. You remember?"

"What about him?"

"They executed him. Tied him to a pole in the courtyard and shot him. I saw it all from an upstairs window."

"When was this?"

"Very early this morning—dawn. It was still pretty dark, you understand, but I managed to see enough."

"And Father Conlin?"

"He was there, too. They made him watch. When I left earlier this evening, he was back on the third level."

"Anything else to report?"

"I don't think so. Oh, yes. The woman—the Vopo lieutenant."

"What about her?"

"She's gone—drove back to Berlin this evening."

Gregor said, "Fifty feet by my reckoning. We're almost at the cemetery boundary, and the sewer pipe is approximately six feet on the other side."

"We could reach it by tomorrow afternoon," Konrad said.

"Easily. Perhaps sooner."

"You're sure of this?" Vaughan demanded.

"I don't see why not. There's the question of breaking into the sewer pipe, but that shouldn't present any kind of difficulties," Gregor told him.

"Which means we could try to bring him out tomorrow night," Konrad said. "Unless you think that too soon for any reason."

"Good God, no." Vaughan shook his head. "The sooner the better. We can't be sure from one day to the next what Van Buren might try with Conlin. The wrong kind of drug, for instance." He turned to Berg. "You go down there again tomorrow with your rat poison and get the padlock off that manhole cover."

"I understand," Berg said. "But at what time will things really start to happen? When do we leave?"

"It must be after dark for obvious reasons. I'd say nine o'clock would be as good a time to strike as any."

"Call in with some milk churns at six," Konrad said. "I'll give you the final details then."

Berg nodded. "Fine. I'll go now."

He went out. Konrad turned to examine the plan again with Gregor, and Margaret Campbell handed Vaughan a mug of coffee without a word. They walked to the door, which was partly open. Rain drifted through the courtyard light outside. It was as if they were alone.

"You look tired," he said.

"Everyone is tired. So much must be done at night, and there's the appearance of things. The milk and eggs to be delivered round the village each day. The cows to be taken to pasture and so on. These things must be seen to be done; otherwise, someone might wonder what's happening."

"How's your leg?"

"I manage very well." Her shoulder touched his; she leaned against him wearily. "Not long now, Simon."

"Not long."

"And then what?"

"You'll be able to go home."

"And where would that be?" There was a bitterness, an anger in her voice that he had never heard before. "If you find out, let me know, Major. I've never been too sure myself."

And suddenly, he was desperately anxious to say the right things, for her, not himself. "You've got to start fresh, Maggie. Unstamped metal. All right, you've had one hell of a life so far, but the kind of knowledge you get from bitter experience has a limited value. It sets your thinking in a pattern built on that experience, and that's no good."

"So what do I do?"

"Practice your trade, I suppose. You're a doctor, aren't you? Pascoe should be able to get you a choice of England or America if you want. Or you could stay in West Germany."

"And you?" The eyes were darkly watchful as if someone were inside looking out at him.

He remembered what Meyer had said about the sniper on the roof and tried hard. "God knows. Something will turn up. It always does for people like me."

"And what kind of person are you? How do you see yourself?"

"Old Chinese saying," he said. "There's always an official executioner. If you try to take his place, it's like trying to be a master carpenter and cutting wood. You'll only hurt your hand."

"And what is that supposed to mean?"

"It means, give it up, Maggie. Let me go."

"No," she said simply. "Which doesn't mean that I approve of you or how you live or what you've done in the past. It simply means I love you."

Her hand was on his arm, her eyes serene, calm. He gazed down at her, suddenly desperate. From behind them in the tunnel came the most dreadful cry he had ever heard.

Franz had turned to take the sheet of corrugated iron from Florian when it happened. There was a trickle of soil on his head. He glanced up.

Florian scrambled back. "Careful, I think the roof goes."

The soil bulged, a rotting coffin appeared. The end broke away and two decaying feet poked through, minus the toes. The stench was immediate and appalling. Franz cried out in horror and tried to scramble back. As he moved, the entire coffin descended, the rotting wood breaking to reveal what was left of the corpse inside.

Vaughan and Gregor slipped through the darkness of the cemetery and crouched by the wall.

"This should be the place," Gregor whispered.

Vaughan switched on his torch. There was a grave—a comparatively recent one. An old man who had died ten months previously. It was more ornate than some, a marble slab on the ground surrounded by railings.

"Is this the one?"

Gregor nodded. "It has to be. Thank God for that slab. Without it there might have been one hell of a hole to explain."

They returned to the farm quickly. There was that smell in the barn again, only worse now, and Konrad and Augustin had the bandaging wrapped around their faces. Margaret Campbell had the medical chest open on the table and was filling a hypodermic.

"I'm going to give everyone a shot. Just as a precaution, and that includes you, Major. The possibilities of infection are appalling."

"Where are Franz and Florian?" Vaughan asked. "Not still in there surely?"

"But of course," Konrad said. "It must be brought out, that thing, before we can break through the final few feet."

There was a movement below, and Florian appeared, pulling a long, sacking-enshrouded bundle. Franz appeared at the other end. Konrad jumped down to help them, and they struggled up the ramp.

In spite of the sacking, the smell was terrible, and he said, "Keep back, the rest of you."

They went into the other room, and Vaughan followed in time to see them drop the body into the well. Konrad poured a sack of lime after it; Florian followed this with a barrowful of soil.

When they returned, Margaret Campbell was waiting to give them their injections. Franz was breathing hard, his eyes wild, and the stench on him was terrible.

Konrad said, "Better go have a bath, Franz. We'll carry on here."

"A bath?" Franz glared at him. "You think I can wash that thing in there off me with soap and water? It will be with me till the day I die."

He rushed out. In the silence, Konrad picked up a shovel and said calmly, "Last lap, my friends, so let's get to it." And he went down the ramp and crawled into the tunnel.

Hartmann was sitting in the sacristy at the table reading the *City of God* by St. Augustine. It was very quiet. There was the lightest of taps at the outside door. It opened, and Sigrid looked in.

"May we come in, Father?"

To his astonishment, he saw that her father was with her. Georg Ehrlich looked embarrassed and thoroughly uncomfortable.

"What is it?" Hartmann asked. "What can I do for you?"

"Go on, father," the girl urged.

"It's my aunt," the mayor said. "She's an old woman. Eighty-two."

"Well?"

"She's dying, Father," Sigrid told him simply. "And she hasn't seen a priest in a long time."

"I'll come at once," Hartmann said. "Is it far?"

"The edge of the village."

He opened his vestment bag and rummaged in it quickly. There was a ciborium from which he took a Host, which he hung in a silver pyx around his neck, and a small silver jar containing holy oil to anoint the dying woman's ears, nose, mouth, hands, and feet.

He threw a stole over his shoulder and picked up his missal. "I'm ready."

The door opened, and Vaughan entered. The mayor was obviously considerably put out. Vaughan said, "What's going on?"

"Herr Ehrlich's aunt is dying, Horst. She needs me. You can come if you want, but we haven't got time to argue."

He took Sigrid's arm and went out like a strong wind. Vaughan said to Ehrlich, "I'm supposed to follow him everywhere, did you know that? Not only the day but half the bloody night as well. I'll be glad when they transfer me to another assignment."

He went out, the mayor hurrying at his side. "She's an old woman, my aunt, and old people, you have to humor. On the other hand, it could be very embarrassing for me in the party if this got out, Comrade. You know what I mean?"

Vaughan turned up his collar against the rain. "Yes," he said sourly, "I know exactly what you mean."

The bedroom was on the ground floor, the door half open. Vaughan could see the old woman clearly, propped up against pillows. Hartmann was celebrating Mass, and she followed every move, hands clasped together. After he gave her communion, she started to cry, and he held her hands at the end.

"*Ite, missa est.*"

"*Deo gratias,*" she said through her tears.

And Sigrid, too, was crying, as she hurried from the room.

As they walked back toward the church, Vaughan explained in detail what had taken place at the Home Farm.

Curiously enough, Hartmann didn't refer to the incident of the body in the tunnel but simply said, "So you could be ready for Father Conlin tomorrow night? That's much sooner than I'd imagined."

"Or any of us did," Vaughan said. "You almost sound sorry."

"There's work to be done here. A real need to be filled." Hartmann smiled. "Remember what I told you in Berlin? One is always a priest before everything else. Still . . ."

They went up the steps to the church, and he opened the door. A man and a woman were sitting in one of the rear pews with three young children. They stood up at once, and the woman pushed the children forward. The eldest looked no more than seven.

"Please, Father," she said. "I'd like them baptized."

Her husband stood at her side, cap in hand, his face anxious. Beyond them Vaughan saw another half-dozen people at the confessional box.

"But it's two o'clock in the morning."

Erich Hartmann smiled. "You see, my friend?" he said. "You see now what I mean?"

FOURTEEN

The Franciscans worked on relentlessly through the night, and it was just before five o'clock in the morning when Franz's shovel sliced through soft earth and rattled against something harder.

"I think we're there," he said to Gregor, who was acting as laborer. He renewed his attack with vigor, pulled the soil away, and the curved side of the great concrete pipe started to take shape.

"I'll be back," Gregor said excitedly, and crawled away.

Franz kept on working, shoveling the soil back into the cart, until the pipe wall was completely clear. Gregor returned with Konrad. They carried a sledge-hammer and a couple of steel crowbars.

"Give it to me and keep back," Franz said.

He took the sledge and, when they had pulled the cart out of range, swung it with all his strength against the pipe. There was a hollow booming sound, but he had made no visible impression on the concrete. He tried again, slightly awkwardly, for because of the confined space, it was only possible to swing sideways.

Gregor crawled forward. "Try it this way," he said.

There was a join where one length of pipe had been cemented to another. He got the sharp end of the crowbar into it and lay flat, keeping his head down.

Franz swung again, connecting squarely with the head of the crowbar, which sank in immediately. He grunted with effort, swinging again with all his strength, and a crack appeared in the concrete and then another.

"I hoped that might happen," Gregor said. "It's prestressed."

Franz swung against the concrete this time, and a large piece fell inward. There was an immediate blast of cold air, a draft sweeping the length of the tunnel. He swung the hammer again and again, Gregor working beneath him with the crowbar, and within a few minutes had made an entrance large enough to pass through.

From the kitchen window of the priest's house, Vaughan could see Berg standing beside his truck outside the inn, talking to Ehrlich. The milk cart appeared from the direction of the Home Farm. To his surprise, he saw that Brother Konrad was pushing it.

Hartmann was at the stove frying eggs. Vaughan said, "That's interesting. Konrad's doing the milk round himself this morning. I think I'll see what's going on."

He found a jug and went out. As he approached the inn, Konrad was helping Berg lift a couple of churns onto the back of the truck. Ehrlich was standing, watching.

Vaughan said, "Good morning, Comrade."

The mayor mumbled a reply and went inside. Vaughan held out his jug for Konrad to fill. "We broke through at five o'clock," he said.

"And how are things?"

"Fine. Gregor, Franz, and I went the whole length of the sewer as far as the exit. The manhole cover is, of course, closed."

"You get down there as soon as you can and get that padlock off," Vaughan said to Berg. "I want you at the farm tonight as late as possible with any news at all on the state of the game up there. Say, seven o'clock."

"All right." Berg climbed into his truck and drove away.

"Anything else you want me to do?" Konrad asked as he picked up the shafts of the cart.

"Activate the transmitter as soon as you get back," Vaughan said. "That will alert them at Bitterfeld to expect something tonight."

The Franciscan moved away, and Vaughan went back into the house. "Anything I should know?" Hartmann asked, passing him a plate with two fried eggs and a slice of black bread on it.

"They've broken through."

"So—tonight it is."

Vaughan found that the eggs were really quite reasonable. "You should be at the farm no later than nine, by the way."

"Why?"

"To get yourself ready to move out with the others."

"We made no such arrangement."

"Good God, you can't stay here, man. You can't stay anywhere in East Germany. Within five minutes of finding Conlin gone, they'll put two and two together and make it five where you're concerned. You've no choice. You've got to leave with the others while you can."

"Yes, I suppose you're right," Hartmann said. "It hadn't really occurred to me before."

Strange how he had suddenly lost his appetite. He pushed the plate away from him.

Berg removed the padlock from the manhole cover, slipped it into his pocket, then picked up his lamp and went to check his poison bait. There were several dead rats and he collected half a dozen and went back up the passage, holding them in one hand by their tails.

As he came to the Vopo outside Conlin's cell, he held them up. "Six at one blow, just like the tailor in the fairy tale."

The young Vopo shuddered. "Stinking things. I can't stand them."

Berg laughed and moved on up the passage to where the next guard stood at the door to the steps leading to the second level.

In his cell, Conlin slept fitfully. He couldn't get the fact of Karl's death out of his mind, and the knowledge, as Van Buren had said, that he could have saved him, just as he could have saved Frances Mary. At the thought of her, all the pain, all the distress welled up in him again, as they had not done for years.

She was his only sister, nine years his junior, and they had always been close, especially after the death of their parents. She had lived with an old aunt during the years of his training, was so delighted when a parish appointment took him back to Dublin.

And then she'd fallen in love with Michael, a young assistant lecturer in history at Trinity College, a Protestant, but a lovely boy for all that. And then there was the child coming.

He could hardly breathe, remembering, his hands clutching at the blanket. That December night, just before Christmas. The car had skidded, overturned, killing Michael instantly. And Frances Mary, seriously injured, had gone into labor.

It was two o'clock in the morning when he'd got there, and the doctor in charge of the case had faced him with a terrible decision. She needed immediate surgery, and under the circumstances, there was no question that she could not be allowed to continue in labor, and in the condition she was in, a cesarean was impossible.

What they wanted was simple: Conlin's permission for them to destroy the child, and that was something he could not give, for such a thing ran contrary to everything he had believed all his life.

"All right," the doctor had said. "If we wait until after the birth, there's a strong possibility your sister will die. The choice is yours."

But as a good Catholic, he had no choice. And he sat and waited until four in the morning, when the doctor returned to tell him they were both dead, Frances Mary and the daughter who had barely lived.

It was snowing when he left the hospital and bitterly cold—almost as cold as it was now. What was it Donne said?

> *Under the rod of God's Wrath having been.*
> *He hath broke my bones, worn out my flesh*
>   *and skin.*

Oh, God help me, he thought. *I killed Karl, just as I killed my own sister out of my own selfish, stubborn pride. The iron conviction that I alone know what is right and true.*

In that moment, he was in total despair, at the bottom of a pit so dark there seemed no way out. He had never felt so totally alone in his life.

"God forgive me," he said, and wept.

A hand reached out to take his, and a fierce, aching excitement filled his heart. It was as if it were the third day and he were waiting for the stone to roll aside.

At Bitterfeld, Pascoe went into the hangar and found Kübel working on the Storch, Meyer sitting on a box watching him. The plane had had a fresh coat of dull black paint and looked remarkably sinister.

"How goes it?" Pascoe asked.

Meyer chuckled. "If he touches that engine once more, it'll complain to the union."

"Half the airmen who bought it during the war weren't shot down by the enemy. They died through engine failure of one sort or another," Kübel said. "That's why I made sure I knew more about them than the mechanics."

There was the sound of running steps, and

Teusen appeared in the hangar entrance, so much out of breath that he could hardly speak.

"What is it?" Pascoe demanded.

"It's come—the preliminary signal. We've just picked it up."

There was silence. Max Kübel walked across to the hangar door and looked out. Gray clouds hung heavily over the airfield, and a curtain of rain swept toward the hangar.

"Ah, well," he said softly to himself. "At least it should prove interesting."

Süssmann and Becker took Conlin into the room between them and sat him down in the chair opposite Van Buren.

"Wait outside," he said.

They withdrew. Conlin straightened himself wearily. "Well?"

"You look tired."

"Yes, I'll admit to that."

"Which isn't surprising. The unfortunate business with Karl. My reminding you of Frances Mary." Van Buren shrugged. "There's a limit to how many stones we can turn over."

"It's no good, Harry." Conlin smiled gently. "You're wasting your time. I didn't kill Karl—you did. And I didn't kill Frances Mary either. It was the circumstance of life that killed her—something I was unable to prevent because of my religious belief. I have no right to judge myself. God will do that for me."

"You still find time for belief?"

"Oh, yes, I think you could say that. In the depths of total despair, I reached out and He was there like a cold wind on the face in the morning. Excitement, Harry—the indescribable, hollow, frightening excitement of knowing totally. I discovered then that nothing could ever touch me again."

"And that's your final word?"

The old man smiled gently. "Harry, your father was a fine man. What happened to him was a terrible thing, but that doesn't excuse you making war on the whole world. Rats aren't people, Harry. A rat in a cage does what you teach him to do, but a man in a cage always has free choice."

Van Buren had gone very pale, his fingers interlocked tightly together. He said slowly, "I have a new drug with me which is used as a muscle relaxant in certain surgical operations, but the crucial point about it is that the patient has to be unconscious. You see, the effect on a conscious person is so horrifying that where accidents have occurred, the standard procedure is to inject scopolamine to erase the incident from the patient's memory."

"You learn something new every day," Father Conlin said.

Van Buren opened a drawer, took out a bottle and a hypodermic syringe, and started to fill it. "Succinylcholine causes convulsive muscular spasms, then leaves the subject totally paralyzed, unable to breathe, in agonizing pain—but conscious. You'll feel yourself dying of lack of oxygen. The effect lasts for only two minutes, but the experience is so terrible that few people can stand the threat of a repeat performance."

And Conlin knew fear then as he had never known it in his life before. His mouth went dry, and his hands started to shake so much that he could only still them by clasping them tightly behind him.

And in the end, can the human spirit be broken

so easily? Did you really intend such a thing, Lord? No, I can't believe it. I stand by my faith, now and always.

He took a deep breath and managed the bravest smile of his life. "Come on, boy. Surely you can do better than that. If the measure of a man is to be decided by which drug you pump into him, then where does that leave you, Harry?"

Van Buren stared at him fixedly, then pressed the buzzer on his desk; the door opened, and Süssmann and Becker entered.

"Hold him," he said.

It was just before seven when Vaughan went up the steel ladder and gently raised the manhole cover. The chamber above was in total darkness. He listened for a few moments, then lowered the cover again and went back down the ladder. Ten minutes later he was crawling along the cemetery tunnel back into the barn.

They were all waiting, and Berg had arrived while he'd been exploring the tunnel.

"Satisfied?" Konrad asked.

Vaughan nodded. "Ten minutes at the outside to get there, five to get Conlin, ten—maybe fifteen—to get back."

"You'll have to carry him," Berg said. "I saw him leaving Van Buren's office an hour ago, over Becker's shoulder, and he didn't look good."

"Had he been beaten?"

"Not that I could see."

Vaughan reached for his leather trench coat and pulled it on. "Probably drugs. There are some pretty nasty ones in use for Van Buren's kind of purpose these days. You get back up to the schloss. Stay there till about eight-forty-five and keep your eyes open. Anything happens before then, get down here with the news as fast as you can."

Berg nodded and went out. Konrad said, "What now?"

"We wait. I'll go and see Hartmann. Fill him in on what's happening, if I can tear him away long enough from his endless confessions and baptisms. The only thing he hasn't done is hold a public service."

As he moved to the door, Margaret Campbell joined him. They crossed the courtyard together, his arm about her shoulder.

He said, "Once things start hotting up I may be too busy to notice what you're doing, so promise me to do as Konrad tells you and get into that truck at the right time like a good girl."

"We could have breakfast together at Bitterfeld," she said.

"I don't see why not."

"And that café on the end of the bridge in Berlin. You'll take me there again if I ask you?"

"We'll see." He touched her cheek lightly with the back of his hand. "Look after yourself." And he stepped out through the gate and hurried away.

It was just after eight o'clock when Hartmann opened the side door and went into the sacristy and found Vaughan waiting for him.

"Where in the hell have you been?" Vaughan demanded.

"Visiting the sick. House calls," Hartmann said. "I told you there was a need here. Why?"

"Because at approximately nine I go in," Vaughan said. "At nine-twenty I come out again with Conlin, and at nine-forty Kübel will pick us up at Water Horse Meadow, and shortly after that, you'll all be on your way to the border in the field truck. So—get together what you want of your things, and you can come back to the farm with me now."

"No," Hartmann said. "I've been thinking about that, and I think I have a rather better idea. My only real purpose in this whole affair was to act as a decoy to a certain degree. It seems to me I'd be most useful doing that right now."

"What in the hell are you talking about?" Vaughan demanded.

So Hartmann told him.

Van Buren was going over his notes when there was a knock on the door and Süssmann entered with Becker.

"Trouble?" Van Buren said.

"In a manner of speaking. I've just had a phone call from the village. An anonymous well-wisher who was in the inn a short while ago when the priest came in and spoke to the mayor."

"And?"

"It seems he told him he intended to bring the Cross of St. Michael back to the church."

"I don't understand."

Süssmann explained briefly. When he was finished, he added, "An act of direct defiance, or so it seems to me. You did warn him."

Van Buren nodded. "Where is this cross?"

"I know," Becker said. "By the Elbe about half a

mile outside the village. I've seen it. I was told the story by Berg, the caretaker, when I first got here." He laughed contemptuously. "Hartmann must be crazy. There's no way he could carry that thing over such a distance."

"If he did, of course, and claimed the right to open the church again for public worship . . ." Süssmann said.

Van Buren nodded. "No, we can't have that." He smiled. "An interesting situation, though. Let's go and see how he's getting on."

At that precise moment, Erich Hartmann was attacking the ground at the base of the cross vigorously with a spade. Twenty or so villagers, women as well as men, some with lanterns, stood in a half circle some little distance away and watched.

Sigrid and her father were closest. The mayor said, "Father, this is madness. When the news reaches the castle, the military will come."

Hartmann said, "You see, Sigrid, we make progress. He worries for me."

"They'll arrest you, Father," Ehrlich said.

Hartmann kept on digging. "Did you phone them up there to tell them what I intended to do? After all, you are local party secretary."

"No," Ehrlich said. "I did not."

"Then they will arrest you, too, my friend. That's the kind of people they are. The kind of society you have." He turned to address the crowd now. "And you use the word *democratic* to describe it."

The cross swayed and started to fall. He threw the spade aside and caught it, easing it down. The evidence of his enormous strength drew an audible gasp from the crowd.

Sigrid ran forward and put a hand on his arm. "Please, Father, don't do it." Her face was strained, pleading. "You'll kill yourself."

"But I must, my child," he said gently. "You see it occurs to me now that this is very likely what it's all about, my life up to now, I mean. What I do now is what gives it purpose."

He looked at the hill, black in the rain, rising up toward the village. "Dear God, give me strength," he murmured.

He hoisted the cross on his left shoulder, braced himself to the weight, and started forward.

Brother Konrad, in the uniform of a Vopo lieutenant, was standing at the table in the barn with Margaret Campbell, examining the sewer plans, when Vaughan came in. He wore dark pants and sweater, and a black balaclava helmet covered most of his face, giving him a sinister and deadly appearance.

Margaret Campbell's eyes widened. "You look . . ." She hesitated.

He scooped up dirt from the floor with his hands and rubbed it over the exposed part of his face. "Look like what?" he demanded.

"Different—another person."

He was filled with a fierce energy that seemed to crackle around him like static electricity. "The real me," he said. "The man I've always been. Rising to the occasion because this is what I'm good at."

There was something close to hurt in her eyes. He turned from it and said to Konrad, "Is Franz in the tunnel?"

"Yes."

Vaughan took a Mauser from his belt, the pre-war model with the bulbous silencer, specially manufactured for the Gestapo and still the best silenced handgun in his experience. He checked the clip, then pushed the Mauser back into his waistband.

"I wonder which Station of the Cross Hartmann's reached now."

There was anger in Margaret Campbell's voice when she said, "He's doing what he thinks is right. It's not proper for you to make fun of him."

"A holy fool," Vaughan said. "Just like Sean Conlin, which is why we're all here if you think about it. God, the trouble the good of this world cause the rest of us." He glanced at his watch and saw that it was a quarter to nine. "To hell with it," he said. "I'm not going to wait any longer."

"And this?" Konrad touched the transmitter, which stood on the table. "What about this?"

"Press that button at ten past nine," Vaughan said. "That should be about right."

"But what if something should go wrong?" Margaret Campbell said in a sudden panic. "The timing is the critical point, you said so yourself."

"Not anymore," he said. "From now on, things just happen. You see, we don't control the game any longer—it controls us."

He ducked into the tunnel and was gone.

At Bitterfeld, Teusen had switched on the outside lights. Heavy mist blanketed the airfield. The Storch was ready on the apron, and Max Kübel, Pascoe, and Meyer stood in the shelter of the hangar.

Meyer said, "Look at the weather. It's times like

these I wonder if there's a God. What a thing to happen."

Kübel wore his old flying jacket, a white scarf wrapped around his neck. He was smoking a cigar and looked enormously cheerful. "Taking off in filth like this is nothing, Julius. It's landing that's the difficulty."

"And if it's like this at Neustadt?" Pascoe asked him.

"Then we have a problem," Kübel said simply.

Never had Hartmann carried such a weight on his shoulders, and as he came up to the crest of the hill, he paused. His entire body was one great ache, his left shoulder was rubbed raw, and the right, to which he had shifted position, was no better.

The crowd had swelled considerably, and people were still arriving. The strange thing was their silence. Only the occasional murmur of a voice, here and there.

He started forward again, giving an involuntary groan of pain as the weight settled on his shoulder. He lost his balance almost at once and went down heavily and lay there, under the cross.

There was a rush of feet as people surged forward to help. "No!" he shouted. "No!"

They paused. He stayed there, on his hands and knees for a while. And then Sigrid started to recite the creed in a firm, clear voice. "I believe in one God the Father Almighty, maker of heaven and earth, and of all things, visible and invisible . . ."

Another voice joined in, hesitantly at first, and then another and another.

Hartmann had never known such joy. "I am not

worthy of this burden," he murmured. "I accept it as a cross."

And then he was on his feet again and going forward over the brow of the hill.

Franz waited at the bottom of the steel ladder with the lamp while Vaughan went up and cautiously raised the manhole cover. It was dark in the chamber, but a certain amount of diffused light indicated the entrance to the passageway. He lifted the manhole cover back carefully, then climbed out, taking the Mauser from his belt and cocking it.

When he peered around the corner, he saw the Vopo guard at once, leaning against the wall negligently, an AK slung from one shoulder. Fifty or sixty feet away and the corridor was well lit, but there was no choice. Vaughan started forward, keeping to the wall, holding the Mauser against his right thigh. It was all a question of how close he could get before his presence was noted.

At that moment, another Vopo emerged from the gloom at the far end of the passage, rifle slung and carrying a jug in one hand. He saw Vaughan at once and cried out in alarm. He dropped the jug and started to unsling his rifle. Vaughan fired twice, both bullets ripping into the heart, killing the man instantly.

Even as the Vopo went down, the Mauser was already arcing toward the other guard, whose AK was just coming up. Vaughan shot him in the right shoulder, the heavy bullet turning him around in a circle. The next shattered his spine, slamming him against the cell door. His greatcoat started to smolder at the point of entry, and there was a tiny flicker of flame as he slid to the floor.

The silenced pistol had made virtually no sound at all, but there was the question of the first Vopo's cry. Vaughan ran along the passage lightly and paused at the door at the bottom of the steps, listening. There was no sound, and satisfied, he came back.

He pulled back the bolts on the cell door and went in. Father Conlin lay on the bed, fully clothed, breathing heavily, apparently sleeping, but when Vaughan shook him, there was no response.

Vaughan pushed the Mauser back into his belt, lifted the priest into a sitting position, leaned down, and took him across his shoulder. He went out and hurried back to the chamber.

Franz was peering over the edge of the manhole as he arrived. "Trouble, Major?"

"Nothing I couldn't handle," Vaughan said. "He's unconscious. Drugged, I think. I'll pass him down to you."

Franz stood at the bottom of the ladder and gently took the old man's weight, cradling him in his arms like a child. Vaughan followed, pulling the manhole cover back into place.

He glanced at his watch. It was just coming up to ten past nine. "Okay, let's get moving."

They started forward and a moment later, Brother Konrad in the barn pressed the button on the transmitter that sent the final vital signal to the West.

At Bitterfeld, Max Kübel boosted power and let the Storch go, the Argus engine responding magnificently. The landing lights had been switched on, but he could see only the first few—not that it mattered.

As the fog swallowed him up, Meyer, standing by the hangar entrance with Pascoe and Teusen, said, "Right, so he made it. What happens now?"

"The worst part, as it always is," Pascoe said. "The waiting."

Even before they got to the square, Van Buren could hear the singing. Becker was driving the field car, Süssmann beside him in the front seat, and when they turned into the square, most of the village seemed to be there. Heinrich Berg saw them at once, standing at the back of the crowd, and he moved back into the shadows.

"We would appear to have a religious revival on our hands," Van Buren observed.

Süssmann stood up, holding onto the top of the windshield. "I can see him now."

Hartmann entered the square on the far side, moving steadily, the crowd surging around him. He kept on coming doggedly, and people started to clap and cheer. As he neared the bottom of the broad steps leading up to the church door, Van Buren got out of the field car and moved to cut him off.

"Father Hartmann!" he called.

Hartmann paused. The singing died away; there was silence. It started to rain, heavily in a great rush, as they confronted each other.

"I told you that if you gave me any trouble, I'd pack you back to Berlin."

Süssmann stood up in the field car to address the crowd. "Go home—all of you. That's an order."

No one moved. Hartmann said, "I'm taking the cross into the church. It is my right."

He started up the steps. Van Buren said to Becker, "I've had enough of this charade. Stop him."

Becker went up the steps quickly and grabbed at one end of the cross, pulling Hartmann off-balance, putting him down on one knee. Becker kicked out, sending him toppling.

"You're under arrest," he said.

Hartmann ignored him completely, got on one knee again, and picked up the cross. Becker took out his Walther and cocked it.

"No!" he said as Hartmann rose to his full height.

The priest stood there, swaying, obviously very tired, and when he moved, he almost lost his balance, one arm of the cross catching Becker a painful blow, sending him back against the church doors. Becker, in a kind of reflex action, fired twice. Hartmann fell back across the steps, the cross on top of him.

There was an immediate uproar. The crowd surged forward, and Sigrid was the first to reach Hartmann, falling on her knees beside him. Süssmann drew his own pistol and fired it into the air.

"Go home!" he shouted. "I order you to disperse —all of you."

Van Buren leaned over Hartmann. The Jesuit's eyes were open; there was a touch of blood at one corner of his mouth. Becker came down the steps.

"You fool," Van Buren told him. "There was no need for this."

"Murderer!" Sigrid cried.

"Oh, no," Van Buren said. "He's still with us, but not if you leave him lying out here."

Behind him, another field car appeared in a hurry,

scattering the crowd. The Vopo driver jumped out and hurried forward. It was bad news, Van Buren could tell by his face, before he even got close enough to start pouring out his story.

When Berg pulled on the bell at the Home Farm, it was Brother Florian who let him in.

"Where's the major?" Berg demanded.

"Left five minutes ago in the field truck," Florian said. "It all worked perfectly. He and Franz brought Conlin out between them, and now Konrad's taken them to meet the plane."

Margaret Campbell appeared in the entrance to the barn. "There seems to be quite a disturbance in the village. What's been going on? Where's Father Hartmann?"

"Dead or dying from what I saw," Berg said, and explained what had happened.

She went into the barn without a word and returned with her medical bag.

"Take me to him."

"Don't be crazy," he said. "Konrad will be back here very soon now, and we've all got to be ready to leave with him." He added desperately, "Look, he was shot twice at close quarters. He must be dead by now."

"Take me to him," she said.

Brother Florian opened the gate. "Hurry. I'll tell Konrad when he returns. We'll wait for you."

Van Buren came out of Conlin's cell and stood looking down at the dead guard by the door.

"Impossible," Süssmann said. "It doesn't make sense."

"Of course it does," Van Buren told him. "There must be another way out of this rattrap somewhere down there in the darkness. If you search, you'll probably find it."

He started to walk away, and Süssmann called, "And you, Professor? Where are you going?"

"To visit the priest. It seems to me a remarkable coincidence that he should be putting on such a conspicuous display at the same time this little lot was going on."

He stepped over the other body and hurried away along the passage.

The field truck was parked at the northern edge of Water Horse Meadow. Brother Konrad was looking after Conlin, while Vaughan, after checking the wind direction, took a half-dozen cheap cycle lamps from his knapsack, switched them on, and laid them out in a row. Then he ran to the other end of the meadow, following the direction of the wind, and laid two more.

Simple, but effective, and Kübel, coming in fast at 600 feet a few minutes later, saw the pattern at once. He'd had an excellent flight on the whole except for that earlier part where things had been so dirty he had been compelled to go up rather higher than he would have liked. Still . . .

As the Storch dropped in for a perfect landing, Vaughan put Conlin across his shoulder and said to Konrad, "Off you go, then. See you at Bitterfeld at about eleven o'clock."

Konrad got in the truck and drove away as Vaughan ran across to the Storch, where Kübel waited for him, the door open. He leaned out to catch Conlin under the armpits to pull him in, and Vaughan scrambled up to join them, slamming the door.

The Storch was already turning into the wind for takeoff. Max grinned. "See, my friend, nothing to it."

He boosted the engine; the Storch surged forward and lifted into the night.

Hartmann was quite dead, Margaret Campbell knew that from the moment she entered the crowded bedroom at the priest's house, but she went through the motions of searching for a pulse and listening for a heartbeat. He looked very calm, very peaceful, and she started to put her stethoscope away.

Georg Ehrlich said, "He is dead, then?"

"I'm afraid so."

Sigrid, on her knees at the bedside, started to weep, and there was a general murmuring among those who crowded into the room.

Ehrlich said, "We haven't met. Are you new to the district, Doctor?"

"Passing through."

She closed her bag, stood up and found Harry Van Buren standing in the doorway.

"Hello, Margaret," he said. "This *is* a surprise."

FIFTEEN

Max Kübel, pushing the Storch toward the border at 160 miles an hour, had been in trouble for some considerable time. On his run in, he had climbed to a height of just over 1,000 feet because of bad visibility. He had been able to go down again within minutes, but during the intervening period, his presence had been noted on the radar screens at Allersberg.

Such a brief appearance could indicate a ghost image or ground clutter due to wave reflection. On the other hand, it could be an intruder, and the chief controller at Allersberg was not one to take chances.

The rain had reduced visibility considerably, and Kübel decided to go up. It was only six or seven minutes to the border now anyway. He pulled back the control column, and the Storch started to climb, emerging into clean air at just over 1,000 feet.

There was a quarter moon, pale, rain-washed, but it touched the low clouds with a kind of luminosity. He turned and shouted to Vaughan across the head of the unconscious Conlin, "Not long now."

There was a roaring that filled the night; the Storch bucked like a wild horse in the turbulence so that it took everything Kübel had to hold it as a dark shadow banked overhead and took up station to starboard.

"What is it?" Vaughan demanded.

"MiG fighter. We've got trouble, my friend."

The MiG waggled its wings. "He's signaling," Vaughan said.

"I know that." Kübel switched on the radio.

Reception was very clear. The voice said, "Adopt course three-four-zero for Allersberg airbase. I will follow you down."

Kübel switched off the radio. "This doesn't look too good. Those cannon of his could blow us to pieces."

"Is there anything you can do?"

"In this kind of contest a jet's speed can be a disadvantage. I'm really too slow for him to handle. I'll go down low and see if I can make him do something stupid."

He banked to port and went down fast, and the MiG banked too in a sweeping curve that would bring him in on the Storch's tail. He started to fire his cannon, too soon, his speed so excessive that he had to bank to starboard to avoid collision.

Kübel was at 600 when the MiG came in again, and this time, the Storch staggered under the impact as cannon shells punched holes in the wings.

The MiG turned away in a great curve, then came in again, and once more the Storch shuddered under the impact of cannon shell. The windscreen disintegrated, and Kübel cried out sharply.

Vaughan said, "Are you all right?"

Kübel's flying jacket was ripped just under the left shoulder. When Vaughan reached over to touch it, he found blood.

"Never mind that, I'll live," Kübel said. "Just hang on tight because this time, I'll show the bastard how to fly."

They were now down to 500 feet, the countryside clear below them, the border very close. The MiG came for the kill, sliding in on their tail perfectly. Pieces flew off the wings as the cannon shells struck home, and Kübel dropped his flaps.

The Storch seemed to stand still in midair, and the pilot of the MiG, totally unprepared, banked steeply to starboard to avoid a collision. Too steeply, and the MiG, with no space to work in, plowed straight into the forest below.

There was a mushroom of flame, spectacular in the night, and then it was behind them, already fading as they pushed on to the border.

The engine seemed to miss a beat, and Kübel worked at the controls frantically. "Come on, you bitch. Don't let me down now."

Vaughan checked Conlin. The old man was still unconscious, but his breathing seemed regular enough.

"Is he okay?" Kübel shouted.

Vaughan nodded. "Are you?"

"So I've taken a little steel in the back. I've had worse, and this time it was worth it." He laughed out loud. "Don't you see, Simon? I've got my one hundred and fiftieth."

A moment later, they coasted across the border, and he banked to starboard and commenced his descent for Bitterfeld.

Franz closed the barn doors and barred them with a balk of timber. Like the others, he was dressed in the uniform of the Volkspolizei. They stood by the field truck in the rain, each man with an AK rifle slung across his chest in approved fashion.

Konrad peered out through the side gate anxiously. "Come on," he whispered. "Where are you, Margaret?"

Gregor moved to join him. "It's no good, we must go. It is only a matter of time before our tunnel is discovered. We can't afford to stay here any longer."

There was the sound of running footsteps, and Berg appeared from the darkness, face distraught, totally panic-stricken. Konrad brought him to a halt and held him at arm's length.

"What is it? Where's the girl?"

Berg, struggling to catch his breath, had difficulty speaking. "He's got her. Van Buren's got her."

Konrad shook him. "What are you talking about?"

"She went to see the priest to see if there was anything she could do, but he was dead. Then Van Buren turned up."

"And?"

"They took her away in a Vopo field car. To Schloss Neustadt."

Konrad gazed at him in horror, still holding onto the front of Berg's coat. Berg said urgently, "We must go, don't you see? It's only a matter of time and they'll be here."

"He's right," Gregor said gently to Konrad. "Remember Major Vaughan's orders? We were to wait for no one."

"But we can't leave her," Konrad said. "We must do something."

"She's at Schloss Neustadt by now," Gregor said.

"We can do nothing." He prized Konrad's fingers away from Berg's jacket. "You get in the back of the truck." He turned to the others. "All of you—mount up."

Konrad said in a dead voice, "What a thing to happen after all this. As if she hasn't suffered enough." He turned, and his voice was savage now. "You know something, Gregor? This God I've been serving all these years—I'm beginning to wonder whether He's at home anymore."

He climbed up behind the wheel, and Gregor got in beside him. Konrad pressed the starter and drove out through the gates.

The sound of the engine faded into the night; the courtyard lay silent and deserted. It was a good twenty minutes before there were the first sounds of movement inside the barn and someone started banging on the door.

"The Resurrection was astonishing," Van Buren said. "If true, that is, which I've always doubted, but your case, Margaret—that's what I call a miracle. Old mother Elbe was supposed to have taken you to her bosom weeks ago."

She sat there beside the desk, hands folded in her lap, very calm. "I've nothing to say."

"Nothing new in that," he said. "You always were an introverted little thing. Understandable, of course, after the kind of conditioning you went through."

The door opened, and Süssmann hurried in. "A manhole cover on the lower level gives access to a sewer pipe from the war days that's never been used. We found a tunnel from it leading under the cemetery, emerging in the barn at the Home Farm."

"The Home Farm?"

"The Franciscans."

Van Buren laughed out loud, head thrown back. "Oh, but that's beautiful. That really is a pearl. They're not there now, of course?"

"No. The place is deserted."

Van Buren turned again to Margaret Campbell. "So, that's where you've been hiding out for the past few weeks?"

She made no reply. Süssmann said, "Berg, the caretaker, appears to be missing, also Schaefer."

"Schaefer?" Van Buren said sharply. "But of course, that would fit very nicely. Schaefer and the priest. I always did wonder about him."

"Another thing. There's been a report of a light aircraft landing and taking off again in the vicinity of the river sometime during the past hour."

"Is that so?" Van Buren appeared curiously indifferent.

"For God's sake," Süssmann said. "What are we going to do?"

"I don't know," Van Buren told him amiably. "Call out the guard. Alert the border. After all, you're the military genius around here."

"But we must get Conlin back again," Süssmann shouted, "or we're all finished, and this bitch can tell us where he is."

"You obviously weren't very good at mathematics when you were at school," Van Buren said patiently. "If a plane landed and took off again within the past half hour, who in the hell do you think was on it?"

Süssmann turned and strode angrily from the room, slamming the door behind him. He went down the staircase quickly and entered his office, where he found Becker waiting.

"What happens now?" the sergeant major asked.

"God knows, Rudi," Süssmann said. "We could all find our heads on the block for this one. Get on the phone to HQ. Send out a red alert to all Volkspolizei units between here and the border to pick up anyone they find on the roads who is in the slightest way suspicious."

Becker went out. Süssmann lit a cigarette and paced up and down nervously.

"Schaefer," Van Buren said. "He has to be the key figure. I should have known after he knocked hell out of Becker so superbly. He won't get far."

"The plane," she said serenely.

"He was also on board, was he? So he's safe, and that pleases you." He leaned back, watching her closely. "Are you in love with him?"

"Too late for games," she said. "You've lost. If I were you, I'd be packing my bags right now."

"But where would I go?" He smiled gently. "I've been everywhere, that's the problem. But to get back to Schaefer. If he was on the plane, that means he left you and that doesn't fit. He isn't the type."

She was silent, and he continued. "You were supposed to leave with the others, weren't you? And then you heard about Hartmann and just had to play doctor. He isn't going to like that, Schaefer, or whatever his name is."

"Vaughan." There was pride in her voice. "Major Simon Vaughan."

"English? Now, there's a thing." He nodded slowly. "He'll come back for you."

"Don't be absurd." She was genuinely alarmed now.

"He'll come back for you, Margaret. That kind of man always comes back. It's my business to know these things," he said cheerfully. "I am, after all, one of the world's better psychologists."

"No," she said. "No!" as if by repetition she could make it so.

He poured himself an enormous brandy. "You've got a problem, I can help you." His grimace was painful. "The only trouble is, and this will make you fall about laughing, I could never understand my own. Problems, I mean."

There was silence while he brooded. For no accountable reason she said, "I'm sorry."

"Well, that's handsome of you. Excuse me for a moment, will you?"

Instead of going out, he simply picked up the phone and dialed Klein's office number. Frau Apel answered at once.

"Working late, aren't you?" he said. "Is he in?"

"I think so, Professor."

A moment later, Klein came on. "Hello, Harry, I was just leaving. What's the news at your end?"

"All black," Van Buren said. "Conlin escaped."

"What?" Klein said. "That isn't possible."

"My dear Helmut, anything is possible in this wicked old world of ours," Van Buren told him. "I'd have thought a man of your varied experience would have realized that by now. The details aren't important at the moment. The fact is that an assorted group, which included that damn priest of yours, got Conlin out of Schloss Neustadt earlier this evening and flew him out by lightplane. For some obscure reason, I wanted the pleasure of telling you all this myself."

"You're sure of your facts?" Klein said. "You're certain he's got clean away?"

"Good-bye, Helmut." Van Buren put down the phone and poured another brandy.

"What happens now?" she asked.

"We wait," he said. "We wait to see if I'm right about this Major Vaughan of yours."

Süssmann was just about to leave his office when the phone rang. When he picked it up, Klein was on the other end.

"I've just heard from Van Buren. I want your version of what's happened there tonight. Quickly now."

Süssmann told him, leaving nothing out. When he was finished, there was silence. He said tentatively, "Colonel, are you there?"

"Yes," Klein said. "I was thinking."

"What do you want me to do, Colonel?"

"You're a promising officer, Süssmann. A pity to see you pulled down by your association with a man who is most certainly a traitor to the state. The only conceivable explanation for this whole sorry affair. I should be there in about a couple of hours to interrogate Van Buren personally. Naturally, if he attempts to leave before I arrive, you would be within your rights to prevent him by any means possible. Such action would rebound to your credit. You understand me?"

"Perfectly, Colonel."

"Good, I'll see you later."

Süssmann put down the phone; then he took out his Walther and checked the clip.

After speaking to Süssmann, Klein turned to the rows of books which lined the wall behind him. He removed several to reveal a small wall safe, which he opened quickly. He took out a very ordinary-looking office file and a set of false identity papers which he had long had ready for such a day. The file contained a list of the identities of all agents of his department at that time operating in West Germany.

He slipped it into his briefcase and checked the false identity papers. A good thing that as a security chief, his face was not generally known to the military. He slipped the papers into his breast pocket, pulled on his coat, and picked up his briefcase.

Frau Apel was still at her desk. She glanced up. "You're going now, Colonel?"

"Yes. Good of you to stay so late, Clara. Get yourself home now, and I'll see you in the morning."

He went out, whistling cheerfully. Twenty minutes later, he passed through a little-used checkpoint near Königstrasse and presented himself to the policeman on duty on the other side with the astonishing request that he be put in touch at once with General Reinhard Gehlen, director of the Federal Intelligence Service.

It was still raining at Flossen, where Bülow paced up and down outside the guard hut impatiently. At nine-thirty he had received the red alert signal from the HQ which meant no traffic of any description was to be allowed through. His wife was already safe on the other side with their child, and all he wanted now was to join them.

Hornstein, who had moved a little way up the road, turned excitedly. "There's a vehicle coming."

He moved to the sergeant's side. They waited anxiously, and then a Volkspolizei field truck moved out of the night and braked to a halt.

Konrad leaned out the window. "I believe you've been waiting for us."

Bülow didn't even bother to reply. Hornstein was already raising the barrier. They both scrambled over the tailgate, helped by willing hands, as the field truck started to roll again, moving across to the West.

Pascoe was in the control room at Bitterfeld on his own when Böhmler came in to tell him that the truck had arrived safely. They went across to the hangars together and found a state of some confusion. The Franciscans were standing by the truck, talking to Teusen and Meyer.

As Pascoe entered, Meyer said passionately, "Madness, that's the only word for it. He goes to his death."

"What's going on?" Pascoe demanded.

"I'm afraid we lost Dr. Campbell, Professor," Konrad told him. "She is now in Van Buren's hands at Schloss Neustadt."

"Simon says he's going back for her," Teusen said.

There was the sound of footsteps. They all turned, and Vaughan entered the hangar once again in his Vopo uniform and dispatch rider's raincoat. The AK was slung across his chest, and he was fastening his helmet strap.

Pascoe said, "There's no point to this."

Vaughan ignored him and said to Konrad, "Is there much activity over there?"

"Oh, yes," Konrad said. "We passed several patrols, but no one bothered us. They assumed we were after the same game."

"So why should they treat me any differently?" Vaughan mounted the Cossack and kicked the engine into life.

Teusen said, "Don't be a fool, Simon."

"You want to do something for me, keep that crossing point open for as long as you can." Vaughan opened the throttle and roared away.

There was silence. Pascoe sighed and turned to Sergeant Bülow and young Hornstein. "It would seem you gentlemen are going to have to return to duty for a while."

"Oh, no," Bülow said. "That wasn't in the contract."

"But, my dear man, you must see the necessity. If your HQ phones through and you're not there to answer, they'll come looking."

"That may have happened already," Bülow said.

"We'll just have to take our chances on that one."

"No!"

There was an AK rifle on the driver's seat of the truck. Pascoe picked it up and cocked it. "I'm not disposed to argue. You go back over there and I'll go with you."

"Let me," Teusen said.

Pascoe smiled wearily. "No, Bruno, for once, this is my show. I was always good at sending other men out into the field, but not this time." He turned back to Bülow. "After you, Sergeant, if you please."

Vaughan drove up the narrow approach road to Schloss Neustadt with care, and when he went over the crest of the hill, he found a sentry standing in a box at the tunnel entrance out of the rain.

Vaughan brought the Cossack to a halt. "Dispatch for Professor Van Buren from Berlin."

The sentry waved him on without hesitation, and Vaughan drove in through the dark tunnel. This time there was no sentry at the other end, and he moved on across the cobbled square past the main entrance, following the narrow passage between high walls that brought him finally into the rear courtyard.

He switched off the engine and dismounted, remembering Berg's description of the private entrance to the commandant's quarters. It had to be here somewhere. He unslung his AK and moved forward.

Margaret Campbell lay on the bed in Van Buren's bedroom in the dark, her eyes open. She was thinking about Vaughan, wondering what had happened to him. But most of all, she was praying that he wouldn't act in the way Van Buren had predicted.

At that moment, the door opened and the light was switched on. Van Buren stood looking at her, a glass in his hand. "Come in here," he said and went back into the other room.

When she joined him, he was standing by the fire, pouring another brandy. He seemed more than a little drunk. "He disappoints me, this boyfriend of yours. Where is he?"

There was a slight creak, a sudden cold draft. They both turned as the narrow door in the far corner swung open, and Vaughan stepped into the room, holding the AK at the ready.

Margaret Campbell ran to his side. "Oh, you fool—you marvelous bloody fool. Wasn't once enough for you? Haven't I been enough trouble?"

He smiled. "I decided to forgive you all that." He put an arm around her.

Van Buren laughed delightedly. "You see, I'm never wrong. The mind of man is an open book to the great Van Buren."

Vaughan said, "If you make a sound, I'll cut you in half with this thing."

"And bring every man in the castle on the run? Don't be stupid, Schaefer or Vaughan or whatever your name is."

"I'm taking her out of here."

"Who's stopping you?"

Van Buren poured another brandy and turned away. Vaughan lowered the gun. "What's going on here?"

Margaret Campbell put a hand on his arm. "Don't argue, Simon. Just go." She turned to Van Buren. "I'm sorry, Harry. In spite of everything you did concerning my father, I'm still sorry for you."

"So am I." Van Buren raised his glass. "*Lechayim.* Now get out of here."

Vaughan led the way quickly down the spiral stone staircase. At the bottom, he opened the door and peered out, but there was no one in evidence. He took her arm and hurried her across to the Cossack.

"You'll have to crouch down in the sidecar cockpit, and I'll cover you with the rain tarpaulin."

She climbed in and, as she settled herself, said, "What was it he said up there just before we left?"

"*Lechayim,*" Vaughan told her. "It's a Hebrew word. It means: to life."

She didn't say anything to that, simply crouched down as he had instructed her. He stretched the rain cover across the cockpit, snapping the studs into place; then he swung a leg over the Cossack and started the engine. A few moments later, the sentry was waving them through the main entrance.

Van Buren stood in front of the fire, staring back into the past. "Well, at least I was a pretty good corporal of marines," he said softly. "Maybe that counts for something."

He emptied his glass, put it down, then crossed to the door and opened it, intending to look for Süssmann. There was a murmur of voices from the hall below, and when he peered over the balustrade, he saw Süssmann and Becker standing down there.

"The sooner it's done, the better," Süssmann was saying. "When Klein gets here, he wants to find him dead. It's important for all of us, Rudi. He takes all the guilt."

Becker took out his Walther and checked it, and Van Buren stepped back into his office. A few moments later, he came out again and stood at the head of the stairs as they started up.

"Ah, there you are, Süssmann. I wanted a word with you."

The two men paused on the landing halfway up the stairs and took out their Walthers. "You're under arrest," Süssmann said. "For treason against the state. You will deliver the woman Campbell into my charge."

"Not possible, I'm afraid," Van Buren told him. "I let her go ages ago."

"You're lying."

"No, my friend, with all my faults that's something I never did do. When does the shooting start?" Becker glanced uncertainly at Süssmann, and Van Buren said, "Shot while trying to escape. Isn't that how it goes?"

"If you say so."

Süssmann fired three times. As Van Buren cried out, he opened both hands, dropping the two Russian pineapple grenades he was holding. They bounced down the stairs, one after the other. Becker uttered a cry of fear and, turning to run, collided with Süssmann. The grenades exploded a second later.

It was half past two when the Cossack emerged from the darkness and braked to a halt where Bülow and Hornstein stood waiting outside the guard hut at Flossen. Pascoe appeared in the doorway, the AK in his hands. Vaughan pushed up his goggles wearily.

"Were you successful, Major?"

Vaughan pulled back the canvas rain cover, and Margaret Campbell sat up. "Are we here?" she asked. "Are we in the West?"

"No," Vaughan said. "But we soon will be."

He drove on, and Charles Pascoe, Bülow, and Hornstein followed on foot. Behind them, the telephone started to ring in the guard hut. It rang for quite some time before it stopped. It was quiet then, only the door creaking a little as it swung to and fro in the slight wind.

SIXTEEN

On June 21 in Rome, Cardinal Giovanni Battista Montini was elected to the papal throne by the Sacred College, taking the name of Paul VI. In a room at the Collegio di San Roberto Bellarmino, Father Sean Conlin was in bed, propped up against pillows and reading a book when Pacelli entered to give him the news.

Conlin said, "So—life goes on?"

"So it would appear."

"But not for Erich Hartmann. Tell me, Father. What was he like? What was he really like?"

"Who knows? A mystery—like all men—known only to his maker."

"A bit of a saint, would you say?"

"Certainly not. Erich was entirely lacking in the kind of humility needed for that office. What he did at Neustadt was magnificent nonsense—but thank God for it."

"Ah, well." Sean Conlin sighed. "I'll remember him in my prayers for the rest of my life."

"I, too." Pacelli smiled. "And now you must excuse me. I have a great deal to do. The work goes on."

He went out. It was very quiet in the room as

Father Conlin closed his eyes, folded his hands, and prayed for the repose of the soul of Erich Hartmann.

On June 26, President Kennedy paid an eight-hour visit to West Berlin. After landing at Tegel airfield in the French sector, he made a thirty-mile drive through the city, accompanied by Dr. Adenauer and Willy Brandt, amid the frenzied cheering of 1,250,000 people.

The party finally reached the West Berlin town hall in Schöneberg, where the President was expected to make the most important speech of his tour.

The room on the first floor to which he was taken was crowded, and among those waiting there were Charles Pascoe and Simon Vaughan. The President moved through the crowd, stopping here and there.

When he got to Pascoe and Vaughan, he shook hands, the smile easy and relaxed, no different from what it had been for the others. It was only in words that carried their own meaning.

"Gentlemen, we are glad, believe me, to see you here today."

He moved out on the balcony to an enormous cheer from the crowd. He started to speak. Pascoe said, "I know I'm getting old, but it's still better to travel hopefully. He could be what we all need, that man. At least he says the right things. The things that should be said."

Kennedy's voice drifted in. "Today in the world of freedom, the proudest boast is *Ich bin ein Berliner.*"

He was leaning over the balcony, touched by

light, and then it was as if a shadow had passed over the face of the sun, and the light on him died, but only for a moment.

For some unaccountable reason, Vaughan went cold. He said to Pascoe, "Let's get out of here. You can read all about it in the papers."

He turned and worked his way through the crowd, Pascoe following him. Margaret Campbell was standing against the wall at the head of the stairs with Meyer.

She reached for his hand. "What's wrong, Simon? What is it?"

"Nothing," he said. "Someone just walked over my grave, that's all."

As they went down the stairs, the President's voice rang out across the crowd like a trumpet blast. "Freedom has many difficulties and democracy is not perfect, but we never had to put up a wall to keep our people in."

The Versatile Jack Higgins

After years of writing thrillers under various names, Jack Higgins (also a pseudonym) hit international bestseller lists with *The Eagle Has Landed*, an edge-of-the-seat story of a wartime attempt to assassinate Winston Churchill. He repeated his success with *Storm Warning*, the dazzling World War II novel of German sailors who navigate the 5,000 miles from South America to their German homeland in a schooner.

Day of Judgment, Higgins' latest bestseller, once again makes fictional use of real events—in this instance, the events preceding President John F. Kennedy's historic visit to Berlin in 1963.

Possessing a world-wide reputation as a captivating storyteller, Higgins uses the device of superimposing fiction on a foundation of historical fact. Readers are enthralled by his ability to portray the intricate planning of a sensational coup as well as the equally detailed execution of a counter-coup.

Higgins' real name is Harry Patterson but he has also written as James Graham. Under these two names he has produced *The Wrath of God*, *The Khufra Run*, *Toll for the Brave*, *Hell Is Always Today*, *A Game for Heroes* and *The Valhalla Exchange*. Another early book, *The Savage Day*, featured Simon Vaughan, who returns as a leading character in *Day of Judgment*.

Before becoming a full-time writer, Higgins was Senior Lecturer in Education at a college in Leeds, England. He is married, with four children, and lives an idyllic existence in the British Channel Islands.

RELAX!
SIT DOWN
and Catch Up On Your Reading!

Bantam Book Catalog

Here's your up-to-the-minute listing of over 1,400 titles by your favorite authors.

This illustrated, large format catalog gives a description of each title. For your convenience, it is divided into categories in fiction and non-fiction—gothics, science fiction, westerns, mysteries, cookbooks, mysticism and occult, biographies, history, family living, health, psychology, art.

So don't delay—take advantage of this special opportunity to increase your reading pleasure.

Just send us your name and address and 50¢ (to help defray postage and handling costs).